WITH OR WITHOUT TRUST

HOT COPS SERIES
Book 2

KAREN LIEVERSZ

SUGAR PUSH PUBLISHING

E-book ISBN: 978–0-6458556-2-3

Paperback ISBN: 978-0-6458556-3-0

Cover design by LJ at Mayhem Cover Creations

Edited by Kelly Rigby at Write with Kelly

Proofread by Jo Speirs at Nurturing Words

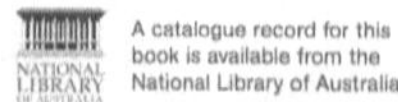
A catalogue record for this book is available from the National Library of Australia

To my sweet but highly strung rescue staffy/kelpie cross, Juno, for whom trust doesn't come easily.

And for everyone (human or furry) looking for love and a safe place to call home.

Author Note

With or Without Trust contains frequent swearing and explicit sex scenes. While there's a lot of humour in this story, it also touches on mental health topics, drug addiction, homelessness, and complicated family relationships that may be uncomfortable for some readers.

Please note that this book is written in Australian English, which differs from US English in some instances.

Prologue

Emily

The obnoxious eighties music flows over me like oil in a non-stick frying pan. Not that I know much about cooking. My determination to prove I could do everything my brother did stepped up several notches when, at ten years old, my mother pulled me aside and suggested a girl's place was in the kitchen and not fixing fences and driving tractors.

I pour myself a glass of bubbles and totter towards the dancefloor. It's swarming with happy couples, so I linger in the shadows and sip champagne. Detective Inspector Jake Matthews and Claire shuffle to the slow tune, their faces shining with mutual adoration, which is only right since this is their party. They've only known each other eight months, but when you know, you know. Or so the inspector said when he proudly announced his engagement to everyone at Parramatta Police Station.

As a civilian intelligence analyst, I have a dotted line of responsibility to the inspector. To be honest, he's a little scary, so it's sweet to see him melt into someone more approachable when Claire's around. She has that effect on people, seeing through my shell the moment we met and making it her mission to be friends. It's amazing she's so welcoming, given everything she's been through. I can't imagine how tough it must have been to be framed for drug possession. Lucky for her, she had Inspector Matthews in her corner. He didn't rest until he found the real culprit. It makes my failure to get accepted into the police force seem like a minor setback. If Claire can rise above what happened to her, then I can too.

I finish my drink as a server walks by and beckon him to top me up. His hazel eyes promise all sorts of decadence as his gaze drifts towards my cleavage. I wish I felt like exploring his less-than-subtle interest, but like all men lately, he leaves me cold. I give him a tight smile and look away. He takes the hint and moves on.

There's only one man who makes my body perk up and take notice—Detective Sergeant Greg Anderson. He glides across the floor with Claire's boss, real estate agent Monica Reynolds. His suit hints at the muscles beneath, his hand resting on the small of Monica's back, lips hovering near her ear. Their bodies are so close a piece of paper wouldn't fit between them. Her slinky red dress displays way too much creamy skin. It's all wrong for a redhead. Where are her blasted freckles? My fingers itch to scratch out her eyes, even though I have no claim on him. And don't want one. I have no desire to be another notch on his bedpost, no matter how prettily he's packaged.

Inspector Matthews growls at Greg and Monica to get a room. From what Claire's told me, they're *only friends*, despite her attempts to set them up. It sure doesn't look like it. Greg flips the inspector off. Our eyes meet, and the music fades. It's just Greg and me and a powder keg of lust. I swear a spark passes between us until Monica whispers to him and he looks away, severing the link.

A sharp pain lodges in my chest. I scull my drink, the bubbles catching in my throat. It's a waste of expensive champagne, but obsessing over a man like Greg is pointless. I hate that I can't take my eyes off him. That I lay awake too many nights thinking about his taut body and wicked smile.

I slip into the bathroom where the mirror reminds me, as if I need it to, that I'm no competition for Monica. Not that I want to be. Or so I keep telling myself. Freckles dot my nose and span across my cheeks, and unlike Monica's sleek updo, my red curls refuse to be tamed by the golden leaf headband I'd bought on a whim.

I finish my business and stumble outside into the balmy summer evening to clear my head. The stone-washed entrance of the stunning hacienda-style function centre gives way to a gravel driveway. Surrounded by bush, it's easy to forget we're still in Sydney. There's an acrid taint in the air thanks to a bushfire burning in the Blue Mountains. It's under control, so the authorities say, but the smoke has drifted across the city, casting an eerie glow. I hope they're right; otherwise, those living near the bush are in for a miserable Valentine's day.

I pick my way along a small, pebbled path guided by a string of fairy lights. I've no idea where it leads, but I need to escape the party. Crickets and cicadas do their best to block out the music and the ringing inside my head, but they're fighting a losing battle. Same as me with the four-inch stiletto heels Claire insisted were *perfect* for my new cinnamon-brown dress. I feel like a little girl playing dress-up next to the sophisticated Monica.

"You couldn't take the racket anymore, either?"

Yikes! I jump at the shadow emerging from the darkness. Greg must have left the dance floor while I was in the bathroom. His suit coat is unbuttoned, and his tousled brown hair looks like he's been raking his fingers through it. A glint of silver at the temples adds to his allure. It should be illegal to look this good!

He gives me his signature sexy smile, the one designed to

melt panties, and I forget why I'm supposed to keep my distance.

"You okay?"

I've been staring, mute. Dammit, I've had too much champagne to deal with him right now. And it's been too long since I've had sex. I need to get out of here before I say—or worse—*do* something I shouldn't.

I straighten my shoulders and try to appear unaffected by his presence. "I'm fine."

I need to remember I love working alongside the drug squad. They're a close-knit team who've welcomed me with open arms. Not like my last posting. I don't want to make things awkward and jeopardise my position by fooling around with a colleague. Especially one reputed to be a ladies' man.

Greg loosens his tie and gestures towards the lights of the function centre filtering through the trees. "According to Jake, Claire prefers the latest hits, but you wouldn't know it tonight."

Music. He's talking about music. I try to think of something to say, but it's like all my brain cells have moved out and my traitorous hormones have moved in.

I nod my head in agreement and immediately wish I hadn't. My limit is two glasses; I've had at least double that. Maybe more. I stumble on the pebbles—stupid shoes—and Greg's hands shoot out to steady me.

"You alright, Em?"

"Nothing some fresh air won't fix." Or smoky air and warm sandalwood and pine. I've only ever caught tiny whiffs of Greg's aftershave, but pressed against him, the spicy fragrance saturates my lungs. I place my hands against his chest. If I don't escape soon, I'll be scaling him like a tree, and that would be a terrible mistake. Especially when he probably has a night of debauchery planned with the sexy Monica. But instead of pushing him away, I find myself clutching his shirt, unable to let go.

Greg tightens his grip, bringing our bodies flush with each other. The unmistakable proof of his arousal juts against my stomach. *Did I cause that?* My nipples bead inside my bra, and my underwear dampens. I smooth the fabric of his shirt and slide my palms across his pecs and along his bulging biceps. Rational thought flees my head, and my hips undulate, seeking more of his delicious hardness.

"Jesus, Em, what are you doing to me?" His voice cracks, and his fingers tighten around my waist.

Him? What's he doing to me? And why is he doing it?

"Shouldn't you be getting back to Monica?" I push off his chest and step away.

He looks pleased. "You jealous?"

"Of course not."

"Monica's a friend. Nothing more." He brushes my cheek with his knuckles, sending a tingle of awareness to my breasts. My core. "You, on the other hand, are so fucking sexy it hurts to even look at you."

Me sexy? Does he mean it? If it's a line, it's a good one.

His brown eyes darken until I can't tell the pupils from the irises. I lick my lips, and Greg tracks the movement, a groan spilling from him. I inhale more of his spicy goodness. Would it be so bad if I took the bait? Maybe this is what I need to get him out of my system.

Greg grazes my other cheek with his fingertips. His touch is light yet firm. Respectful while hinting at all things carnal. My resolve buckles as the champagne I've drunk tells me hooking up with him is an infinitely better option than spending another restless night with my vibrator.

I can't let this moment pass. I'll worry about regrets tomorrow. He's over a foot taller than me, so I loop my arms around his neck and jump, my legs circling his waist and my dress sliding up to my hips. Not very ladylike. Greg seems momentarily shocked but then grabs my butt and holds me in position.

"You're full of surprises." He bends his head, his breath tickling my face. "I like it."

My lips part on a sigh. Greg accepts the unspoken invitation, his mouth plundering mine again and again. He tastes like honey and whiskey, and I can't get enough. I kiss him back, our tongues tangling as I explore his mouth. His flavour, scent and incredible strength fuel the fire whipping through my body.

When Greg pulls away, I whimper.

"One moment, little vixen. Let's go somewhere more private."

Thank God he's thinking. I'd tear my clothes off here and now with no thought of who might stumble along. Why he would pass up the gorgeous Monica for me is a mystery, but I won't overthink it.

Greg carries me into a secluded section of the garden where a large, white gum tree stands sentinel. His muscles flex beneath my hands and thighs as he moves. He must be wickedly strong. Warning bells go off in my head. He's a flirt. A player. We're colleagues. *All reasons to stop.* But the scrape of his stubble against my neck is electric. There's no way I'm rejecting his attention when our bodies feel so right together. I hope he has a condom because I haven't needed one in too long. Then again, a man with his reputation would have a whole wallet full of them.

That thought jumps up and down, trying to catch my attention, but my raging hormones drown it out.

The music is a dull thud in the background, the shadows bathing us in privacy. Greg touches his forehead to mine. His face is flushed, eyes hooded. "You sure about this, Em?"

Yes.

No.

God, I can't think when he's this close. His very essence

surrounds me. I can't see anything but him, and while I know I'll be another notch on his belt, I don't care. In the morning, yeah, I probably will. And when we're back at work. Definitely. But now? Hell no.

I run my fingers through his hair. "I've never been more sure of anything."

Greg rewards me with another drugging kiss, then continues down my throat and along my collarbone. He slides the spaghetti straps of my silky dress off my shoulders, revealing the soft pink demi-cup bra. He groans his appreciation and licks the exposed curve of my breasts. I arch towards him, my nipples desperate to be enclosed in his wet, hot mouth. He shifts, keeping one hand splayed across my butt, while the other one slips between us, cupping my underwear. We both moan as his knuckles brush against the damp fabric.

I dig my fingers into his biceps. If he loosens his belt and undoes his trousers, I could have him inside me in seconds.

"Patience." He nips at my bra, biting my nipple between his teeth.

"Oh, God." I arch my back and shove my hips against his waist.

"Shh …" He sucks on the silk, soothing the sting. "Or I'll have to gag you."

Moisture floods my underwear. A little kink. I like it. "Anything you say, Detective."

Greg goes rigid, and the air around us shifts. Shit. I've said the wrong thing. I rub against him, but he doesn't move. Instead, he loosens his hold on my butt and pushes my legs down. My feet hit the ground.

No, no, no.

Greg squeezes me tight and buries his face in my hair. "We can't do this."

"Yes, we can." I sound pathetic, but my body's on fire, and Greg must be too because the hard length of his erection prods my stomach.

"I'm sorry, Em. This is my fault."

"But ..."

He presses a finger to my lips. "You deserve more than a quickie against a tree." He gives me a sad smile. "And that's all I can offer you."

Greg lifts the straps back over my shoulders and smooths the fabric. He then buttons his jacket, concealing the bulge in his pants. He drops a chaste kiss on my forehead. "It's better this way."

He strides away without a backwards glance. I crumple to the ground with no thought for my dress.

What just happened? I know he was into me. There was no hiding his desire. Heat floods my cheeks. It seems I'm no match for the sexy Monica, after all.

I hang my head. Blasted champagne. I should be grateful Greg stopped things before they went too far, but I'm annoyed that he showed more restraint than me. And mortified.

I punch the ground with my fist. How am I ever going to look him in the eye again?

Chapter One

Greg

The Parramatta River gleams under the full moon, exposing discarded rubbish on its shadowy banks. Drug deals have been going down on this deserted stretch of land, and while that's not a new occurrence, three lives lost in as many days are. General duties police have already combed the area looking for clues, but my gut says they missed something. What, I don't know. But my gut's never let me down yet. Hence why I invited myself on this search, despite it being a Sunday night. Losing myself in an investigation is a much better option than staying home and dwelling on a woman I should never have touched. Or tasted.

It's been two months since Em and I kissed. Two months of pretending I don't get hard every time I see her. Two months of cold showers. A year ago, I wouldn't have hesitated to accept what she offered at Jake and Claire's engagement party. But a constant stream of women no longer has the same appeal as it once did. And I have Em to thank—or blame—for that.

I kick an empty beer can across the concrete path. The rattle is jarring in the eerie quiet, pulling me away from tempting thoughts. Now is not the time to think about how the sexy analyst's curves are the perfect fit under my palms. Against my chest. My groin. Not while I'm trawling through garbage.

"Sir, I've found a piece of clothing."

My bones creak, a reminder that I join Jake in the forty club next year. I'm surprised tendons don't snap as I turn towards the young constable. Isabelle's eyes brim with enthusiasm like this is the best night ever in her short, twenty-something years.

A garish red, white and green scarf dangles from her gloved fingers, dark crimson staining the edges. It's a thick, knitted monstrosity. It's one of those pieces of clothing you never forget once you've seen it. And it's the last thing I expected us to find.

The God-awful service station coffee burns a hole through my gut. "Stay alert, Constable. We might have another victim." Jesus, I hope not. But, homeless Jimmy, the owner of the ugly scarf, is never without it. Winter. Summer. It doesn't matter. He's never told me why the scarf is important to him, but I'm sure it's got something to do with his life before the streets.

The hairs on the back of my neck stand to attention as we approach an array of dumped shopping trolleys. Grass rustles. My heart rate kicks up a notch, and I lower my hand to my gun holster.

I gesture to Isabelle to stay to the left. I circle to the right. A soft groan emanates from the darkness.

"This is the police," I say. "Come out with your hands up."

Another groan answers.

I shine my torch towards the sound. My stomach clenches as I shove the trolleys out of the way and kneel next to the bloodied face of homeless Jimmy. He peers up at me with red-rimmed, shimmering eyes as his furry companion lands a sloppy kiss on my cheek.

Fuck. I wipe my face and ruffle the matted fur of Silas, the one-eyed mutt. The hair is coarse and sticky, but I can't get angry. Jimmy's alive, and that's a good thing. "What happened?"

His eyes bulge like he's too scared to move.

I turn to Isabelle, but she's already on the phone, calling for an ambulance. I remove my disposable gloves and slip on another pair. Run my hands along Jimmy's body, checking for any other sources of injury than the one to his head. The shattered remains of a glass bottle lay nearby. I don't need to check it out to know it's cheap whiskey. "Have you been drinking?"

He shakes his head, but his eyes can't lie.

I swallow my urge to lecture him. No point getting into it now. "Why aren't you at the shelter?"

He glances towards the mutt.

Of course. He adopted the stray nine months ago, twenty years fading from his face with the discovery of his new friend.

The distant sound of sirens draws closer. The dog curls into Jimmy's side.

This is going to be tricky.

Jimmy seems to sense his dog is in danger. Bony fingers wrap around my wrist with surprising strength. They're like blocks of ice. "Look after Silas." The words are raspy and worn.

That ain't happening.

"We'll sort him out, Jimmy," I say soothingly as I try to extricate my wrist. Jimmy hangs on for dear life. He's a strong old fella when he wants to be.

The ambos arrive with a stretcher. Jimmy trembles. "Please, Officer Anderson. Silas means everything to me."

I swallow. Jesus Christ. I know next to nothing about dogs.

The fear swirling around the old man's eyes undoes me. Pissing off my father might be the reason I joined the force, but making a difference to the most vulnerable in our society is what keeps me here. Keeps me hunting down and locking up the oxygen thieves in Sydney's west.

I pat Jimmy on the shoulder, a bit like I patted his filthy mutt. "Don't worry. I'll take care of him."

The dog perks its ears up and gifts me with another one of his slobbery kisses. At least this time it's on the hand, or more precisely, my glove, and not my cheek. The ambos check Jimmy's vitals and whisk him away, leaving me holding a ratty nylon lead and forty kilos of shaggy-coated mongrel.

The young constable does a piss-poor attempt at hiding a grin. "Do you need any help, sir?"

The dog cocks its leg, and I jump back to avoid being hit by a stream of pungent urine. "Nope. All good."

What the hell do I do now?

&a.

"What the fuck is that?"

Jake stands in the doorway of his house in a pair of homey flannel pyjamas, eyes glued to the mutt at my feet.

I attempt a smile, but it probably comes out a grimace because my senses are still reeling from the dog's farts in the car. With any luck, Claire will feel sorry for the dog and take him. "You remember Silas."

Jake cocks his head at me like I've had one too many whiskeys, but the only hangover I'm nursing is the kind you get from working late nights.

"You know ... Old Jimmy, the homeless man on Church Street. He was taken to hospital."

Jake straightens, his expression becoming serious. "What happened?"

I glance past him, knowing Claire will be sticking her nose in at any moment. "Nothing I can talk about here. I'll brief you at the station in the morning."

"So why have you got the dog?"

"I told Jimmy I'd take care of him." I suck in a deep breath. All I want is a long shower and sleep. "I didn't know where else to go."

Jake wrinkles his nose as he glances at Silas. "The RSPCA?"

"They'll be shut. Besides, I can't do that. I promised Jimmy."

Jake crosses his arms, his eyes narrowing like he knows where I'm headed. "I'm not taking him." He closes the door and lowers his voice. "The last thing we need is another dog."

"Come on. What am I going to do with him?"

"You've got a house. A fenced yard. I'll give you some dog food. You'll be fine."

The door swings open and Claire peers out dressed in the fluffiest white robe on this side of the Antarctic. Her gaze drops to the mutt, and a one-hundred-megawatt smile beams on her face. "Oh, my. Who is this gorgeous creature?"

Jake and I exchange a look. *Is she blind?*

I pull on the lead to stop Silas from jumping up on her. "He belongs to a homeless man."

"Oh, Greg. You're such a good person for taking him in."

"No, I …"

"A dog is just what you need." Claire pats me on the forearm like I'm five years old. "It will help you find yourself a nice girl to settle down with."

Ouch. Claire sounds like someone's mother. I'd feel sorry for Jake, except he walks around looking like every day is Christmas now—and if anyone deserves happiness, it's him.

"Ah, thanks, Claire." I clear my throat. "But all the good women have partners. Now"—I give her a wink—"if you ever get sick of Jake, then maybe I'd reconsider my bachelor status."

An adorable blush creeps up her neck. "Very funny."

Jake pulls her into his arms. "Bugger off and find your own woman."

The mutt nuzzles my leg. "What do I do about the dog?"

"I can give you some of Ruby's food to tide you over." Claire snuggles into Jake's side.

"Thanks." I sigh as Claire and Jake share one of those annoying couple looks. Seems like I'm not getting rid of Jimmy's fleabag any time soon. "That'd be great."

Claire disappears inside. Jake grins, obviously enjoying my predicament. Prick. There's got to be someone who can help me.

Flirty red curls and a mouth designed for kissing spring to mind. She's the last person I should approach, but Jake said to find my own woman. "Em's a farm girl. She must know about dogs."

Jake's grin vanishes and the vein at his temple pulses. "That's not a good idea."

"I'd only be asking for help with Silas." It's my turn to grin. There's nothing like pissing off Jake to distract me from the fatigue headache looming behind my eyes. "Not getting her naked."

"Don't bullshit me." Jake's jaw stiffens. "I've seen how you ogle her when you think no one's watching. She's too young for you."

"She's only a few years younger than Claire."

The pulsing vein at Jake's temple kicks up a notch. Shit. I might have pushed him too far. He won't do me any favours if he blows a gasket.

"Alright, alright." I throw my hands in the air. "It's not smart to fool around with colleagues." I cross my fingers. The less Jake knows about what went down at his engagement party, the better.

Jake regards me with that steadfast glare he gives criminals in the interrogation room. It's chilling, even for me, and I'm his best mate.

He nods. "I hope you mean it, Greg. Messing with Emily could backfire. You can't afford another mark on your record."

I give him a tight nod. He doesn't need to remind me of my fuck ups. "I know. And that's why I'll keep my hands to myself. I am capable of self-control."

Jake's expression says he's unconvinced, but he doesn't call bullshit.

I rock on my heels and focus on the charcoal-grey tiles of the patio while we wait for Claire—one of many improvements Jake's made to the house since he moved in with her. It's clear he would have my balls if he found out I've already sampled Em. Luckily, there's no risk of that happening because Em's been the consummate professional, pretending nothing happened. The trouble is, I'm not sure I want to keep pretending. And that's a problem. A fucking big one.

Chapter Two

Emily

I push back from the computer screen and stretch my arms in front of me. Roll my shoulders. Wiggle my bare feet. It's only six am, and I've been pouring through crime stats for the last hour. I like to get in ahead of the day shift. That way, I have time to analyse the data and give a detailed report at the morning briefing. I learnt early on that Inspector Matthews has a low tolerance for latecomers or incomplete analysis. Disappointing him means disappointing my boss, Sergeant Jacobs. The high opinion of both of them is critical for a good performance review.

A few heads bob above the grey partitions of the open-plan office area. Soon it will be teeming with people. I smother a yawn and rub my eyes. Looks like I need another pot of tea to wake myself up. I lock my computer and slip my patent leather court shoes on. They seemed comfortable in the shop but pinch my toes to the point of numbness. I've persevered, hoping to wear them in, but it's not looking promising.

My tailored navy skirt limits my stride as I walk down the station corridor, the two-inch heels clicking along the tiles. Having lived in jeans all my life, wearing skirts and blouses—

not to mention toe-crushing shoes—to work takes some getting used to.

I feel like a different person.

Who am I kidding? I am a different person. Thanks to a manager at my last placement.

He told me I needed to dress the part to get ahead. And act more feminine. Jerk. When I complained to my boss, she advised me to ignore him, but she also suggested I consider replacing my faded jeans and Doc Martens with more businesslike attire if I wanted to be taken seriously. And I do.

After acing my psychology degree, where I majored in criminology, I had dreams of joining the NSW Police Force, but they rejected my application. Twice. The first time, I underestimated the level of fitness needed to pass the physical. On my second attempt, the psychometric test let me down. I was told I had impulse control issues, which is ridiculous. How the results gave that conclusion is beyond me. I squash the memories of scaling Greg at the party two months ago. Alcohol was to blame for that indiscretion.

The academy advised me to take some time to reassess my goals, which is how I ended up as an intelligence analyst at NSW Police. I figure a few years proving I'm capable with the drug squad and regaining my confidence, and then I'll reapply. Next time, I'll whip both the physical and psych testing.

Sergeant Seymour saunters towards me, a cup of coffee in his hand, his beady grey eyes zeroing in on my chest. I have little to do with him, and I prefer it that way. I always feel like sandflies are feasting on my skin when I'm near him. And even though we're inside a police station, being this close is unsettling.

"Emily." He stops, and there it is, the creepy smile that has you wishing for a hot shower. Good manners have me slowing my pace.

"Morning, Tom."

He hitches his utility belt and licks his lips.

Oh God. He's so repulsive. He's the reason Claire was thrown in jail after being caught with drugs at her office last year. It's a long story. Obviously, she wasn't guilty, but Seymour got a kick out of locking up Inspector Matthews' girlfriend. He seems to hate the drug squad. I have no idea why.

I brush past, a sickly metallic odour nearly gagging me. What an awful cologne, or deodorant, or whatever it is he's wearing. At least I don't have to deal with him on a daily basis. Otherwise, I might give in to the desire to kick his arse, and that would hardly be conducive to the cool, calm and professional image I'm trying to convey.

The lunch room is empty except for two round tables, chairs and the kitchenette. The aroma of coffee fills the air, but that's not my caffeine of choice. I scoop tea leaves into the small pot I brought from home when I first started at the station and fill it with boiling water.

Greg shuffles in a few minutes later, his usual mask of cocky playfulness absent. Tie askew, hair ruffled, he looks like he climbed out of bed after a night of steamy sex. My chest tightens. I remind myself to be grateful he came to his senses when we nearly hooked up. After all, he goes through women with the same frequency other people go through tissues.

I pour myself a cup of tea and take a sip to wet my dry throat. "Big night?"

He glances down at me, his pupils widening ever so slightly. My breath hitches the way it always does, and the tension clogs my lungs, making it impossible to draw in much-needed oxygen. But I school my features into a pleasant mask.

Greg scrubs his face. "You could say that."

He stands next to me and slips a pod into the coffee machine. There's no ignoring the raw power beneath his dark-grey suit or how tiny he makes me feel, the top of my head barely reaching his breastbone. His woodsy cologne tickles my nose. Fresh. Virile. Expensive. Why does he have to smell so good?

I sip my tea and lounge against the counter. My brain is screaming at me to run away from temptation, but it's hard to ignore the way my body perks up at his nearness. I just feel so … alive.

"Maybe you should keep your extracurricular activities to the weekend?" I bite back a curse the moment the words are out.

He stops pouring his coffee, his jaw tightening. "Does it bother you thinking I was out with another woman?"

"Nope." I give him my best haughty glare. "I have standards."

He surprises me by tucking a wayward curl behind my ear. "They seemed to be missing at Jake and Claire's engagement party."

My fingers clench around the teacup. I can't believe he went there. We never mention that night. It's an unspoken rule. He must be even more exhausted than he looks. "We all make mistakes."

Greg flinches. "Yes. And you can do a lot better than the likes of me." He grabs his coffee and slumps into a chair at the nearest table. "I was out in the field till late. Old Jimmy was attacked."

"Oh no." Now I feel like a shrew for jumping to the wrong conclusions. I slide in next to him. "Is he okay?"

Greg's shoulders sag, giving me a glimpse into his inner turmoil. "He has a head injury. They've put him in an induced coma."

"I'm so sorry." My fingers itch with the sudden urge to hug him, which would be asking for trouble, so I pat his shoulder instead. I know how much he cares about the homeless, especially Jimmy. What I don't know is why.

He covers my hand with his. For a tiny moment, I allow myself to imagine his touch means more than it does. Which is stupid. He's a distraction I can't afford if I'm going to excel in this job.

"Save your concern for the arseholes who did it." Greg scowls. "When I find the bastards—"

"Good morning." Inspector Matthews strolls into the lunchroom, his gaze narrowing on where I'm touching Greg. Even though it's innocent, I snatch my hand away.

"There's nothing good about it," says Greg. "Three hours' sleep is bullshit."

"Your new bedfellow keep you awake?"

I wrap my arms around my waist. Greg said he was working last night. Did he lie?

Greg gives him the bird.

Inspector Matthews glances at me, then back at Greg, his expression hardening. Uh oh.

"I'm going to let that go, *Sergeant,* since I know you've had a tough night." His irises turn the deepest blue grey and the vein at his temple pulses.

I will myself into the floor. The inspector is a stickler for formality. Greg making a lewd gesture at him in front of a lowly intelligence analyst like me is a huge no-no.

"Sorry, Jake." Greg shakes his head. "It's just, I don't know what to do about the mutt. He kept me up all night whining and barking at God knows what."

Tension buzzes between them. I paste on a big smile, hoping to defuse the situation. "What dog?"

"Old Jimmy's dog, Silas. He's very fond of it." Greg rests his elbows on the table, and there's a weariness to the action that reignites my urge to hug him. "God knows why. It's ugly as sin and smells worse than a men's urinal."

I snort laugh and cover my face. "It can't be that bad."

"Trust me, Em. It is."

Inspector Matthews still looks like a lemon has wedged itself in his mouth, but his lips twitch, so I figure he must agree with Greg's assessment of the poor dog.

"I'm sure a good bath would fix him," I suggest.

Greg gulps his coffee. "Well, it'll have to wait 'til the weekend when I've got time to find someone to do it."

"I could help." *What am I thinking?* I need to keep my distance from this man. Maintain a professional relationship and control my wayward hormones. But the thought of a dog in need gets the better of me.

Inspector Matthews clears his throat. Greg meets his gaze, and just like that, the air in the room vanishes in a whoosh, like the waves rushing out from the beach, pulling unsuspecting grains of sand with it. I don't know what's going on between the two men, but as my dad always says, never get between two bulls. Or a rip tide and the shore.

I scrape my chair back, eager to escape. Greg breaks the stand-off with a lopsided grin and squeezes my fingers. "Thanks, Em. That'd be great. Would tomorrow after work be okay?"

"Sure," I squeak out. His grip is impersonal, but electricity still zips up my arm and settles between my legs as I get to my feet.

Inspector Matthews gives me a smile that doesn't reach his eyes. "Have you got your reports ready for the intel briefing this morning, Emily?"

My knees shake, and not for a sexy reason. I might be friends with his fiancé, but the inspector still scares the bejesus out of me. "Almost, sir."

His eyebrow lifts.

My face burns as I lower my gaze. "I'll get right on it."

I flee the room. This infatuation has to stop. Inspector Matthews isn't stupid. He picked up on the vibes between me and Greg. If I want to advance in my career, I need to act the part, not just dress for it. Which means no more sexy thoughts about the rakish detective.

Chapter Three

Emily

Greg lives in the exclusive North Shore suburb of Cammeray. It's a world away from Parramatta. I was surprised when he gave me the address. I imagined him living in a high-rise unit, but his home is a quaint Federation house with cream brick walls and a wrought-iron fence. Police sergeants get paid well, but a property of this calibre requires serious money. I feel a little underdressed in my old jeans and light grey T-shirt.

I knock, every nerve ending alive. I hope I'm not making a big mistake helping him with the dog. My brain short-circuits whenever he's near, and I can't afford to do something stupid, like throw myself at him. He rejected me once, which, I have to keep reminding myself, is a good thing. Only a fool would go there again. And I'm no fool. Not anymore.

The door swings open, and a scruffy blur leaps up, rough paws landing on my thighs and nearly pushing me over.

"Silas, no." Greg pulls on the dog's collar, almost choking the poor thing as he wrenches him away. I dust myself off.

Silas wriggles from Greg's grasp and runs back the way he came. Greg stumbles. "Fucking dog will be the death of me."

I suppress a giggle. Greg's wavy hair sticks up at all angles like he's been stabbing it with his fingers.

"Quick, come inside. The bastard's probably ripping up the lounge."

Greg darts through the door. I follow, warmth filling my chest. It's quite gratifying to see the unflappable cop messed up by one innocent animal.

A low growl leads me into the kitchen. Like my flat, the living area is open plan, but unlike my place, it's spacious. My unit would fit inside three times over. Silas' front feet are on the white marble bench top, a small piece of bread hanging from his mouth. His one eye blinks at Greg. Greg warned me about Silas' missing eye, not that he needed to. Some people might be uncomfortable, but all I see is an adorable, happy dog.

Greg glares at Silas, hands on hips like he's ready to tear the poor animal limb from limb. "That was my dinner, you stupid mutt."

"Oh, no." This is one reason my mum always told us never to leave food on the edge of a bench. Dogs can be resourceful devils. I pad towards Silas. "What was it?"

"A hamburger."

I squat and prise Silas' jaws open, but his mouth is empty. "Did it have onion?"

Greg shakes his head. "Nah. I'd buttered the bun and put the mince patty on it when I heard the knock on the door. Why?"

I tickle Silas behind the ear and straighten. "It's toxic to dogs."

Silas licks his lips and saunters to a plastic container on the floor where he laps up water, while Greg leans against the counter. "This was a mistake."

His black T-shirt stretches across his chest, reminding me how firm the muscles felt beneath my fingers the night we almost hooked up. I swallow, heat prickling my skin. I've been here five minutes and I'm already too aware of him. Of the fact we're alone. In his house. Just the two of us. And one dog.

Silas pads over and presses his nose against Greg's leg.

My heart melts at the affection and trust. "Aww. He's a sweetie."

"He's filthy." Greg straightens and runs his hands up and down his jeans. "Thanks for offering to help. I'd understand if you'd rather not, given …"

Heat fills my face. I don't want to talk about that night ever again. Nope. Never. It's bad enough I think about it. Constantly. "That's okay. I love dogs. I'm here for Silas."

"Gotcha." He clears his throat. "Even so, thank you."

The temperature in the room seems to have simultaneously gone up and plummeted twenty degrees, tension stretching between us like a living creature. Helping him out is going to be so much harder than I thought.

I hold up a cotton tote bag. "I brought a few things to help with his bath."

"Excellent." The tension snaps, and Greg's eyes light up. "He'll never fit in the laundry tub, and there's no way I'm putting him in the ensuite spa. The tub in the main bathroom should be big enough. Guess I can disinfect it afterwards."

I smile as Greg's nose scrunches up. His kitchen is spotless, and the timber floorboards are shinier than a new car. Given his apparent attention to cleanliness and order, he's doing well to accept an unwashed street dog in his house.

Greg carries a wriggling Silas into the bathroom and dumps him into a pristine free-standing tub that's more than big enough for two people, let alone one dog. "Thanks again for doing this. Call me when you're finished and I'll get him out for you." He backs away, dusting his hands as if Silas has given him an infectious disease.

Silas looks up at me with a soulful eye like he knows what's about to happen. I remove the frayed collar from around his neck, slip the hose I brought onto the tap and test the water. The bathroom is floor-to-ceiling white marble, with a rectangular skylight making the space even lighter. It seems a crime to sully the room with grime, but I have no choice. Silas needs to be cleaned up, and Greg's clearly not up to the challenge. I hadn't realised how prissy he is when it comes to germs.

For a dog who's spent God knows how long on the street, Silas surprises me by behaving like a prize poodle and the wash is over in no time. His coat, a muddy brown before the bath, is a mottled grey and white by the end. I'd guess there's a generous dose of Irish wolfhound in him.

"Who's a good boy?" I rub Silas' ears and give his snout a quick peck, lifting him out of the tub. I don't need a man to help me. Silas is no heavier than a bale of hay. I clip on a new collar I bought at the pet shop. It was too darn cute to leave behind. And just as well. There's no way I could put the old one back on Silas now he's all cleaned up.

Silas scampers off, and I'm left with a warm fuzziness spreading through my chest, which is not all because of the dog's cuteness. The sandalwood and spice of Greg's cologne permeates the bathroom, making my skin all hot and tingly. I ignore the inappropriate reaction, fold the wet towel over the side of the bath, and walk down the hallway to the kitchen.

Greg's denim-clad bum pokes out, his upper body buried in a cupboard as he mutters to himself. My fingers itch, remembering how firm those muscles are. I clear my throat.

He bumps his head and twists around. "Fuck."

"Sorry. I didn't mean to startle you."

"No problem." His gaze dips to my breasts, then it slowly lifts, like his eyes are stuck in something sticky.

Heat surges through me. I'm torn between punching him in the nose for his rudeness and swooning like a heroine in a romance book. I look down. Oh. Washing Silas has soaked the front of my shirt, the lace of my apricot bra visible, together with my erect nipples. I cross my arms.

Greg gives me a sheepish smile. "Sorry. I'll get you something to change into."

He brushes past me and strides down the hall. When he returns, he throws a T-shirt at me. "It'll be way too big, but at least it's dry."

I catch the shirt. "Is it clean?"

He laughs. "Of course. I'm only dirty on the inside."

There's a boyish charm about him I can't help but respond to despite his reputation. And his rejection. "I'll go change."

Onion and garlic greet me as enthusiastically as the dog's wagging tail when I return to the kitchen. But Greg's face isn't so welcoming.

He points to Silas. "What's that around his neck?"

"It's a new collar."

"It's bright purple." Greg spits the words out like purple and sewerage are interchangeable.

I smother a smile. "So?"

He shakes his head and mutters, "Women."

"Men …" I start to reply, but my growling stomach drowns out the words. Even Silas cocks his head at me.

My cheeks burn. "Sorry. I haven't eaten since breakfast."

"You should have said something." Greg returns to the stove and starts stirring a large pot with a wooden spoon. "Would you like to stay and have dinner with me?"

"I thought Silas ate the food?"

"He did. So, I'm making a creamy vegetarian fettuccine instead." He glares at Silas, who sits nearby, his attention riveted on Greg and the stove. "Since it's got no meat in it, I'm hoping it will be of no interest to thieving dogs."

The traitorous tingle running through my body wants to say yes. But I can't risk my career by getting too close to Greg and doing something I'll regret. "Thanks, but I'll take a raincheck."

He lowers his head and gives me the saddest puppy dog eyes. "You sure I can't tempt you? For Silas' sake?"

It's surprising he's so persistent, given how we've been avoiding each other for the last two months. Is there a catch? Or am I being overly paranoid? Silas doesn't make it easy, scampering across to nudge me like he knows I'm about to leave. He sits to attention, his one brown eye mirroring Greg's.

Damn their cuteness. It's only dinner. No booze. It's not like it's a date or anything. I can control myself despite what that stupid psych test said about my so-called impulsive tendencies. "Okay."

❧

"Can I help you with anything?"

Greg rinses the pasta and glances over his shoulder. "You could open a bottle of wine? A Verdelho will bring out the flavours in the sauce."

Has he forgotten what happened the last time we drank together? "I'm not sure that's a good idea."

"Worried you won't be able to keep your hands off me?"

He's spot on, but there's no way I'm admitting it. "Absolutely not."

He winks and turns away, tossing the pasta in the colander, his wrist flicking with ease.

I can't ignore the challenge in his eyes. "Alright. But only one glass. A small one. I have to drive." I'll stay under the limit, so I'll still be in control.

Like the bathroom, marble bench tops and sleek white cabinetry complete the kitchen. The difference here is the shiny, state-of-the-art appliances. A black leather sofa and a massive sixty-inch screen dominate the combined lounge/dining room, but I barely notice them as I look through the glass sliding door to the small, manicured back-yard and stunning harbour view.

How does he afford this on a sergeant's salary? I'm itching to ask, but it's none of my business.

Greg pulls a bottle of wine out of the fridge. I open it and fill two glasses. "How long have you lived here?"

"About three years."

He's been working in Parramatta longer. I thought he might have moved closer to the station. "It's quite a distance from work."

"I prefer to be near the city." He shrugs. "That's where the action is on the weekends."

Of course. My stomach drops. It'd be an all-you-can-eat buffet for someone like Greg.

We sit at the round teak kitchen table, Silas tracking our every move.

Greg places tongs next to the bowl of fettuccine. "Help yourself."

I transfer pasta onto my plate and follow it up with a generous sprinkling of parmesan cheese. The moment I take the first mouthful, I know I'm in trouble. Flavours explode across my tongue. This man can cook even better than my mum, and that's saying something.

"It's amazing."

Greg grins. "You like?"

"Like? No. I love. What brand did you use?"

"Brand?"

"Yeah, the sauce."

Greg looks insulted. "I don't buy bottles. It's a special recipe, made from scratch."

I drop my fork. "No way."

He crosses his arms. "Are you saying I can't cook because I'm a bloke?"

"No. Not at all." Well, maybe a bit.

"I think you're telling fibs, Miss Saunders, but I'll let you off." He picks up his glass and points it at Silas. "Since I'm giving you a restaurant-worthy meal, any chance you can take this monster home with you?"

"Nice try, Sergeant Anderson." I laugh. "Even if I wanted to, I can't. I only rent. No dogs allowed."

He strokes his chin. "You could claim it's an assistance dog."

"Are you telling me to break the law?"

"Not at all. You'd be assisting me if you took the dog."

I scrunch up my eyes and groan. "I hope you don't use that sort of logic to solve crimes."

"Whatever gets the job done." He takes a long sip of his wine and smacks his lips.

The pasta congeals into a heavy mass in my stomach. What does Greg mean by that?

Greg must see the shock on my face because he rests his hand on mine. "I'm joking. I'd never break the law, Em, but there's a shitload of grey in the real world that's had me skirting close to the edges from time to time. I'm careful not to cross it." His expression hardens. "The last thing any cop wants is the pricks from internal affairs getting up in their business."

The venom in his tone has me wondering if he's ever been investigated. 'Internal affairs', or the 'Professional Standards Command' as they're officially known, is whispered in hushed tones at the station or with language colourful enough to make a sailor blush. Cops hate them. Fear them.

Silas nudges my knee. I welcome the distraction and rub his head. He's a sweet boy. As clueless as Greg seems about dogs, I'm confident Silas is safe. However, I won't be if I don't leave now.

I rise to my feet. "It's been a lovely meal. Thank you. But I'd better get going."

Greg winks. "We could finish that bottle of wine together?"

"That's not a good idea." I back away. "I have no desire for a repeat of what happened at Inspector Matthews' engagement party." A lie, of course, but I can't admit the truth. That I like him more than I should. While there are no rules against relationships at the station, my boss has made her disdain for them very clear. I don't want to get on her bad side. No man is worth ruining my career over, no matter how mind blowing the sex might be.

I grab my bag and rush to the door before I succumb to that sinful baritone voice.

Chapter Four

Greg

"Get your dog off me, Dylan, or I swear I'll do something we'll both regret."

I shoo Milo, Dylan's drug sniffer dog, away from my trousers. The stupid mutt must smell Silas on me. Or maybe it's the blood from the scratches Silas gouged across my shins that's attracting him?

"Sorry, sir. I don't know what came over him." Dylan yanks on Milo's lead and ties him to the table.

I stab the button on the espresso machine and pour a coffee. It's not Dylan's fault I've got the worst case of blue balls. That's the real reason I'm in a foul mood. Seeing Em last night with those delicious nipples poking through her wet T-shirt, I nearly blew my load on the spot. Which is why I should heed Jake's warning and stay away from her. She's like sunshine on the beach while I'm washed-up detritus on the sand. I shake my head. That's a big fucking word for me after the night of tossing and turning I've had.

"Sounds like you didn't sleep very well again last night, Sergeant." Jake struts in with a massive I-get-laid-every-night grin on his ugly mug.

"No. I didn't."

I grind my teeth. I almost prefer Jake the way he was before he met Claire. Grumpy, boring. A pain in the arse. Now he's a royal, smiling pain in the arse. "That crazy dog of Jimmy's wouldn't stop whining until I let him into the bedroom. Then he snored worse than you when we're on a stakeout. And smelt just as bad."

"Did Emily help you with the dog?" Jake's voice drops to a soft growl, and the warning is obvious.

"Yeah. She washed him for me and left." A little lie. I seem to be telling a lot of them lately. Jake doesn't need to know she had dinner with me. That I deliberately cooked a second meal that was vegetarian to entice her to stay longer. She doesn't make a big deal about being vego, but I notice. I notice a lot of things about Emily Saunders.

I flop down at the table and change the subject before Jake asks more questions. "So, onto police matters. The hospital says Jimmy's stable, but they've got him in an induced coma until the swelling on his brain eases."

"Don't worry." Jake slides in next to me. "We'll catch the cowards who beat him up."

Dylan clears his throat, his eyes wide like saucers. "*You're* looking after Jimmy's dog?"

I straighten in my chair and pin him with a glare. "Yeah. You got a problem with that, *Constable*?"

"No, sir." Dylan swallows and shakes his head. "Just …" He glances at Milo and lowers his voice. "I didn't think you liked dogs."

I laugh. Dylan is besotted with his canine and thinks anyone who doesn't fuss over it like it's a four-legged, hairy child must be a dog hater.

"It's not that I don't like them. I don't have time for them." Not to mention, when my father walked out on us, his girlfriend left the gate open and my dog, Buster, escaped. When I finally found him, he was dead. A homeless bloke I'd seen my old man abusing for daring to pollute the streets of our 'prestigious' suburb had pulled Buster to the side of the road after he'd been hit by a car. His actions saved Buster's body from being trampled and showed a homeless stranger cared more than my own flesh and blood.

Tears prick my eyes at the memories, and I blink them away. It forever changed my view about what constitutes good and bad people. I never forgave my old man, and I swore I'd never get another dog. Never get attached again. To anyone. Human or animal. It only ends in heartbreak.

Jake gives me a look like he's going to call bullshit on me, but he holds his tongue. This is the problem with having a boss who's also your best mate. He knows me too well. There's no way I'm continuing this conversation.

"Alright, gentlemen." I scrape my chair back. "I'm heading out to the park to see if any of the other homeless saw or heard anything the night Jimmy was bashed."

"Isn't that for the criminal detectives?" Jake regards me over the rim of his coffee cup.

My jaw clenches. Jesus, he'd better not pull rank on me. I need to be a part of this investigation. Need to bring Jimmy's abusers to justice. "I've spoken with Inspector Olsen. He was okay with me checking it out."

"And *your* boss. What did he say?" Jake's voice is soft, but there's fire behind it, waiting to be released on my sorry arse.

Again, this is the problem with being best mates. I tend to forget my place. "Sorry, sir. I was going to ask you."

Jake's lips press into a familiar thin line. "I know you're worried about Jimmy, so I'll let it go." He gestures to Dylan. "Take Constable Longhurst with you."

Dylan and the chocolate labrador at his feet both sit taller.

I shake my head. "This isn't a job for a drug sniffer dog."

"No. But he could do with the experience."

I groan. Just what I need. A wet-behind-the-ears constable and his annoying dog traipsing after me.

Dylan's head bobs up and down. "I can leave Milo here, sir, if he's not needed."

Jake's eyes bulge. I turn away so he doesn't see the grin on my face. It's obvious what he's up to. He wants Dylan *and* the dog out of his hair. It's the least I can do for him.

"Nah." I wave at Milo. "Bring him along."

I rip off my tie and throw it on the driver's seat. Leave the coat behind. A casual look is best when visiting the homeless. I saunter across the park, burnt grass and thirsty trees a reminder of how hot and dry the summer was. Even now, in the middle of autumn, the days are unseasonably warm. That's why we drove instead of walking the short distance.

Milo strains at the lead and makes a bee-line for Ian, one of the long-term homeless. Dylan dangles behind him. The only reason the stupid dog hasn't been sacked is he's the best we've ever seen at sniffing out drugs, no matter how well hidden they are. He plops his butt down at Ian's feet.

Interesting.

Ian's always come across as clean. No alcohol. No drugs. Not even cigarettes. He found himself on the streets ten years ago after getting cancer and losing his job. The good news is he beat cancer. The bad news is he's forgotten how to function in society.

"What's the meaning of this, officers?"

"You tell us." I gesture towards Milo, drool dripping off his jowls, his gaze trained on Ian.

"Dogs like me," he says with pride.

"Sure." I nod. "Then you won't mind if we search your bag?"

"Knock yourself out."

I slip on a pair of gloves and squat. Thank fuck, I didn't

wear my best trousers. I don't want to think about what's mixed in with the dirt and sparse clumps of grass.

A putrid stench smacks me in the face as I unzip the bag. It's almost as bad as Silas' farts. Almost. But Ian has nothing to hide. I only find dirty tracksuit pants, a shirt and a few toiletries. I straighten, slip off the gloves and dispose of them into a plastic bag.

Milo looks on, his eyes bright and totally focused on Ian. That's when I notice. Ian's shirt is clean. Like brand new, clean. It's still got creases in it from being in a packet.

"Where'd you get the clothes?"

He crosses his arms. "They were a gift."

"Really?"

"Yeah. Really." He gives me his toothless smile. "I'm not too proud, especially when the offer's being made by a smokin' hot chick."

Odd. "Can you describe her?"

His grin widens. "Tall, blonde hair, big tits."

I scowl at him. "I hope you treated her with respect."

"Of course. I'm not an animal." He smooths his hands down his shirt. "Doesn't mean I couldn't appreciate how sexy she was." He picks at his teeth, extracting God knows what and wipes it on his clean trousers.

"Was there anyone else with her?"

"Yeah. There was some burly bloke, but she did all the talkin'." He picks at his teeth again, this time flicking whatever he finds onto the ground.

I take an involuntary step backwards. "So, she gave you new clothes. Just like that."

"Yep."

"When?"

"A few days ago. Before we went to the church for dinner. Jimmy was preening the whole time." His grin fades. "I heard what happened. Is he gonna be okay?"

"He's stable for now." But a long way from being out of

danger. I drop to my haunches so I'm not lording it over him. "When did you last see Jimmy?"

"Whoa!" Ian's hands shoot up. "I had nothin' to do with it."

"I'm not saying you did. But it's odd that he strayed away from the park. He knows there's safety in numbers."

Ian stares at the ground.

I wait. People always fill the spaces in the silence.

Milo breaks his sit and sniffs the grass nearby, his furry tail whipping back and forwards.

Ian tracks the movements. His head jerks up. "What about Silas? It'd gut Jimmy if anything happened to his dog."

"He's safe."

Ian continues staring at Milo, his throat working. "Jimmy got spooked around eight that night."

"Spooked?"

"Yeah. Some teens wandered through, kicking our stuff, shouting a lot of bullshit. They were off their faces. I kept my head down, but Jimmy gave them a mouthful when they had a go at Silas."

My fingers clench. "What did they do?"

"Nothin'." He glances at Dylan and Milo, then back to me. "Just accused Jimmy of doing unnatural things with his dog. If you get my drift."

Dylan's face turns bright red as he pats Milo's head. I take a deep breath. Release it. Even Ian recognises the kid is just that. A kid. I've been mentoring Dylan for a year now, but I'm still not convinced he's got what it takes to make it on the force.

"What did Jimmy do?"

"He grabbed his stuff and stormed off with Silas."

We talk for a few more minutes about the other people who were in the park at the time. When it becomes obvious Ian has no further information, I give him a couple of chocolate bars and a bottle of water and return to the car.

On the drive to the station, Ian's new clothes nag at me like they mean something. I'm familiar with all the volunteers who help with the homeless. None of them are big busted or what I'd call hot.

Milo pants the entire way. The noise carries through from the back of the van. Despite his uncanny ability to sniff out drugs, I still question for the hundredth time how he ever graduated dog sniffer training. He's the most annoying dog I've ever encountered. Except for Silas.

Fuck.

Silas.

I locked him in the laundry. Didn't I? I chuck a U-turn at the next intersection and slam my foot on the accelerator.

Dylan screeches, drowning out the squeal of the tyres. "What are you doing?"

I risk a glance at him. Any whiter and he'd be a corpse. "Silas might be loose in the house."

Dylan stares at me like I've lost my mind, but he has no idea just how destructive that dog can be. I've already had the legs of two chairs chewed and one of my favourite pairs of shoes ripped to shreds.

"We're making a detour."

Home is thirty minutes away outside peak hour. I join the motorway and hit the accelerator. Luckily, there are no uniformed cops around, except for the white-knuckled kid beside me.

"Ah, sir, the speed limit is one hundred." Dylan's voice comes out all scratchy.

"Yep. I know." I switch on the lights and siren.

He wisely says no more. My stomach churns. The more I think about it, the more I'm certain I didn't close the laundry door properly. This is what I get for fixating on one sexy little redhead.

The moment we reach my house, I turn off the ignition and charge inside, and that's when the world morphs into one of those weird slo-mo videos. My brain takes a few seconds to catch up with my eyes … to the crime scene in front of me. The insides of my brand new, ten-thousand-dollar soft leather sofa are strewn from one end of the lounge room to the other. Metal springs lay exposed like bones picked clean by a ravenous predator.

But the carnage doesn't end there. Pottery pieces, clumps of dirt and pulverised leaf matter—the remains of a large potted lily—litter one end of the room. It's as if some weirdo with an axe to grind has broken into my house. But I already know who the culprit is.

I stomp into the kitchen, ready to rip the dog a new one and stop. Bloody paw prints stain the white tiles. Silas gazes up at me, a paw in his mouth.

The fire burning my face extinguishes. I'm the worst human ever.

Dylan scampers in behind me. He's smart enough to keep his trap shut. I feel bad enough as it is without having some kid barely out of the academy telling me I screwed up. I'm not capable of speech right now. Memories of Buster lying on the side of the road, his black fur matted with blood, blur my vision.

I squat next to Silas. He lets me hold his paw, total trust in his big brown eye. I smile to let him know it'll be alright. And it will be. The bleeding has stopped, and I've seen plenty of trauma cases to know it's only a flesh wound. Still, I'll feel better if a professional confirms it.

I glance at Dylan, who's keeping his distance. "Can you google the number for a local vet?"

He takes his mobile out of his pocket. "Yes, sir."

I ruffle Silas' head, and he rewards me with what Em would call a kiss, but I call a life-threatening infection waiting to happen. But I'll let him have it. His hair is soft against my fingers. Much more pleasant since Em bathed him. Although, the purple collar will take some getting used to. I shake my head. It was a mistake to promise Jimmy I'd care for his dog. I'm not cut out for looking after another living creature. Work and fucking are the only things I'm good at.

Chapter Five

Emily

After spending the last two months trying to forget our near-hook-up, I can't believe I'm on the doorstep of Greg's house for the second time in only a few days. He asked me if I could finish work early, something I wouldn't normally do, but there was a panicky tone to his text. A Silas emergency, he called it.

Like me, Greg has swapped his crisp suit for faded jeans and a T-shirt, and he's wearing the same dazed expression he wore the first time I visited. "Thanks for coming."

"No problem. I'm happy to help."

He gestures inside, and I follow him. Silas barrels towards me like a torpedo, making me relieved I swung by my flat and changed into jeans.

Before he can bowl me over, I squat and hold my hand out. "Hey, gorgeous." He leans into me, and I rub his fur. It's so silky now he's all cleaned up. He seems healthy and happy, except for a bright orange bandage on his paw. "What happened?"

Greg sweeps his arm towards the lounge room.

Oh. My. God!

Silas wags his tail as if to say, *pretty awesome, isn't it?* It's as if he knew exactly which furniture to target to inflict maximum damage. The couch had designer label written all over it when I glimpsed it earlier in the week, and even the shattered pot looks like it cost upwards of four figures. I'm surprised, and relieved, that Silas is still breathing.

"I don't know what to say, Greg."

My estimation of him rises tenfold. Many men would have lost their cool and taken it out on the dog. But Silas shows no fear as he nuzzles Greg's leg.

Greg shakes his head. "It's my fault."

"I don't see how. Obviously, Silas isn't used to being inside."

Greg drops his chin, looking like a lost little boy in desperate need of a hug. My fingers itch to soothe him. "I don't know what I'm doing here. I'm not fit to look after a dog."

I tiptoe through the mess. "On the contrary, I think you're doing a wonderful job."

Greg's eyes widen. "Are you kidding me?"

I rest a hand on his forearm, a jolt of electricity zipping through my fingers. We both jerk back. I wipe my palms on my jeans. Ignore the chemistry buzzing between us. "You need to keep him in a safe place while you're at work. Why didn't you leave him in the backyard?"

Greg slides the back door open and beckons with his finger. The garden bed next to the side fence looks like a tornado has swept through and uprooted every plant.

"Silas did that?"

"Yep."

Silas bounces past and pounces onto the luscious lawn.

Greg curses, but he doesn't call the dog back. We both watch on as Silas sniffs around the clothesline before making a decision, cocking his leg and dousing the steel pole in pee. He finishes with a flurry of foot scraping that sends several tufts of grass into the air.

Greg sighs and scrubs his fingers through his hair. "I should take a photo of the lawn to remind me what it looks like. Crazy dog will destroy it in no time."

He's right. And he's being calm for someone who claims he's not a dog lover.

I walk into the yard and look around. "What if you put up a temporary enclosure next to the deck? It would shelter Silas from the elements but still give him access to a small amount of grass to do his business. What do you think?"

Greg hooks his fingers into the front pockets of his jeans. "It would be easier if you took him."

I shake my head. "I told you, I can't. I rent."

"You could ask for an exemption to have a dog. Extenuating circumstances."

He won't sweet-talk me into this. "You know I live in an apartment. My landlord would never agree with it."

"So, you think I should waste a day erecting an enclosure for a mutt who'll be gone soon?"

I pace out the distance to determine how much material would be needed. "I'm sure it wouldn't take more than a few hours. In fact, if we go to Bunnings now, I reckon we could have it done before dark."

Something flickers behind his eyes. Not surprise but something else. "You'd do that for me?"

Yes, I would. But I'm not admitting it. "I'd do it for Silas."

He lowers his gaze. "Of course."

Silas gives a little bark and scratches in the dirt.

Greg jabs his finger at the ground in front of him. "Silas, get back here."

The dog lifts his nose from the soil.

"Now." Greg's voice is all authority. The sort I can easily imagine him using with the criminals he deals with.

Silas turns and bounds towards Greg, his tongue lolling out happily. Greg squats and inspects his front feet. Surprisingly, the bandage is still intact. "Good boy." He ruffles Silas' fur. "The vet told me to keep his paw clean and come back tomorrow if there's any sign of infection."

The total lack of fear in Silas' eye, together with Greg's determination to keep him safe, undoes me. Greg might deny it, but there's genuine affection between him and the dog. I draw in a deep breath. This attraction is playing havoc with my brain. How do I help Greg with Silas without ending up in his bed?

Chapter Six

Greg

"What about here, Greg?"

Em taps a star post into the ground with a mallet. Her short bob of curls gleams in the sunlight, and a sheen of sweat coats her chest, the thin pink T-shirt doing nothing to hide the treasures underneath. I'm going to hell. I'm sure of it.

"Yeah," I croak. "That should be enough."

Enough grass for Silas to dig up, pee and shit on. And isn't that a bucket of cold, dirty water to my privates? Em's only here for him. I need to remember that.

"Go!" Em throws a ball, and Silas races after it. She claps her hands and jumps up and down on the spot, her chest jiggling.

Well, fuck me. Having a dog isn't all bad.

Silas returns and plops the ball at Em's feet. "Aren't you a good boy?"

Em drops to her haunches and gives him a pat and me an eyeful of her perfectly rounded arse. She turns and looks up, her brow furrowing. "How's old Jimmy going?"

The stirring in my jeans deflates, and I shake my head. "Still in a coma."

"Oh." Her eyes glisten. "That doesn't sound good."

"No, it isn't. The doctors are still waiting for the swelling on his brain to ease."

"Will he make a full recovery?"

"Possibly." I grab another post, avoiding her watery gaze. Avoiding the uncomfortable sense of failure in my gut, as if I could have prevented Jimmy's bashing. "Or he might never wake up."

"The poor man." She scratches Silas behind the ear, and he nuzzles her leg. "Does that mean Silas could be with you long term?"

"Nope. No way." Although, I'd be lying to myself if I didn't admit that despite the destruction, my home no longer feels empty with Silas running rampant in it.

"What would you do with him?"

"Take him to the RSPCA." The words taste like dirt as they leave my mouth.

Em kisses the top of Silas' head. "They might put him down."

That's my thought too, which is why I didn't take him there. The shimmer in her eyes does weird things to my insides. They're a striking blue, a rare colour for a redhead, one that's fast becoming my favourite. "It won't come to that. I promised Jimmy I'd look after his dog, and I never go back on my promises."

Em straightens and tips her head up, exposing the creamy length of her throat. "Never? That's a bold statement."

"And true." I curl my fingers into tight balls by my sides. The biggest risk to Silas is being under my care. I'd never forgive myself if anything happened to him.

"Right." While Em's tone is playful, there's a subtle accusation behind the words.

"I'm many things, but a liar isn't one of them."

Her cheeks bloom, turning the same colour red as her curls.

I stare her down. "When have I ever lied to you, Miss Saunders?"

She parts those sweet cherry lips and pulls on the bottom one with her teeth. "Umm …"

I step closer. She tips her head back further, maintaining eye contact.

"I'm waiting, Emily."

She huffs. "Sometimes not saying anything is a lie."

I uncurl my fingers. She's got me there. I respect her too much to mess with her, but the sexual tension between us is like a living creature. One that's proving impossible to ignore.

"True. But it's safer."

She draws in a deep breath, her breasts straining against the T-shirt. "You're right. Safe is better." She juts her chin out, then picks up the drill. "Come on, Mr Lazy Pants. Let's get this fence built."

Emily's attempt to defuse the tension does nothing for the half boner in my jeans because Em wielding a drill is one of the sexiest things I've ever seen. Her inner farm girl shines, revealing a confidence I don't see at the station. There, she's like a mouse, whereas here, she's in her element. All she needs is blonde hair and a pair of tiny shorts, and she'd be the spitting image of Jessica Simpson from *The Dukes of Hazzard*. But hotter.

In a couple of hours, we've fenced off a quarter of the yard. It's not pretty, but it's solid. Silas will have room to run around without risk of damaging the garden or himself. He cocks his leg against a post and grins at us.

I grab his collar, grimacing at the grime. He had a bath a few days ago. How could he be dirty already? I give him a light rub between the ears. "No pissing on my fence, you cheeky mutt."

He wriggles from my grasp and darts under the house. Shit. Was I too rough? "Silas, come here." I lower my voice. "You're not in trouble."

"I don't think he's scared." Emily squats and points. "He's digging a hole."

I peer under the floorboards. "Come on, boy. Get back here."

He ignores me, his paws scratching at the earth. The bandage is long gone. Guess I'll be making a trip to the vet tomorrow, after all.

Em sighs. "We might have to fence this off, too."

The part of me that died when Dad abandoned us springs to life when she says 'we'. I'm used to being a team at work but not at home. My mother became obsessed with yoga and all things hippy. My brother, Troy, buried himself in school, and our sister, Rachel, joined Mum in her alternative lifestyle. I learnt to rely on no one else until I teamed up with Jake at the police academy.

I'd been looking forward to watching the footy, but now I don't want to be alone. "Let me cook you dinner. It's the least I can do."

Em opens her mouth as if to say no, then closes it. "That would be nice. I'm not keen on another frozen meal tonight."

"You do that a lot?"

"Yeah. More than I should, but cooking isn't my thing, much to my mum's disgust. Eating, on the other hand ..."

I keep my gaze on her face, resisting the urge to give her curvy body a once-over. She's soft and full in all the right places. Jake would be proud of my restraint. Hell, I'm proud of it. "Food suits you."

Her eyes widen.

Fuck. Was that insulting? "I mean, you ... you look good."

"Oh, okay. Thank you." Her shoulders straighten, stretching the fabric of her T-shirt enough to have my dick stirring again. "I'll go wash up."

Silas scampers after her, no doubt hoping for a treat. That makes two of us.

As the shadows lengthen and the air cools, Em's nipples put on quite a show through the thin material of her shirt as we eat our dinner on the back deck. But when I see the goose-bumps along her arms, the gentleman in me wins out. Who knew I could be chivalrous? And who knew doing the right thing could be so rewarding? Turns out, Em looks even more fuckable wrapped in one of my jumpers.

She finishes the last of the pizza and takes a swig of beer. For a tiny woman, she has quite the appetite. And as I learnt during our almost hook-up, that appetite definitely extends to the bedroom … or, in our case, the garden. I adjust myself. Thank Christ she can't see under the table. She'd think sex is all that's on my mind. Which … yeah, maybe that's not far from the truth.

"I'll never be able to eat normal pizza again." Em pats her stomach. "That was incredible, Greg. Have you got Italian blood in you?"

"Not that I know of. But you can thank my mum. She said no son of hers would be useless in the kitchen." A not-so-subtle dig at my father's chauvinistic ways and about the only time she ever noticed me.

Silas' ears prick up as if he knows we're talking about food. Once he realised there was no getting scraps from us earlier, he settled down on his bed. One of them. There's another one in the house. Manipulative mutt.

Solar lights illuminate the garden and the fence we built. It's quality work. Em clearly knew what she was doing.

I sip my beer. "How are you finding life in the big city?"

"It's different, that's for sure."

"Would you go back?"

"Nope." Emily shakes her head. "There are no jobs there. And as much as I loved growing up on the farm, it's not what

I want. I enjoy working at the station. The city is where I belong now."

"Did you ever think of being a cop?"

Her shoulders tighten. Interesting. I've hit a sore spot. She looks sideways at me. "I'm five feet two in heels."

"There's no height restriction anymore." Although she's right, she's so short she'd be a target for all the arseholes out there. "And you wield a mean drill."

"That's because I had to keep up with my brother and cousins."

From what I've seen so far, I can imagine her giving the men in her family a run for their money. "What about helping your mum with baking cakes and stuff?"

Her knuckles go white around the beer bottle, and she juts her chin at me. "Girls can be more than pretty housewives."

Whoa. I've hit another sore spot. "Absolutely. That's not what I meant. You can bring your tools here anytime." I wink.

A delicate rouge spreads across Emily's cheeks. "I should get going."

"Stay." My tone is more forceful than intended. For the first time in my life, I'm enjoying the company of a woman outside the bedroom. Even if we don't have sex, I don't want her to leave.

She glances at the door and back at me. "Do you think that's wise?"

"Nope. But do it anyway."

Em focuses on the beer bottle she's holding, peeling the label off, one tiny piece at a time. It's annoying as fuck, and I'm sure I'll find scraps on the floor later, even though I can tell she's trying to keep the mess on the table.

I still her hand. "Can I ask you a question?"

Her stunning blue gaze snaps to mine.

"Do you ever wonder what it would be like if we didn't stop at Jake and Claire's engagement party?"

She looks away and tips her head back, swigging her beer

like a bloke. Memories of how sweet she tasted send a rush of blood south. "It shouldn't have happened."

"But it did." Do I tell her I haven't stopped thinking about her since? Would that change her mind, knowing she's ruined me for other women? Bugger what Jake says. Maybe if we give in to this attraction between us, we can move on.

Em shakes her head. "Greg …"

"What's the harm? We're two consenting adults who are attracted to each other."

"We work together, and I don't want to be another one of your conquests."

Her accusation cuts deep. For all my flirting, I've never taken advantage of a woman. It's been a mutual understanding. Except that one time when it all went south. But Em doesn't strike me as the stalkerish type.

I stroke the back of her hand. It's smooth and trembling ever so softly. "I like you, Em. And that's not something I usually say to women."

She pulls her hand away and crosses her arms.

Shit. I rake my fingers through my hair. That was a stupid thing to say. So much for my legendary charm. "What I mean is, you're different. I enjoy spending time with you. As ridiculous as it sounds, I had fun building the fence this afternoon."

"You want to build more fences together?" A smile dances on her lips. Cheeky woman.

"Christ no. Can I take you out to dinner? On a date?"

She scrapes her chair back. Shit. I've fucked this up. "I offered to help with Silas. That's all."

She's not making this easy for me. I can practically smell her arousal. I know she wants me. "What if I told you there's been no one else since Jake and Claire's engagement party?"

Emily's jaw drops. "You expect me to believe you haven't had sex in *two* months?"

"Yes."

She hugs her arms around her waist, and I can see she's weighing up whether or not to believe me. "Why?"

Because I'm tired of meaningless hook-ups, and Em is like the proverbial breath of fresh air, filled with country goodness.

"I can't get you out of my mind. That floral perfume you wear, the cute blush that fills your cheeks when you're embarrassed, the way you felt so perfect in my arms that night." I scrub my face and stand. "Give me a chance. Please."

A frog croaks somewhere in the distance. It's a rare sound these days. I take it as a positive sign, but my skin still prickles with anticipation as I wait for Em to respond. She wants to say yes, I can feel it.

Em leans against the deck railing, giving the appearance she's relaxed, but the tight expression on her face says otherwise. "What if I said there'd be no sex after this dinner date?"

"I'd be okay with that." I'd have to be an idiot to answer any other way. I can't remember the last time a date didn't end in sex, but I'd settle for a kiss from Em. She's worth waiting for. And doesn't that thought whack me in the balls? I'm not sure how I went from wanting to have sex and getting her out of my system to a date with no sex, but for some reason, I don't care. I just want her to say yes.

The air is charged as I wait for Em to answer, every nerve in my body on high alert. After what feels like hours but must only be seconds, Em pushes off the railing and takes a step towards me. She tucks a stray curl behind her ear and gives me a shy smile.

A rattling sound intrudes on the moment. What the hell? Silas springs out of his bed, barks and disappears down the side of the house.

"Anyone home?" comes a deep voice from the shadows.

You've got to be kidding me.

"Down." Jake's distinct growl has Em freezing like a deer in headlights. Seconds later, he and Claire stroll into the yard, their young son, Oscar, between them. His eyes narrow on Em. Fucking fantastic. "We knocked, but you mustn't have heard."

Em glances at me, and I can tell from the stiffness in her body that I've missed my chance. Mother fucking Jake and his shit timing. I shove my hands into the pockets of my jeans.

"We didn't know you'd be here, Emily. What a wonderful surprise." Claire's smile is like a warm summer sky alongside the thunder in Jake's eyes.

"I helped Greg build a fence to keep Silas off the garden."

Claire's smile widens, and her eyes sparkle. No doubt she's putting two and two together and coming up with a wedding and four kids, while Jake's probably planning my castration.

"You have a dog, Uncle Greg?"

All attention turns to Oscar. Perfect timing. I kneel so I'm at eye level. "I'm looking after him for a friend."

Oscar's the only kid I have anything to do with. My two nephews don't count since I can't remember the last time I saw them. My brother is my old man's clone, or will be soon the way he's headed. The less I see of both of them, the better.

Silas joins us and licks Oscar's face. "Why's he only got one eye?"

"He lost it saving his previous owner."

"Wow. That's awesome. He's a superhero." Oscar pats Silas' head. For a six-year-old, he's surprisingly gentle. Jake's done an excellent job bringing him up, and Oscar clearly adores his new mum, Claire. And dogs. I still don't see why Jake couldn't have taken Silas.

"You can play with him if you want." I glance at Jake. "As long as your dad says it's okay."

Oscar tugs on Jake's leg. "Can I, Dad?"

Jake wrinkles his nose at Silas.

Em wraps her arms around her waist like she's holding

back a laugh. "He's had a bath, Inspector. I promise you he's clean."

Picking a leaf off Silas' back, Jake holds it up between two fingers.

Em exchanges a look with me, one that burrows deep, touching places that have never seen the light of day. She obviously finds Jake's reticence funny, but she'd never dare laugh at him. "Well, he might have rolled in some dirt since then, but he's much cleaner than he was."

Jake nods, and Oscar tears down my small backyard with a whoop. Silas scampers after him.

Jake looks pointedly at the empty beer bottles on the table.

I see my chance with Em fading into the darkness. "How come you're out on a weeknight?"

Claire yawns and covers her mouth. "We took Oscar to Taronga Zoo for a school excursion to see the nocturnal animals."

Jake glances towards the back door and then at me. Subtle as ever. Guess I'm not kicking him out yet. "You want a drink?"

"Thought you'd never ask." Jake's voice drips with sarcasm. Prick.

Claire glares at him. "Just a cup of tea for me, Greg, if it's not too much trouble. I know it's getting late."

"For you, Claire, no problem." I retreat to the kitchen, but there's no reprieve from Jake's disapproval because he's right on my heels.

"What the hell are you doing?" Jake hisses, his face one giant scowl.

I fill the jug with water and switch it on. "Nothing."

Jake pinches the bridge of his nose. "Don't nothing me. You and Emily look mighty comfortable. What did I tell you?"

"It's none of your business what happens off the clock,

Inspector." I turn my back on him and pull a small black teapot out of the cupboard.

"Jesus, Greg. She works with us."

"I know."

"Have you forgotten what happened with Senior Constable Lovedale?"

I grit my teeth. He just had to go there. "Of course not. She nearly cost me my job."

"She thought she was in love with you, you idiot, until she saw you with your tongue down some other woman's throat at a nightclub." Jake slaps his hand on the bench. "Have you learnt nothing?"

The jug boils, and I fill the pot. Water splashes on my fingers, but I'm too angry to care. "Em's not the type of person to cause trouble."

"That's not the point. She doesn't strike me as an experienced woman. You could break her heart. And if she filed a complaint, Commander Gordon would be all too happy to haul your arse in for sexual harassment—even if it was consensual."

"You're having a coronary about nothing. I asked Em out. She said no." At least, I'm pretty sure that'll be her answer now that the moment has passed.

Jake slumps onto a stool. "Thank Christ."

Jake's been my best mate for twenty years. He's my only real friend. His disapproval cuts deep. "Geez. Tell me what you really think of me."

He shakes his head. "I don't mean it like that. You're the best friend I could ever ask for, Greg. You've been there for me in my darkest days." Jake stands and clasps his fingers on my shoulder. "But you have a reputation for good reason. Emily deserves better than that."

Shit. Jake's pulled out the big guns. My throat swells, and I blink to hold back a couple of stray tears that leak into my eyes. "I agree."

The lines in Jake's forehead crinkle into deep furrows. He opens his mouth to respond, but the last thing I need is touchy-feely bonding. I fill two cups with tea, add a dash of milk, and shove them at him. "This is for Claire and Em. I'll get the beers."

Jake mumbles something incoherent as he juggles the cups and saucers, spilling the contents of one. He curses and tiptoes out the door like he's carrying live grenades. That was one way to shut him up.

Beer bottles in hand, I linger in the doorway. Oscar and Silas chase each other around the yard. By the way he's panting, I'm guessing the dog will conk out long before the boy. Em and Claire chatter at a hundred miles an hour while Jake sets their cups on the table. He glances at me and gives me a look that says, 'Get your arse out here and save me from estrogen overload.'

I saunter out, pleased to see Em pause for breath and sweep her gaze over me. Jake's eyes narrow. He still doesn't trust my intentions. And he shouldn't. That's why he's the boss. He reads people too well.

Because despite what I told him, what I keep telling myself, I can't walk away from her. I won't be satisfied until I have Em under me. Over me. Completely consumed by me. The question is, will she consume me?

Chapter Seven

Greg

The hospital doors slide open, and Jake and I stride into an empty reception area devoid of life. It's barely seven am, too early for visitors, but the rules don't apply here. I hit the elevator button, and we head up two floors to Jimmy's ward. He came out of his coma three days ago, but he hasn't been well enough to see us until now.

The smell of antiseptic chokes the small space, leaving a nasty taint in my mouth. Jake's fingers curl into fists by his side. If we weren't blokes, I'd hug him or something. He had his fill of hospitals with his first wife's illness, so it's surprising Jake insisted on coming along today. As you'd expect, he hates hospitals, and this interview is way below his pay grade. Hell, it's below mine too. It's the sort of case we'd normally let general duties take care of, except Jimmy's one of those people who's managed to get under my thick hide. The furry proof is sunning himself on my back deck right now. Or digging a hole in the tiny patch of lawn he has access to. But it's not the only reason we're here. Jake and I both feel there's more behind Jimmy's bashing than an old homeless man in the wrong place at the wrong time.

Intensive care is an organised chaos of beeping machines

and bustling nurses. The mood is sombre, but the competency of the medical professionals shines through in their every movement. It takes a special person to deal with illness, bodily fluids and death on a daily basis. Give me the dirtbag criminals any day.

A buxom brunette mans the front desk, her shirt straining against the buttons. "Can I help you?"

Jake flashes his badge. "Detective Inspector Jake Matthews and Detective Sergeant Greg Anderson to see Jimmy Sharmon."

The nurse, or rather Nursing Unit Manager, by the look of her identification, nods. "Of course. We were expecting you. The swelling on Mr Sharmon's brain has receded. The doctors are very pleased with his recovery." She taps the keyboard a few times. "I'll show you to his room."

My gaze drifts to the snug fit of the nurse's blue scrubs around her arse as we follow. She has a sexy sway to her hips that would've had me asking for her number a few months ago. Now? All I can picture is how well Em fills out a pair of jeans. That image gets the blood pumping south. Until I remember why we're here and the arousal dies a quick death.

The Nursing Unit Manager gestures towards a doorway. "He's very weak. You have ten minutes."

Jimmy's room is all white walls and white sheets. I'm not prepared for the sight of him in the hospital bed. It punches my gut and scrambles my internal organs. The staff must have shaved his face. The bruises have faded to a mottled purple, drawing attention to wrinkles so deeply etched it's like someone's taken a carving knife to his flesh. His eyes brighten and a tear slides down his cheek.

"Silas?" The word slips from his mouth in a croaky whisper.

I eat up the distance between us and touch his forearm, avoiding the cannula in his hand. His skin is colder than I expected. "He's good. Taken over my house."

Jimmy's lips part, revealing a toothless, watery smile. My free hand clenches by my side. The cowards that bashed him will pay.

I yank my mobile out of my pocket and bring up the photos. "Take a look." I move the phone so Jimmy can see Silas curled up on a grey, fluffy, doughnut-shaped bed.

"He looks good." Jimmy's voice trembles and his eyes are glossier than when we walked in.

"Yeah, he does. A friend gave him a bath." I flick to the next photo of Silas chewing on a rope toy, a goofy, contented expression on his ugly mug.

Jimmy reaches for my hand, his bony fingers weak against mine. "Thanks, Sarge."

A lump forms in my throat. "No problem."

Jake steps closer. Jimmy tenses beneath my palm. His chequered past means he's leery of cops, but he's trusted me from day one, thanks to Silas. The first time I came across them both huddled against a shopfront, Silas rubbed his snotty nose and slobbering mouth all over a new woollen suit. There was something about the pair of them that reminded me of my dog, Buster, and the homeless guy who dragged him off the road. So, instead of walking past, I bought Jimmy a coffee and sandwich and Silas a puppuchino before taking them to the shelter to get cleaned up. Jimmy couldn't stay because of the no-dogs rule, but he got a shower and clean clothes. He's treated me like a God ever since.

"It's okay, Jimmy. This is Detective Inspector Jake Matthews. He's my superior and best friend. You can trust him."

Jimmy licks his lips. They're cracked with fissures almost as deep as the wrinkles on his face. I've seen a lot of shit during my time on the force, and one thing it's taught me is there's a mighty thin line between having and not having. A line that's easily broken by circumstances, by illness, addiction or sheer bad luck. Jimmy fell on the wrong side of that line.

Jake lowers himself into a chair by the bed. Smart move. Makes him less intimidating. "Can you tell us what you remember of the night you were attacked, Mr Sharmon?"

Jimmy stiffens and glances at the door. I close it and return to the foot of the bed.

Jimmy sinks into the mattress. "I was at the river."

We already know that. "What were you doing there?" It's been bothering me why he stayed away from the park after the incident with the rowdy teens. There's safety in numbers.

He lowers his gaze, his fingers working up a fast tap on the edge of the bed.

The guilt on his face says it all. "Were you buying drugs?"

He closes his eyes as if that will shut out the truth.

I smother the lecture I want to throw at him. He's suffered enough.

His eyes open. "I'm sorry, Sarge. My back was hurting so bad."

"How did you pay for it?"

He slides his gaze to Jake. I know before he opens his mouth, he's going to lie. "Some people can be generous."

"Really?" I have a hunch this is related to the mysterious woman Ian told me about. "Were these people a pretty young woman with long blonde hair?"

His head whips towards the door and his fingers white-knuckle the sheets. He attempts a smile, but it's overshadowed by the fear swirling in his irises. "I don't remember."

What's he frightened of? "We didn't see any drugs at the scene."

Jimmy tugs the sheet up his body. "The guys who jumped me must have taken them."

"And the whiskey we found nearby?"

"Weed's harsh on the throat." He shrinks under the sheet

and averts his eyes. "Needed somethin' to wash it down with."

Jake adjusts his jacket and leans forward. "Do you remember anything about your attackers, Mr Sharmon?"

Jimmy shakes his head. It's a slow movement, his eyes scrunching up with obvious pain. An alarm sounds, and the monitor shows his heart rate rising. I pat his shoulder. "It's okay if you can't."

"It happened so quickly. Silas growled and then ..." He coughs.

The door swings open, and two nurses and the unit manager charge in. I step back, and Jake jumps off the chair.

"I'm sorry, officers, but that's enough for today."

"But—" Jake interjects.

"No more, Inspector." The Nursing Unit Manager fixes a glare on Jake that would have most men shitting themselves. It slides straight off him.

"Just a few more minutes." Jake turns to Jimmy. "Is there anything else you can tell us? Anything at all?"

Jimmy crosses his arms over his chest, his eyes pleading just like Silas does when he's begging me for food. "No. Nothin'." He's lying. Another cough wracks his fragile body and bloody spittle sprays across the bed.

"Officers, I won't tell you again." The nurse in charge jabs a finger at the door. "Out!"

We back out of the room. I sift through the evidence in my mind. No doubt, Jake does the same as we return to the lift.

We buy coffee in the café on the ground floor and settle at a corner table. Jake kicks back in his seat and loosens his tie. "Sounds like Jimmy got on the wrong side of some drug dealers."

"Yep." I squeeze my fingers around the cup, spilling half the contents as the recycled cardboard folds in half and burns my skin. I ignore the pain. It's nothing compared to what Jimmy's been through. "And it made him expendable."

"I'll arrange for a police guard while he's in hospital."

"Thanks." I sip what remains of the coffee, the bitter taste of burnt milk coating my mouth. "And when he gets out?"

"We'll worry about that later."

The Nursing Unit Manager walks into the café, her nose scrunching up when she sees us.

Jake elbows me in the ribs. "Looks like she's immune to your charms."

"Ha!" I crack my knuckles. "More likely it was your surly face that got her back up."

Jake's expression darkens. "This is what I was talking about yesterday. You can't keep your eyes off any woman over the age of eighteen."

Not this again. I grind my teeth. "I told you I'd stay away from Em. What more do you want from me?"

"Your word."

"Jesus, Jake." I shuffle in my seat. "You're not gonna let this go?"

He pins me with his steel blue gaze. "Nope."

"I can be friends with a woman after fucking." I throw my hands in the air. "Look at Monica."

"Monica doesn't count. She's cut from the same dubious cloth as you."

"Fine." Time I got his sanctimonious arse off my back for good. I hold up my right hand. "I, Gregory James Anderson, promise that I will not seduce Emily Saunders."

Jake scowls. "You're being a child."

I ignore his comment. "Happy?"

He nods. "Yes."

Thank Christ. I uncross the fingers on my other hand, the one sitting in my lap. I've never outright lied to Jake before. My stomach growls at the deception. If Em keeps the boundaries in place, I'll respect her wishes. And Jake's. But if she lets me in, I won't be saying no. I'll just have to make sure Jake never finds out.

Chapter Eight

Emily

Thwack. Thwack. Thwack.

Endorphins sing through my veins as the slap of flesh on flesh rings in my ears. There's nothing like fighting to take my mind off sexy cops with dirty mouths. I'd be another notch on Greg's playboy bedpost if Inspector Matthews hadn't interrupted us. Instead of being grateful, I'm pissed off because a wicked, irresponsible part of me yearns for a repeat taste of those firm fingers and sinful mouth. Which means I'm doubly pissed off at myself for wanting the one man I have no business getting involved with.

"Easy, Emily. Don't get too cocky." The trainer, Scott, circles me and my sparring partner, Natalie.

Leather and the salty tang of sweat tease my nostrils as I bounce on the balls of my feet. The mat beneath my soles gives me the illusion of walking on water, but I know from experience that it still smarts when you hit it with force.

Natalie rubs her forearm where I smacked her hard and crooks her finger. "Is that all you got, little rocket?"

I grin and dance around her. Along with Claire, she's the closest thing I have to a friend in Sydney. While she beats me with size, I'm all over her when it comes to speed.

"Come on, you tease," she growls. "Face me like a grown-up."

Ah, Natalie. She should know by now I don't respond to taunts. Well, most of the time. I skip to the side and feint a couple of punches. She strikes fast, but not fast enough. Her glove grazes the top of my arm as I spin away. I thrust my leg out at full force, slamming against her thigh. She stumbles and shakes her head, beads of moisture flinging into the air.

I rub clammy hands on my shorts. Time to put Natalie out of her misery. My leg sweeps low, bringing her down.

Thump.

Natalie bounces on the thin rubber mat with a thud and a curse. I stand over her, one foot on her lower rib cage. "Yield."

My ears roar with the blood rushing between them. The euphoria of winning never gets old. After three gruelling years, I'm now a black belt. There's no way I'll fail my physical for the police force next time I apply.

Natalie shakes her head and raises her hands off the floor in surrender. "I yield, you crazy bitch."

I give her the finger and do a victory dance around her prone body.

Scott crosses his arms. "Emily, that's not very sporting."

Natalie coughs. "Never argue with a pissed-off woman."

"I'm not pissed."

"If you say so." Natalie climbs to her feet.

There's a snigger from across the room where three guys have stopped practising their kicks to gawk at us.

Arseholes.

I stand taller as if another inch will make all the difference, square my jaw and glare at them. They give me mock salutes and return to their moves, all lean muscles and lightning-fast reflexes as they slam against the massive teardrop bags hanging from the ceiling.

Show-offs.

I spin and confront Natalie and Scott, my hands planted on my hips. "I'm not pissed."

Scott grunts, his eyes twinkling.

I step forward and punch his shoulder. Not too hard, but enough for him to rub it.

"Okay, okay. Everything's fine. Got it." Scott backs away, a stupid smile on his face. "I have another client, so I'd better get ready. See you ladies next week."

Natalie pulls up her T-shirt and peels the top of her shorts down to reveal an impressive foot-sized bruise on her hip. Shit. I didn't mean to hit her that hard. "My husband might ban me from coming to the gym when he sees this."

"Sorry."

"I've been hurt worse." She smooths her shirt down. "So, what's going on, Emily? Those cops giving you a tough time?"

My shoulders tense. "It's nothing."

Natalie's brow furrows into deep lines, making her look older than her thirty-five years. She's no fool. That's what makes her a formidable sparring partner. She reads people, recognises the intent behind the moves. "Is it man trouble?"

"Of course not." I grab my bottle of water and chug it down.

"Liar." Natalie clamps her arms around my waist and hoists me off the ground. The bottle goes flying across the room. "You have the same look my husband gets when he can't decide whether to pull me into the bedroom or dig a hole for my dead body in the backyard."

"Put me down, you big oaf." I slap her chest. I swear there's Amazon blood in her.

"When you admit it."

"Admit what?"

"That you've got man trouble."

She's impossible. "Alright. Fine. I've got man problems."

"Yes!" Natalie swings me around, sending my stomach

into a series of somersaults and sets me down. The room spins. This is the problem with being short. Even at twenty-five years old, people are fooled by my tiny stature into thinking I'm weak. My boss says being underestimated is my biggest asset.

Natalie cracks her knuckles. "So, what's wrong with this guy? Do you need me to sort him out?"

I grab my sports bag and throw it over my shoulder. "I can handle him myself, thank you very much."

"That you can." Natalie slaps me on the back. "Time to hit the showers."

We head to the bathrooms, where we have our pick of cubicles. I shrug off my clothes and turn on the taps. The hot spray soothes my sore muscles. Natalie's not the only one sporting bruises. She got a couple of good kicks to my right thigh. We don't always spar that hard, but I was spoiling for a fight, and Natalie rose to the challenge like I knew she would.

I shampoo the sweat out of my hair. My hairdresser says I shouldn't wash it every day, but there's no way I'm leaving it caked in grime. I'd end up with limp noodles instead of springy curls.

My thoughts circle back to Greg and his proposition. What do I do?

I'm not the same naïve country girl who was played for a fool at uni. While I was far from innocent, thanks to my high school boyfriend, Matt, and more than a few trysts behind the sports oval and in his car, our relationship didn't prepare me for the sharks in the city. The first guy I hooked up with turned out to be the worst kind of player, winning a bet with his mates on who could nail the nerdy tomboy. It was a tough lesson, but one I learnt well. No fooling around with guys in class or at work. It's been an easy philosophy to maintain ... until Greg. I know the score this time, yet I still find myself irrationally tempted.

Closing my eyes, I massage conditioner into my hair and

scalp. Next, I smooth on creamy body wash, the refreshing citrus notes cleansing my mind and easing the tension in my heated flesh. My body knows what it wants, my nipples hardening to small pebbles despite the warm water as memories of Greg's confident hands and mouth surface. Damn, I can't stop thinking about him.

What if we did hook up? We'd need to keep it a secret; otherwise, my reputation would be forever tarnished. I'd find myself doing the equivalent of the walk of shame every day at the station, bowed down by the judgement that comes with stupid double standards. The humiliation I felt at being exposed for a gullible fool at uni still simmers in my DNA. Besides, my boss has already warned me about the perils of workplace relationships and made it clear she doesn't condone them. Would she punish me by marking me down in my performance assessment? And would it count against me when I reapplied to join the police force? It shouldn't, but the cop world is incredibly insular. I'm not sure if it's worth the risk.

Argh! What do I do?

"What are you ranting about?" asks Natalie through the door.

"Nothing." I shut off the water and grab my towel. It scrapes along my bruised flesh. I welcome the pain.

Dressed in fresh underwear, leggings and a T-shirt, I emerge from the shower cubicle. Natalie leans against the sink, hip cocked, her expression calling me out.

"We've only known each other a short time, Emily, but I've never seen you this worked up before." She pushes off the vanity. "I'm here if you want to talk."

The warmth in Natalie's turquoise eyes nearly undoes me. I've been so focused on my career plans that my friends have drifted away. I try not to fixate on it, but my life can be lonely. When Greg devoured me with those warm chocolate eyes at Inspector Matthews' and Claire's engagement party, I realised

I was tired of being alone. Tired of lusting from afar. And finding out he hasn't been with anyone since our near hookup makes me crave him even more.

Natalie continues to watch me, her gaze steady. She's a social worker and used to talking people down from agitated states. But I'm not ready to untangle the jumble of thoughts and feelings I have about Greg, let alone verbalise them.

I grab my bag and hold it in front of me as if it can shield me from the truth. "Thanks, but I'm good."

She opens her mouth. I expect her to tell me I'm full of crap, but she doesn't. "Okay. But if you change your mind, please call. You're not alone."

Natalie's words pierce that empty place inside my chest like bullets. She's even more insightful than I thought. I nod and escape the bathroom. If I stay, I'll turn into a blubbering mess. The best thing I can do is retreat to safety. To the four drab walls of my apartment.

Chapter Nine

Greg

I hate it when Jake's right. Sanctimonious prick. Em never said yes to a date, and I won't ask her again. She deserves better than the likes of me, so I need to stop fixating on her and get laid. Which is why I'm perched at what used to be my favourite bar in the city, letting the bass of the DJ's music pound through me while I check out the attractions. The strobe lights are annoying as fuck, and the gyrating, half-naked bodies that should have my dick perking up leave me cold.

"If that scowl is meant to scare off the ladies, it's not working."

The soft, sultry words tickle my ear as a woman slides onto the seat next to me. A deep slit in her slinky red dress accentuates the length of her toned legs. A hint of exotic perfume designed to bring men to their knees wafts through the air. It's too over the top for my taste, but my dick has woken up, and that's enough to make me swivel and drink her in. Her long, straight blonde hair floats around her face, giving her an angelic look, but there's nothing chaste about the gleam in her eyes.

I throw back my whiskey, the fiery burn spreading

through my body and down to my groin. "Guess I was waiting for the right woman to show up."

She responds to my obvious pickup line by tossing her hair over her shoulder and batting long, obviously fake, eyelashes at me.

I gesture to the bartender. "Can I buy you a drink?"

She nods and flashes me perfect white teeth. "A gin and tonic, please."

I paste on a smile and hold out my hand. "I'm Greg."

She takes it; slim manicured fingers weighed down with gold and diamonds stroke my palm. "Julia."

Instead of imagining those scarlet-tipped nails raking down my back while I pound into her, I'm reminded of Em's short, practical nails, devoid of jewellery, when she drilled screws into the fence.

Stop it. Em's off limits.

I take Julia's hand and bring it to my lips. Kiss her fingers. The inside of her wrist. Her breath hitches as I knew it would. "Nice to meet you."

We engage in my least favourite conversation—small talk. She's an advertising executive. Throws around famous names like I should be impressed. I'm not. I tell her I'm a cop. She can't hide her surprise or how her eyes rove over my bespoke suit and Rolex watch. Yeah, sweetheart, I bet I could match you dollar for dollar and then some.

When Julia disappears to the bathroom, I check my watch. Nine pm. Silas would be sound asleep. There's plenty of time to fuck and still be in bed by midnight. Alone. And finally put to rest my infatuation with one sexy little intelligence analyst.

I slide off the seat as Julia returns and pull her in close, bringing her hips flush with mine. My erection's only flying at half mast, but it's big enough she gets the message. "How about we go to your place?"

She clutches my shirt, her caramel eyes darkening. "I'd

love to, but my housemate is having a party. It'll be noisy and not very private."

Looks like a hotel will have to do. "Okay." I step back and pull out my phone. "Let's see if we can get a room nearby."

Julia pouts. "That's so seedy. What's wrong with your place?"

Nothing. Except I don't want her and her cloying perfume clogging up my space. But I also don't want to fuck her with a party going on nearby. "Fine."

Her eyes glaze over, and she rubs against me. I capture her mouth with mine. Her breath is fresh; she must have popped a mint in the bathroom, and yet it's stale at the same time. Fake. Still, my dick enjoys the way her mound nudges it and her breasts flatten against my chest. I can make this work.

We pull apart. Her cheeks are rosy and her eyes bright and full of decadent promise. "Why don't we take this somewhere more private, Detective?"

And just like that, my hard-on withers. Em was the last woman to call me that while climbing me like a jungle gym.

Still, I'm determined to shake the curse of Emily Saunders. We exit the club, hail a taxi, and arrive at my house in no time. It's risky bringing a random home. You never know if you'll end up with a class one clinger. But I checked her out online while she was freshening up. She seems legit, with a LinkedIn profile and photos of herself plastered across Facebook and Instagram pages. Another high-powered woman looking for fun—the perfect hook-up.

Julia wraps herself around me as we tumble out of the taxi and walk up the front path. I palm her arse while she rubs my arms and back with the confidence of a woman who knows she's about to get lucky. Her perfume chokes my every pore. She must have spritzed herself with it again before leaving the nightclub. My insides recoil. There's a queasy sensation in my stomach and a decided lack of interest in my trousers. For the first time in my life, I'm not sure if I can go through with this.

Crickets chirp as I unlock the front door and flip on the light. Julia wanders up the hallway ahead of me, her head swivelling side to side, taking in the decor and clearly liking what she sees. She lets out a squeal when she reaches the living area. "What in the world is that?"

I stand behind her and chuckle. Silas strains at the bars of his dog crate, his enormous tongue hanging out. I bought the crate so he can sleep inside at night without destroying the furniture. "It's my dog."

"Can you put it outside? Or in the laundry?"

My jaw locks. No way. This is Silas' house now. I tuck her into my side. "Don't worry. He's harmless." I nuzzle her cheek. "And it's not like he can get out of there."

"What happened to his eye?"

"He lost it protecting his previous owner." I don't mention Silas is only with me temporarily. It's none of her business. Her position is even more temporary.

"Oh. That's sweet." She waves at him. "Hey there, doggie."

Silas looks at me and then barks. Julia shudders. "I guess he's cute."

"He's ugly as sin, but he's friendly." When he's not digging up my garden or destroying the house. "Would you like a coffee?"

Julia curls her arms around my neck and mouths my throat. "How about we skip the drink and get onto the good stuff?"

Normally my dick would think this is an awesome plan, but it's gone into hibernation, and the churning in my stomach has grown into a category-four emergency. If I'm not careful, I'll be barfing all over Julia's dress.

Silas must sense my unease because he growls. It's a gravelly warning that has Julia plastering her sickly sweet body against me. His accusing gaze lifts to mine, and I know what he's thinking. *This isn't Em.*

Christ. I scrub my face. He's right. I don't want any woman. I want Em. I'd rather lie on my new sofa with Silas and text her photos of the goofball than get a random stranger naked.

Julia nuzzles my ear. "How about you show me that king-size bed of yours, Detective?"

Not detective again. That phrase is Em's and Em's alone. There's no escaping the truth. The pint-sized redhead that is Emily Saunders has bewitched me and this clusterfuck of a night needs to stop. Now.

I peel Julia's fingers from my neck. "Sorry, sweetheart. I don't think it's gonna work."

She reaches for my hands, but I shrug her away. "What do you mean?"

"Look, I thought I wanted this, but now I realise I don't."

She crosses her arms, her eyes narrowing. "You can't invite a girl home and then say no."

"Ah, yes, I can."

She swats my chest. "You pig."

She's got that right. "I'll call you a taxi."

"Don't bother." She flounces to the front door. "I'll get an Uber."

The door bangs shut, and I'm left with Silas watching me, his head cocked to the side, that soulful brown eye brimming with condemnation.

I stride to the front door and open it. Julia's talking on her mobile phone. She raises her middle finger. I just nod. It's a safe neighbourhood, but you can never be sure, so I keep watch over her until her ride turns up. Thank Christ it's here in less than five minutes. She gives me another shot of her middle finger before sliding into the car.

What a night. I lock the door, kick off my shoes, remove my coat and then let Silas out of his crate. He tries to lick me, but I sidestep him and sprawl on the lounge. "I did the right thing, mate."

Silas glances towards the hallway like he knows what I've said and flops at my feet. The sick feeling in my stomach has faded, but there's no getting away from the fact that Em's got me by the balls.

I bend down and scratch the scraggly mutt behind his ear. He leans into my hand. "What do I do?"

Silas' one eye opens, and he regards me for a few seconds. Before I can stop him, he jumps onto the lounge and settles next to me.

"Whoa, buddy." I point at the floor. "Off."

Fucking dog ignores me and plops his head on my lap. On my pure wool Armani trousers. Jesus Christ. Both Em and Silas have me well and truly whipped.

I sink further into the leather and stroke his ears, playing over the mess I've got myself into. Within minutes, Silas is snoring, oblivious to my inner turmoil.

Since I'm clearly a goner for Em, I need to convince her to go out with me. Prove I'm capable of having a relationship that's more than sex. Which means I've got to treat her differently to other women. Flowers and dinner would be too cliche. If I'm going to capture her attention, it needs to be a date she wouldn't expect. One that shows she's more than a conquest. For the first time all night, a genuine smile teases my lips. After watching the pleasure on Em's face while she helped build the fence, I know exactly where to take her.

Chapter Ten

Emily

The sun hasn't even thought about making a show for the weekend and I'm showered and eating breakfast. It's a legacy of growing up on the farm. No sleep-ins for me. I sip my tea and scroll through news updates on my phone—a one-punch incident in the city overnight, politicians hitting the campaign trail, another murder near the river. That last one gets my attention. No doubt there were more incidents in western Sydney that didn't make the news. I'll be busy mapping and analysing trends when I get into the station on Monday. It's also a reminder that I need to stay focused on my career.

My mobile rings, and my brother's name pops up. He often calls me early morning for no reason. He misses me, but he'd deny it if I called him out on it.

"Hey, Ethan."

"How are you, sis?"

I glance around the dirty beige walls of my tiny living room. It's a world away from the luxury of Greg's house. "Good."

"Caught any bad guys yet?"

I shake my head. My brother is four years younger and

loves to stir me. "I'm an intelligence analyst, not a cop." And it still stings to say that. Thank God I kept my applications to the police academy secret. I was going to surprise my family. Now, they need never know that I failed. That I wasn't good enough.

"At least tell me you've found yourself a boyfriend amongst all those hot cops."

"That's none of your business."

"Ah, so you have?"

"Bugger off, Ethan."

"You're too easily riled, Em." He chuckles. "Just remember, any bloke you bring home will have to be strong enough to survive Dad. He keeps a set of shears sharpened, ready for the occasion."

I grimace. "And that's why I won't be introducing anyone to Mum and Dad in a hurry. I'm not a little girl anymore."

"You try telling our parents that."

I swallow a groan. Ethan's being groomed to take over the farm when Dad retires. Meanwhile, he and Mum are waiting for me to get this 'silly career thing' out of my system and come back and marry a nice country boy. Give them grandkids. They think that's all I'm good for. I'm determined to prove them wrong.

I pour myself another cup of tea. "Did you ring for a reason, little brother, or to annoy me?"

"Just wanted to tell you Simon finishes his apprenticeship this month and has been offered a job to stay on."

"That's awesome." Simon and Ethan have been dating for a year now, and I could tell when I saw Ethan at Christmas that he'd fallen hard for the ink-covered mechanic. "And what about Mum and Dad?"

"Soon, Em. Soon. I know I can't keep our relationship secret much longer."

"I'm sure they'll understand."

He gives me a non-committal grunt.

We chat for a few more minutes about the weather and how the crop planting is going, and then Ethan suddenly remembers he's supposed to be at the neighbour's farm helping them with a broken tractor, and we say goodbye.

I pull up the roller blind to find darkness has given way to pale grey with a splash of pink. I'd unlatch the window and inhale the brisk morning air, except it'll be tainted with petrol fumes. Nothing like the fresh, grassy notes of the country. I grab my keys. Time to greet the dawn with a jog.

My mobile dings. I unlock it, expecting it to be a silly text from Ethan, but it's not.

Greg: Are you busy today?

Butterflies take flight in my tummy. It's been two weeks since Greg asked me out. I figured he'd changed his mind, and while a part of me was disappointed that he gave up so easily, the responsible part of me knew it was for the best.

Do I respond? Ignore? My fingers answer for me.

Me: Depends

The cursor blinks. What's he up to?

Greg: How about an unconventional date?

Huh! Not what I expected. I should decline for all the reasons I've been fixating on, but he's piqued my interest. No doubt that's his intention.

Me: I didn't say I'd go out with you.

The cursor blinks again. Keeps blinking. My throat closes up. I'm on edge, wanting him to keep trying, wanting him to stop.

Greg: Would you have said yes if Jake and Claire didn't turn up?

Yes. Yes, I would have. But I'm not answering that question.

Me: What did you have in mind?

Greg: Rock climbing.

I burst out laughing. Luckily, I didn't have a mouthful of tea. Is he kidding me?

Me: Why would you ask me to rock climb on a first date?

He responds quickly.

Greg: Means I'll be too sore to put the moves on you.

This time, I choke on my saliva. He's impossibly cocky.

Greg: Pick you up at 10?

The smart thing to do would be to say no. If this got back to the station, to my boss, it could ruin everything I'm working towards. But I want to get to know Greg better because, so far, I've liked what I've seen of him outside work. It's admirable how well he's caring for Silas. Not to mention, I can't resist the challenge of wiping off the smug smile that's undoubtedly on his face right now.

Me: See you then.

The cursor blinks. And blinks some more. Then it dings with a winking emoji.

I giggle and drop the phone on the table. This man. His arrogance is expected, but the proposal isn't. I thought someone like him would try a fancy dinner—that would have been much easier to reject. But rock climbing … wow.

He probably thinks he'll be teaching me the ropes, getting in a few feels under the guise of helping me. Is he in for a surprise.

❧

A cool breeze scatters leaves across the path outside my block of units and teases my curls. They're in a mad riot around my head today. Nothing seemed to tame them, so I gave up. An exuberant Belgian shepherd mix scampers past. I smile at the man clutching the lead and jogging behind the dog. He gives me a frantic wave as he's pulled down the next street. It reminds me of Greg. I bet it hasn't occurred to him to walk Silas.

A sleek silver Audi pulls up, the exact type of car I'd expect Greg to drive. He peels out of the driver's seat. The sensors in my brain overload as he comes into view—charcoal climbing pants, matching sleeveless shirt, and arms of pure muscle and sinew. He's never looked hotter. I squeeze my thighs together. Why did I assume rock climbing would be safer than dinner?

Greg makes no secret of checking me out, his gaze slowly taking in my purple leggings, fitted black T-shirt and jacket. I'd normally wear my climbing pants, which happen to be the same brand as Greg's, but I don't want to show my hand too soon.

I tug at my jacket. "I hope what I'm wearing is okay."

"Yep." His throat moves up and down. "But I might have to punch out all the blokes leering at you."

A flush of heat spreads across my chest. Greg's reaction pleases me more than I'd like it to. But I can't let myself get too attached. Whatever happens, this can only be fun. Nothing more.

He helps me into the car. The simple gesture is a reminder that this is not work nor Silas related, but a date. His arm brushes against mine as I slide into the passenger seat, sending a jolt of electricity to my core. He winks as he shuts the door, and the scent of new leather, sandalwood and spicy man envelops me.

I'm in so much trouble.

The climbing gym is one I'm not familiar with, but it's obvious Greg's a regular as he waves to a couple of people in the car park. Large glass doors open to a vaulted ceiling and a blast of warm air.

"You brought a friend." The woman behind reception regards me with narrow eyes, her nose twitching like there's a foul odour in the air.

"Yep." Greg's hand rests on the small of my back, warmth radiating through the thick fabric. "This is Emily. I'm going to show her the ropes."

The receptionist wrinkles her nose faster like the odour has reached noxious levels. "I see."

Greg guides me into the gym, seemingly oblivious to the daggers the woman is throwing at me.

I pull on his arm. "Have you gone out with her?"

Greg stops midstride. He swallows and glances at the receptionist, who's still giving us the evil eye. "Why do you ask?"

"She doesn't seem happy to see me with you."

He rests his hands on my shoulders. "She's in my past."

"So you've slept with her?"

He grunts. "You ask too many questions."

And he dodges them, which means I'm right. "Sorry. It's none of my business, and here I am behaving like a jealous girlfriend on our first date."

He tucks a curl behind my ear. "It's all that red. Makes you feisty."

I roll my eyes. "If I had a dollar for every time someone said that, I'd be sipping cocktails in Hawaii."

A lean man with short blonde hair strides towards us. Uh oh. It's my trainer, Scott. What's he doing here? I'm going to be busted. I widen my eyes at him and shake my head ever so slightly, hoping he gets the message. His brow furrows, and then he turns his attention to Greg. "Hey stranger, haven't seen you for a few weeks."

"Nah. Work's been keeping me busy." Greg wraps his arm around my waist. "Scott, this is Em. It's her first time."

"First time?"

I give him a wink, which Greg can't see because he towers above me, and stick out my hand. "Nice to meet you, Scott."

He hesitates for a moment and then takes my fingers in his. "And you too, *Em*." He squeezes harder than is polite. Bastard. But at least he doesn't rat me out.

Scott turns back to Greg. "So, what do you have in mind?"

"Let's start on the short bouldering wall so she can get a feel for it."

Scott makes a show of looking me up and down. "I don't know, Greg. I reckon you could start her on the ropes. She's so tiny; she'll have no problem with her centre of gravity."

I smother a smile. Thank you for playing along with me, Scott.

Greg tightens his arm around my waist. "I don't want to scare her."

This is what pisses me off about men. They assume I'm not capable because I'm a woman and a tiny-arsed one at that. Greg saw what I did with his fence. He should know by now that I'm not a fragile wallflower.

"Please, Greg." I pout up at him. "I was hoping to climb with the ropes."

"Em ..."

"It's settled then," says Scott. "I'll get you our extra small harness and hire shoes." He pivots and strides off, not giving Greg a chance to respond.

Greg cups my chin. "Are you sure about this?"

"Of course. You'll be holding the ropes. I trust you not to let me fall." But I don't trust myself. I could like Greg a little too much if I'm not careful.

We watch a beginner video on the basics of rock climbing and the key commands. I pull on the shoes while Greg hovers to ensure they're firmly on my feet. Scott gives me the harness, and Greg bats him away. "I can do this."

Scott grins and stands aside. "Fine. But for safety, I need to supervise since Emily's new and all."

Greg's the consummate professional as he fits my harness correctly, touching me only when necessary.

Once he's finished, he looks me over, his gaze lingering on my arms. "You obviously work out, Em, but lifting a few weights at the gym is nothing like rock climbing."

"Of course." I nod, trying not to smile.

"Even though the video went through it, I'd like to demonstrate the three basic techniques again." Greg steps towards the wall, lifts his arm and grabs a hold. The cool mask of a professional slips into place. "First, keep your arms straight. Then imagine pushing yourself up with your legs rather than pulling with your upper body."

"I can do that." Guilt prickles at the back of my neck. He's taking this so seriously. Has no idea I could scale this beginner wall with my eyes closed. I should tell him I'm a rock climber, but I've been hiding my 'tomboy' ways for so long the lies come easily. Besides, he needs teaching a lesson about making assumptions.

Greg then places a foot onto a hold, keeping his leg bent. "Now, the second point is to find your centre of gravity. Rotate your hips so your torso is closer to the wall."

He swivels his hips from left to right, showing me how to keep my body centred. My mouth goes dry at the way his climbing pants tighten across his butt. Not to mention the yummy bulging of his arms. It makes him even more attractive, knowing rock climbing has contributed to his muscles rather than simply pumping iron in front of a mirror.

He drops back onto the floor. "As the video said, remember to use the toe of your shoe, not the full foot. You'll be able to reach higher if you do that." He looks me up and down. "And you need all the help you can get to find those extra inches."

Arrogant bastard. Any guilt I feel for tricking him disappears. "Great. My turn now."

Greg does a safety check on our harnesses, then attaches the rope. "I'll be your belayer. As they said in the video, that means I keep the cord taut as you go up, and if you slip, don't panic. I won't let you fall. You'll just hang, suspended. Okay?"

"Okay."

I do my own checks on the harness, deliberately stumbling through it.

Greg smiles indulgently. "Impressive, Em."

Wait till he sees me in action. "On belay," I say.

"Nice, Em." Greg double-checks that the rope system is locked in place. "Belay on."

I face the wall. "Climbing."

"Climb on." Greg's voice is full of authority, of certainty. I'd be lying to myself if I didn't admit it feels nice to have a man as capable as Greg watching my back.

I grab a hold and hoist myself up, perching my left foot on another hold. I twist and smile down at Greg. "How's that?"

"Not bad." His gaze drifts down my body. "But as much as I love looking at your rear end, Em, you don't want to leave it hanging out. Remember to swing your hips in so you can better centre your gravity."

Scott sniggers. Arses. Both of them. Time to show Greg what I can do.

I push up, grab the next hold, and swing my hips to the right. Push up again. Reach for the next hold. I hear Greg's intake of breath as he must realise I'm not a newbie. But I don't look down. I focus upward and scale the wall.

It's short, maybe five or six metres. I reach the top. It was too easy. Doubt creeps in. I hope Greg isn't angry about my deception.

"Take," I yell, which means I'm ready to be lowered.

When my feet hit the ground, Greg looms above me, his face grim. "You little liar."

The twinkle in his eyes tells me he's not mad, and the tension in my muscles eases. "I didn't lie. I just didn't tell you everything."

He slaps my butt. "That's for making me look like a fool."

Scott high-fives me. "She played you good, mate."

"You knew?" Greg jabs a finger at Scott. "You could have given me a heads up."

"Where's the fun in that?" Scott saunters away, chuckling.

"You are quite the surprise, Emily Saunders." He scratches his jaw, drawing my attention to the fine stubble. "I've underestimated you."

People always do. "Just because I'm short doesn't mean I'm less."

"I've never, *ever* thought you were less." Greg pulls me flush against his body, his erection prodding my stomach. Whoa. That's unexpected. He whisper growls in my ear. "There's nothing sexier than a woman who knows what she's doing."

I wrap my arms around his waist to stop myself from sliding to the floor. What have I got myself into?

I keep asking myself that question when I get into Greg's car a couple of hours later. When he rests his palm on my thigh. Squeezes. My body succumbs to the practised seduction, but my brain rebels as it lists all the reasons why getting involved with him is a bad idea.

Greg pats my knee. "Stop thinking so hard, Em."

"What do you mean?"

"Your nose is all scrunched up. You do that when you're concentrating."

He slows down as we approach the pub where he's promised me a no-strings lunch. "I said your virtue would be safe rock climbing, and I meant it."

"Why?"

"Because I want more than one date. And, contrary to your assumptions, I don't always put out the first time."

"Really?" I'm not sure whether I'm relieved he's treating me differently from the long line of women who've shared his bed or disappointed he won't be the one to ease the ache between my thighs tonight. "And how many times has that happened?"

"Not counting today?"

"Yeah."

Greg's jaw tightens. "Never."

Chapter Eleven

Greg

Sunlight streams into the little café, bouncing off the eclectic decor—purple, green and hideous golds that work together to create an offbeat atmosphere. Not that I usually notice that sort of crap, but I'm doing my best to keep my mind from drifting to other things. Like one sexy redhead. Hence why I walked the forty minutes here instead of driving.

My fingers drum on the tabletop. It's a miracle I kept my hands off Em yesterday. She was primed after the rock climbing. If I'd pushed, I'm sure I could have convinced her to come home with me. But a quick fuck isn't what I want from her, and that scares the shit out of me.

My phone dings. Monica better not be cancelling on me. I need to talk to her, and I'd rather do it face-to-face. But it isn't her; it's a text from Troy, saying we should 'catch up'. We never 'catch up', which means he wants something. I ignore his message and slide my phone into my pocket when Monica appears in the doorway. I'll deal with him later.

"Hey, stranger." Monica pecks me on the cheek and slides into the chair across from me. She's all sophistication in black leggings, a soft woollen jumper and long red curls. It's not the same shade as Emily's. It's more burnished iron, whereas Em's hair is like a raging fire. One I'm dying to burn in.

"Morning. Thanks for meeting me."

"How could I not?" Monica grins. "It's not every day an old flame calls me up and invites me to brunch." She pats my arm. The blood red of her long nails contrasts with the smooth porcelain of her fingers. Em's skin is smattered with freckles. Where Monica is all feline sensuality, Em is passionate cuteness. Funny how I haven't noticed those things about Em until I find myself looking at her polar opposite. I had no idea I had a thing for freckles.

Monica withdraws her hand. "So, I'll cut to the chase. What's wrong?"

That's what I like about Monica. Straight to the point. She's the only woman I've slept with whom I've maintained an ongoing friendship, which is lucky. She's Claire's boss and good friend, so if things had ended up messy, it would have made running into each other awkward as hell.

I pick up the salt shaker. Consider my response. Place it back on the table. "Does anything need to be wrong?"

"Yes."

The waitress hovers. "Are you ready to order?"

I nod at Monica. She scans the menu. "I'll have the granola and coconut yoghurt and a decaf soy latte, please."

"And you, Greg?" The woman brazenly looks me up and down despite the fact I'm not alone. It's hard to say if she's sizing me up for sex or a body bag. And she addressed me by name. Do I know her? "The big breakfast, thanks. And a double espresso."

The waitress flounces away. Weird.

Monica's gaze narrows. "What's going on?"

"I've got a dog."

She raises an eyebrow. "You invited me to brunch to tell me you bought a dog?"

"No. He belongs to a homeless man. I'm looking after him

for a while." I scrub my fingers through my hair. "It's a long story."

"Okay. And in this long story, you met someone?"

"Why do you ask that?"

She waves at me. "Because you've got a little boy lost look going on."

Jesus. Am I that obvious? I cross my feet, then uncross them. Sit up straighter. "I had a date yesterday."

She taps her nails on the tabletop, her emerald gaze pinning me to the seat. "And you want to see the woman again?"

I straighten my shirt. "Well ... yeah."

Monica gives me a Cheshire smile any cat would be proud of. "Let me guess. You were the perfect gentleman and kept your pants zipped on this date."

This is why Monica and I have remained friends. She's my female equivalent. She understands me in a way even Jake doesn't because he's always been a forever kind of guy.

"Em works at the station. Jake would have my balls if he knew I asked her out, so I took her to the climbing centre and then lunch. Nothing more."

Monica's mouth drops. "You went rock climbing for a first date?"

"Yeah. Turns out Em's a better climber than me." I smile at how she played coy about her ability. "She was at Jake and Claire's party. She's an intelligence analyst at the station." I don't tell Monica what Em and I got up to in the garden. That's between us.

"I know who she is. She's a beautiful woman." Monica crosses her arms and smiles. "I never thought I'd see the day."

"What do you mean?"

"The player meets his match."

Monica's insightful gaze makes me want to hide under the

table. She's nailed it. I want more than a fling with Em, but am I capable of giving her more?

I'm given a reprieve from answering when the waitress arrives with our food. She dumps the plates on the table and backs away, scowling at me. I'm guessing that means I should know who she is.

My stomach rumbles at the sizzling bacon, fried eggs and toast. A little girl at a nearby table giggles. I rub my belly and wink.

Monica leans across the table. "Seems like you care about Emily."

"I do." I pick up my cutlery. "And I have no idea what to do about it."

"What does she want?"

"I'm not sure. She's helping me with the dog, and we have wicked chemistry. But she's fighting it."

Monica shakes her head. "I'm still having trouble imagining you with a dog. It'd mess up your yard."

"You should see what he's done to my lounge room."

She looks aghast. "You let it inside?"

"Yeah. Bastard wrecked my sofa."

Monica rubs her hands together. "Oh dear, Greg. I have to see this."

"You want to meet Silas?"

"Is that the dog's name?"

"Yeah. He's ugly as sin, but Em washed him, and he smells pretty decent now. Although, I'm gonna have to get my cleaner to come twice a week. He drops hairs everywhere."

"It seems that both Emily *and* Silas have you running around in circles," says Monica cheekily. "And I think you like it."

I stab a piece of bacon with my fork and chew. She's right. I am enjoying it. Now that Silas isn't wrecking my furniture, it's nice to come home to someone, even if it is a dog. And having Em over to help has felt right.

What am I doing?

I'm not capable of having a relationship. They never last. My parents taught me that.

Monica taps the table. "Stop overthinking it, Greg."

I chew and swallow the meat down with some coffee. "Alright. Time to change the subject, then. What's happening with you?"

"Same old things." She shrugs. "We've got more work than we can handle. I've just signed a contract to sell a property in Oatlands." Her eyes light up. "It's a divorce settlement, which is sad, but it's an exciting opportunity—architect designed with all the extras."

"Good for you. And what about *your* love life?"

Colour floods Monica's face, and her gaze dips to the table. Interesting. "Spill."

"It's nothing."

"You're sporting a shade of red I've never seen on you before, so don't give me the brush off."

"There really is nothing to tell, but ..." She looks around the room as if to check there are no eavesdroppers nearby. "There is someone. He's a client. It would be terribly unprofessional."

"But you want to fuck him?"

"Greg!" Monica nods her head at the child. If she's worried, she shouldn't be. The girl has her head down, colouring in a picture. "I forget how crass you can be sometimes."

"Just calling it as I see it."

She sighs. "There's something about this guy that makes me wonder what it would be like to settle down."

Jesus. Who'd have thought? "That's serious."

"Yeah." Monica wipes her mouth with the napkin. "But enough about me. Let's finish eating so I can meet this dog."

Ten minutes later, our plates are empty. Monica gathers up her handbag and we stand. Despite the waitress' surliness, I leave a large tip.

Monica sucks in a breath. "That's too much, Greg."

"I'm feeling generous." And a little guilty. I have a vague memory of doing shots with the waitress and then doing each other. No idea when. They all blend into each other after a while, which is why the whole scene has become tiresome. Empty.

Monica drives us back to my house in her new BMW convertible. I climb out and stretch my legs. "Jesus, when are you going to get yourself a bigger car?"

She slaps my back. "You're getting old, Sergeant."

"Ha! You're not that far behind me, Miss Smarty Pants."

A familiar fiery halo catches my eye. Em? She stumbles into a beat-up red sedan.

"Em. Wait," I yell, but the car burns rubber and accelerates down the street.

"Fuck!"

Monica grabs my arm. "Greg?"

"That was Emily. She saw us get out of your car together. She must have assumed ..." I choke on the words. Fuck. I slap my palm against my forehead. She'll think that I've been playing her.

Chapter Twelve

Emily

I dodged a bullet on the weekend. That's what I keep telling myself as I work through the latest intelligence data. Allowing myself to be seduced by Greg's charms was a mistake. One I won't be repeating. He's an unacceptable and unprofessional distraction.

I sense his presence behind me. I almost called in sick to avoid him, but I'm stronger than that.

"You haven't been answering your phone." The low rumble of Greg's voice sends a flurry of tingles through my body. Add in the sensual woody fragrance of his cologne, and I need to fixate on the memory of him and Monica so I can stay angry with him. I won't be fooled. Not again.

I hit save on the keyboard and turn. Desperate brown eyes stare back at me. "What can I do for you, Sergeant Anderson?"

"Silas missed you yesterday."

"I'm sure *Monica* made up for it."

"She's a friend. Nothing more."

A beautiful, Goddess-like creature with legs that go on forever. *Friend,* my arse. "Sure, she is."

He leans closer and whispers. "I've told you before, Em, I'm many things, but a liar isn't one of them."

"What's going on here?"

The tightness in my stomach lessens. I've never been happier to hear Inspector Matthews' grumpy voice.

Greg clears his throat. "Nothing important."

Yeah. Nothing important. Just another silly girl thinking she can play with the big boys and getting her naïve butt handed to her. It's the university pricks all over again. When will I learn? No man is worth risking my career over.

Inspector Matthews' eyes narrow to tiny slits. "My office, now, Sergeant. I need a word with you."

Greg hovers over me, a tic in his jaw pulsing erratically, his hands clenched into fists. For a moment, it looks like he's going to defy the inspector, but he slowly straightens, gives me a lingering look, adjusts his jacket and strides off.

I sink into my seat, ignoring the questioning stares of the few people who've arrived early to work. Thank God Sergeant Jacobs isn't here yet. I return to the map I'm creating and add the locations of all recent drug overdoses and arrests. It's a meticulous task and, to date, hasn't elicited any obvious pattern that may be helpful for the team. But some unusual correlations might be relevant.

When I walk into the meeting room, tension hits me like a blast of hot air. Greg lounges in the back corner, a scowl on his face, while Inspector Matthews paces at the front. I avoid eye contact and slink into a seat in the corner opposite Greg.

As the room fills up, Inspector Matthews settles himself in the front row and Sergeant Jacobs stands at the front and begins the briefing. She runs through the PowerPoint presentation I prepared, skipping past the slide where I noted some vandalism incidents.

"Hold on." Inspector Matthews raises his hand. "What vandalism?"

"It's not important." Sergeant Jacobs gives a dismissive wave.

"I'll be the judge of that. Tell me more."

Sergeant Jacobs returns to the slide, but there's no detail. Oh no. I must have sent her the wrong version. That's not like me. It's because thoughts of Greg had scrambled my brain. She swallows and takes a sip of water. Nudges her glasses. Her expression is desperate as she looks at me. "Emily, can you elaborate?"

"Um ..."

Inspector Matthews gestures for me to stand. I smooth my hands down my dark brown skirt, straighten my jacket, and walk to the front of the room. It's only a dozen steps, but I'm hyper-aware of Greg tracking me with his eyes the entire time.

I point to the presentation, my hand shaking more than I'd like. "I noticed a cluster."

The inspector peers at the map on the screen. "Are you sure? I can't see anything."

A few officers smile and whisper to each other. I can't hear them, but I doubt it's complimentary.

A flush of heat floods my cheeks. I can't believe I stuffed up. "The detail's missing from the slide, sir." There's a loud snigger in the crowd, followed by more twittering. Inspector Matthews' expression darkens. He turns to face the room, and the chatter stops.

My fingers tremble as I attempt to salvage the situation. "Seventy percent of the drug overdoses over the last month have occurred within a hundred metres of a recently vandalised building. And in each instance, expensive cigar butts were found discarded on the footpath. It might be nothing, but I thought it was odd."

Inspector Matthews scratches his jaw as he continues to stare at the presentation. I clasp my fingers tightly in front of me while I wait for him to say something. Anything.

"You're right; it could be nothing. Or it could be everything." He turns his piercing blue gaze in my direction. "Well done, Emily."

I let out a long, slow breath. Sergeant Jacobs beams at me. Anything that reflects positively on me is good for her, too.

When the briefing finishes, I slide off my seat eager to return to my cubicle and dig out the missing slide, but Inspector Matthews stops me. "Emily, could you come to my office?"

"Of course." My mouth goes dry. He must be very impressed with my analysis.

I follow the inspector down the hallway. He ushers me inside and shuts the door.

"Please have a seat."

I perch on a chair, a fluttery sensation in my stomach. I'm not sure I'll ever be fully relaxed in his company.

The inspector sits and shuffles the papers on his desk. Tugs at his tie. His shirt. He looks even more nervous than me. Oh no. This isn't about my report. It's about Greg.

I glance at the door, wishing I could escape. "You didn't ask me here to talk about the intel, did you?"

"No." He clasps his hands on the desk and regards me with unblinking eyes. I refuse to crack. There's no rule forbidding staff from having relationships, despite Inspector Matthews and my boss being against them.

I clench my fingers tight to stop from fidgeting. Is this how cops make people talk?

The inspector clears his throat. "Emily, you're a good friend of Claire's."

Okay. That's not where I thought this conversation was going. I nod because I have no idea what to say to that.

He taps a finger on the table. "Sergeant Anderson is my best mate."

My heart rate speeds up. My fingers go numb from how hard I'm squeezing them.

"What I'm trying to say, Emily, and not doing a good job of it, is I don't want to see you hurt." He gives me the barest hint of a smile. "You're the best intel analyst we've had. You proved that yet again at this morning's meeting. I'd hate for it to become awkward for you if things went sour with Greg."

He can't possibly know anything's going on between us. Besides, it was one date. I need to play it cool. "They won't. Greg's a friend, that's all." Or was. Until I saw him with Monica.

Inspector Matthews' Adam's apple bobs up and down. His steady gaze tells me he doesn't believe me, but he's respectful enough not to call me out. "Okay. I know what you do in your own time is none of my business." He gestures to the door. "Obviously, this discussion is confidential."

"Of course, sir."

After several seconds of awkward silence, he nods. "My door's always open."

I mumble my thanks and flee the room. If Inspector Matthews is already suspicious, how long would it be before the rest of the station realised something was going on between Greg and me? I should thank Monica for saving me from a terrible mistake. Why, then, do I still want to tear her perfect, shiny red hair from her scalp?

Greg's kept busy in the field all week. I'm grateful for the breathing space, although it doesn't stop him from sending me texts each day, reiterating that Monica is only a friend. When I don't answer, he starts messaging me about Silas. Despite the cute pics accompanying the texts, I hold my ground. Even if Greg's telling the truth, it's better this way. I can't risk my job for a man.

Friday night rolls around and Inspector Matthews issues an open invitation for drinks at the pub as a thank you for another drug bust. He mentions that Greg and Dylan are out on a job and unlikely to make it. I'm tempted to go, but what if Greg still turns up? I'm not ready to see him in a social setting. It's safer to go home. Before I can decline, the inspector tells me Claire will be joining and would love to see me. How can I say no to that?

The pub thrums with energy, like a live animal, one with stale beer breath. It gobbles me up as I enter. Inspector Matthews offered me a lift, but I'd rather have my car, so I'm free to leave when I'm ready. I head towards the corner the gang usually hangs out in, dodging and weaving groups of office workers and tradies in animated conversations that apparently need both arms waving in the air, drinks spilling, to get their messages across. My pulse, which had been beating erratically, calms when I see no sign of Greg.

"Emily!" Claire jumps up from the table and greets me with a hug. "It's so good to see you."

She pulls me onto the bench seat beside her and scoots beside Inspector Matthews to make room. Any closer and she'd be sitting on his lap. My chest aches at the obvious love and affection between them.

Inspector Olsen, who's in charge of the station, and three drug squad detectives are seated across from us. The general duties guys and girls are at a different table. They're all in their twenties, and from some groans I've heard from Inspector Matthews at the office, I imagine he's thrilled to be out of hearing distance of their inane chatter. Given I'm a similar age, I wonder if he finds me just as annoying.

"Wine?" asks Claire.

"Yes, thanks."

"We've ordered garlic bread and a bunch of pizzas," says Inspector Matthews. "They shouldn't be too long."

Laura Nielson, one of the detectives, laughs. "Lucky Greg's probably out on the prowl; otherwise, we'd need to order twice as much food." Her barb hits home. My throat goes dry, and the sip of wine I was about to take becomes a gulp. Yep. Very lucky Greg isn't here. No doubt he's on a date with *Monica* at a fancy restaurant before taking her back to his place and doing what he does best.

I can't let on that Laura's comment bothers me, so I focus on the detectives across from the table. Laura's a tall woman, Amazonian in physique. She reminds me of Natalie. Except where Natalie's eyes are warm and welcoming, Laura's are cold and grey as granite boulders. She's always been friendly to me, but there's an intensity in her gaze that makes me uncomfortable. I wouldn't want to cross her.

"And don't forget beer," says Bryan, one of the other detectives. He's a sweet, quiet man who looks and sounds more like a church minister with a penchant for oversized suits.

The other detective, Jane, pipes up, pointing at the table of general duties cops. "Even Greg couldn't eat or drink as much as that lot. If we were worried about the cost, we shouldn't have invited them along."

Inspector Olsen grunts. "Hey, none of this, us and them."

It's like a switch flips and the five cops enter into a good-natured ribbing contest.

Claire nudges me with her elbow. "I don't know how you put up with them all day."

I laugh. "They're usually a lot more serious at work."

Claire leans closer. "They don't scare you?"

"No. You get used to them." Although, the steel blue of Inspector Matthews' eyes can be pretty scary when he's not happy.

Claire squeezes my hand. "Maybe one day I'll feel like that, but the memory of being locked in a jail cell is still too fresh."

"Of course. It must have been awful to be accused of something you didn't do."

"Yep." She glances at Inspector Matthews and rests her

hand on his thigh. "But Jake looked after me. He's such a sweetie."

Sweetie? I can think of many adjectives to describe the inspector, and that is not one of them.

The pizzas arrive, and we dig in like vultures fighting over their last meal. Claire cajoles me into drinking another glass of wine, and a pleasant lethargy seeps through my body. Looks like I'll be catching an Uber home now. But it's worth it. While a few officers treat me like a subordinate not worthy of their time, the people around this table embraced me from day one, making me feel part of the team. Over the past year, I've gotten to see beneath their austere exteriors and like what I've seen.

After a trip to the bathroom, Claire and I return to the group, and my stomach plummets. The very man I've been avoiding all week, the one responsible for a sudden surge of heat through my body, approaches the table, beer bottle in his hand. Damn.

Our gazes collide and a myriad of expressions flit across his face: longing, sadness, regret. Too late. I won't be played for a fool again.

There's a flurry of goodbyes as Inspector Olsen and the other three detectives depart. Part of me wants to bail with them, but why should I leave when my wine glass is full and Claire and I are having such a lovely time? Greg's appearance shouldn't ruin my night. Claire and I return to our seats and Greg sits across from us. Inspector Matthews joins him.

The Inspector gives me a funny look, then turns to Greg, a deep crease marring his brow. "What are you doing here?"

"I was invited."

"I thought you were too busy to come."

Greg shrugs. "Dylan and I finished up earlier than I expected."

Claire glares at the inspector. "You're being rude, Jake." She leans across the table and pats Greg's arm. "I'm glad you could make it. I feel like all our friends have been avoiding us since our engagement party."

"We're giving the newly engaged couple space." Greg winks. "The last thing I want to do is turn up unexpectedly and see something I shouldn't. Jake would deck me."

A deep shade of pink stains Claire's cheeks.

"You're not funny." Inspector Matthews' jaw tightens. "It didn't stop you from dropping in and trying to foist that mutt on us."

Greg chuckles, but it seems forced. Like he's trying too hard. He turns his attention to me. Dark flecks swirl amongst the molten chocolate. A girl could drown in those eyes.

Two can play at this game. It's best to show I'm not affected by his philandering. "How's Silas going?"

"He's good." Greg takes a sip of his beer. "I even walked him yesterday without scaring the neighbourhood kids with my swearing."

It's too easy to imagine Silas dragging Greg along. Greg suffering the indignity of picking up dog poop. I take a large gulp of wine to hide my smile. I mustn't forget what he's done.

"Would you like me to bring over a few more of Ruby's toys for you?" asks Claire.

"That's okay. I went and bought him a bunch of stuff from Pet Barn. Gotta stop him from destroying my things somehow."

For someone who claims to hate dogs, Greg's doing an impressive job of pretending otherwise. It makes it hard to stay mad at him.

Inspector Matthews slaps Greg on the shoulder. "I still can't believe you've got that dog." The inspector's phone rings. He pulls it out of his pocket. "Sorry. I have to take this."

I feel Greg's gaze on me, but I avoid its seductive power. Being good to Silas doesn't make him any less a womaniser.

The inspector ends his call with a frown. "That was my

parents. A large branch from the old liquid amber tree in the backyard fell at their place after a freak wind gust."

"Oh, no." Claire clutches her throat. "Are they okay?"

"Yeah. It didn't hit the house, but Oscar's upset."

Claire slides out of her seat, her expression reminding me of my mum whenever she tended to the many grazes and cuts I got as a child. "We'd better get home, then."

Inspector Matthews stands, his gaze flitting between me and Greg. "We can give you a lift if you like, Emily."

I shake my head. "I'll catch an Uber."

"You sure?"

"Yeah. I'll be fine, sir."

"*Sir?*" Claire digs me in the ribs.

"Ouch." I give her a playful shove. "Your fiancé will always be Inspector Matthews to me."

The inspector's eyes twinkle. "One day I'll get you to call me Jake."

Nope. No way will I be calling him Jake anytime soon.

"I'll make sure Em gets home safely," says Greg.

I grit my teeth and say nothing. I don't want to delay Claire and Jake, but I'm a big girl. Perfectly capable of looking after myself.

Inspector Matthews gives Greg a long, hard glare before taking Claire's hand and leaving. I should follow them, but some perverse part of me wants to have it out with Greg. The anger I've been suppressing all week rises to the surface.

"So, who's the lucky girl to grace your sheets this weekend, Greg?"

"Don't be like that." Greg runs his fingers through his hair. "I told you, Monica's an old friend. Nothing happened."

He sounds sincere. But Monica is so beautiful. And he's well … him.

"Why should I believe you?"

"Because I don't lie."

There's no hint of deceit in his voice or his expression.

Still, I remember how close they danced at Claire's engagement party. There was a familiarity between them that suggested they were well acquainted with each other's bodies.

"Have you slept with her?"

"Yes."

I gasp, somehow surprised at his quick admission.

"But it was last year."

"Do you have breakfast with your 'friends you once slept with' often?"

"No." Greg stretches a hand towards me, then pulls back. "Monica is different. She really is just a friend now. All I did was talk about you."

I look away and take a sip of wine. Despite my best efforts to focus on my anger at Greg this week, in my heart, I still want to believe it's the truth. "Why would you do that?"

"Because I like you, Em. I wanted a woman's opinion on how to be a better man for you."

Oh. That admission burrows deep inside, warming my ovaries. But I can't let him sweet-talk me. "You could have asked Claire."

"Yeah, right." He snorts. "She'd tell Jake, and he'd bust my balls for getting involved with you. No way I'd confide in her."

"And that's why it's best we end things now."

Greg clasps his fingers around my hand, stroking the wrist with his thumb. It's both erotic and comforting. "Is that what you want?"

Everything about Greg's body language tells me he's truthful—his eyes burning into mine, the openness of his chest and shoulders. I chew the inside of my cheek. Detecting lies is something I've always been good at. An innate ability, so my dad said. It's what led me to study psychology. I wanted to understand more about what made people tick. The only times I've been wrong are when I haven't listened to my gut. Like with Jared, the arsehole at uni who slept with me to win a bet. Focused on my studies, I hadn't realised rumours were circulating about me being a hillbilly cold fish. All the warning signs had been there, but I'd ignored them when he asked me out. The humiliation still smarts.

But Greg isn't Jared. And while my brain is freaking out at the thought of dating him, my gut says to give him a chance.

"I'll go out with you again."

Greg's face breaks into a megawatt smile.

I hold my hand up. "But this needs to stay between us. I won't be fodder for the gossipers at work."

The smile wavers. "Of course. You can trust me."

It's still risky. If Sergeant Jacobs finds out we're in a relationship, or whatever this is, I'd lose her good opinion. I can't risk it influencing her assessment of my performance. Not to mention, I refuse to be the laughing-stock of my peers ever again.

Can I trust Greg to be discrete? It's clear Inspector Matthews and my boss are on the same page when it comes to fraternisation, so yes, I can. Greg will be as invested as I am in keeping things secret.

Decision made, I slide out of my seat. Greg places his hand on the small of my back, a solicitous and respectful move that has my body perking up while my brain does a private freak out. I hope this won't be something I'll regret.

Chapter Thirteen

Greg

This is madness. Why did I suggest Em choose the location for a second date?

Guilt.

Even though I've done nothing wrong, the insidious emotion has been sitting like a lump of grey metal in my stomach for the hurt I caused her through the misunderstanding with Monica.

I yank at the waistband of my jeans and shake. A trickle of sand escapes through the legs, but I'm sure some grains have ended up in my jocks. I glare at Silas. He stares back with a lopsided grin, unrepentant for the mountain of sand he's scraped all over me with his digging.

"Look at that sunrise, Greg. It's perfect." I'd rather bask in Emily's smile. She's brimming with vitality. "And Silas is so happy to be here."

I grunt. Lucky Silas. What about me?

Em runs ahead barefoot, the dog on her heels. We have the place to ourselves. Not a surprise when the sun is a shimmer of gold on the horizon. Who in their right mind would think breakfast on the beach at dawn, in late autumn, with a mangy mutt as a chaperone was a great idea for a date?

Emily.

I follow behind, my joggers squelching in the soft sand. Fantastic! They'll probably be ruined after this. A couple of seagulls glide past, checking us out. No doubt sensing the food in my backpack. The ball of the sun rests above the horizon when we finally stop. Em flops on the sand, looking barely legal with her windswept hair and rosy cheeks. But the hipster jeans hug a woman's hips and arse, not a girl's. And if she ever takes off the navy-blue puffer jacket, the grey long-sleeve T-shirt underneath contains shapely breasts that I had a hard time keeping my eyes off while driving.

"This is a perfect spot for breakfast, Greg."

"Yep." I hope I sound sincere. We're in a private area, hidden from the rest of the beach by the natural topography. It'd be romantic. If we'd left the dog at home. And it was summer.

I slip off my backpack and withdraw a picnic rug. Spread it out. Em jumps up and kneels on the material, scattering sand everywhere. I grit my teeth. This is why I don't do beaches unless it's sitting on the shore with a beer and enjoying the scenery. Between Em and Silas, we'll drag half the beach home in my car.

Em scoots closer. "Can I help?"

"You sit back and relax. I've got this."

"Thanks for agreeing to the picnic, Greg. I know you're not real keen on it."

"Not at all." Lie. "I just thought it might be a bit chilly."

"I love the beach, but I only saw it once a year growing up. It's so vital. Energising. Very different from the farm." Em stares at the waves and a tear slides down her cheek. I catch it with my thumb. The city might be where her life is now but she clearly misses home.

"Maybe you need to move closer to the coast?"

She huffs. "Not all of us can afford water views."

If only she knew. Those views come with their own

emotional baggage. I wouldn't wish it on anyone. "Well, you're here now. How about you take Silas exploring, and I'll set breakfast up?"

"Thank you." She kisses me on the cheek, lingering for a second. Or do I imagine it? I lean into her sweet perfume, and then she's gone, Silas trotting alongside her up the beach.

I shake the gingham rug to remove the sand, place a handwoven rattan plate on it and spread out the food: mini quiches, croissants and fresh fruit salad. Next is a handful of pink rose petals. Some escape on the breeze, but most remain. I might not be keen on breakfast on a beach in the cold … alright, I've been bitching like a whiny brat in my head ever since we hit the sand … but I like the challenge of wooing Em. She's nothing like the other women I've known.

The wind settles, and the sun's rays reduce the chill enough that I shrug off my jacket. I sit and pull out two thermoses: coffee for me and Lavender Earl Grey tea for Em.

Em and Silas return wearing massive smiles and a hint of mischief in their eyes. Em's jaw drops. "Wow. I wasn't expecting all this."

"When I take a lady out, I do it properly."

Her eyes mist. "That you do." She turns to Silas. "Sit."

He assumes the position, his adoring gaze fixed on her. She rummages in her backpack and retrieves a black rug. Then places a huge bone on top of it. Half a cow's leg. Jesus Christ. I'm surprised it didn't stink out the car.

"Don't pull that face, Detective." Em shoves at my arm with a giggle. "It'll keep Silas busy so we can enjoy this beautiful picnic." She unwraps the plastic covering and hands the bone to Silas. "Here you go, boy."

Good point. I like her thinking, although we could have enjoyed the morning even better if we'd left the smelly hound at home.

Em rubs her hands with sanitiser, then sits next to me. I

give her the mug of tea. She brings it to her mouth, sniffs and her eyes widen. "How did you know?"

"I take notice." It's all she drinks at the station. Turns out you can't buy that sort of tea in a supermarket, but I found it online and express shipped it so it would arrive before our date. The pleasure in Em's eyes tells me it was worth sourcing it for her.

She closes her eyes and breathes in the tea again. "Thank you."

My chest tightens. There's a vulnerability in Em's expression that makes me want to haul her into my lap and hug it away. At the same time, she has steel running down her spine. Jake assumes Em's would be hurt in a relationship with me, but I'm starting to think I'm in more danger.

We enjoy the food in silence, except for the background roar of the waves. Em lets out an unladylike burp and slaps her hand over her mouth. In anyone else, I'd find it gross. With Em, it's adorable.

"So, what made you decide to be an intelligence analyst?"

She stares at the ocean and chews on the inside of her cheek. She does that when she's nervous. "I majored in criminology at uni, so it seemed a good fit. Why'd you join the police force?"

Her question doesn't fool me. She's diverting the conversation away from herself. What isn't she telling me? "To piss off my old man."

"Why?" She looks confused.

"He expected his sons to follow in his footsteps and become politicians." Controlling bastard. I glance down at the sand so she can't see the depth of my resentment. "I had no intention of selling my soul."

"Not all politicians are corrupt."

"No, they're not. But my dad is all for progress at any cost. If he had his way, all remaining heritage buildings in Sydney would be torn down and skyscrapers built in their place." I admire the pristine shoreline and straw-coloured sand as far as the eye can see. My father would allow this piece of paradise to be desecrated with concrete monoliths if he could.

Em winces at the harsh note in my voice. I don't want her to think I'm heartless, so I clasp her hand and say, "I don't mean to be abrupt. Dad left us for a woman half his age when I was fourteen. I guess it's a sore point. He could be a benevolent doctor saving starving kids in a third-world country, and I'd still hate him."

"I'm sorry, Greg." She squeezes my hand, and I love how small and soft it feels in mine. "That must have been tough. How did your mum cope?"

"She did her best, but she never got over the bastard." That's why I've avoided relationships. Someone always gets hurt. *No, don't think that. Enjoy the date.*

Em scoots closer to me until our hips and legs brush against each other. Her desire to connect with me is intoxicating. I shove the empty rattan plate to the side and pull her onto my lap. She doesn't resist, allowing me to settle her between my thighs.

Silas glances at us but returns to gnawing his bone. Good boy. Em nestles into me, her back against my chest, legs draped over mine. My dick stirs. I ignore it and bury my face in Em's hair and the sweet smell of apples. Further up the beach, a few surfers brave the cold water in wetsuits. Otherwise, we have the place to ourselves.

My dick refuses to get the message there'll be no action, at least not here. I give up trying to will it down and just enjoy the warmth of Em's body, the pressure of her soft curves on my thighs and chest. The gentle in and out of her ribcage. The painful pooling of blood in my crotch. It's a first for me— cuddling for the sake of it. Not as a prelude to sex. I find it's not unpleasant.

Em burps. "Oops. I might have eaten too much." She wriggles on my lap. Then stills. I guess she's noticed the hard rod in my pants. She adjusts her position to avoid pressing down on me. I suppress my disappointment.

Her cheeks are flushed, and her blue eyes are brighter than the sky. "How about we take Silas for a swim?"

And here I was, hoping she'd suggest we return to my place. Get naked. "You want to get him wet?"

"Of course. I've brought a ball. Dogs love chasing them into the water."

I shake my head. My poor car will need premium detailing after this. I might even have to sell it.

Em's smile is infectious. I can't say no. So, against my better judgement, I agree.

Silas isn't too happy to give up his bone. He falls short of growling, but he gives Em quite the stink eye. For once, the mutt and I are in agreement.

"I'll pack up the picnic. You play with Silas."

"Okay." She doesn't need further encouragement, stripping off her jacket and throwing the ball towards the water. Silas cocks his head and stares at her like she's lost her marbles. Drool slides down his jowls as he stares longingly at the backpack she put the filthy bone into.

Em flaps her hands. "Off you go, Silas."

He continues to stare at her. I clamp my jaw shut to stop myself from laughing.

"Huh!" Em's hands slide to her hips. "He enjoyed chasing the ball in your yard."

I chuckle at her screwed-up button nose. "I think he'd rather eat his bone." If given the choice, Buster always chose food, too.

"I'm sure he'll change his mind when he gets in the water." She trots towards the sea. Silas runs after her. I pack up the picnic and shove everything into my bag. If only it was as easy to lock up my growing feelings for Em.

By the time I stroll to the water's edge, Em's rolled up her jeans and is knee-deep in the water, begging Silas to join her.

If dogs could stand on tippy toes, that's what he'd be doing. I burst out laughing at his expression—abject horror. It's like he's asking himself why she's intent on drowning him.

Em flicks the water, trying to entice Silas to follow. He backs away as the remains of a wave skim his paw.

"Come here, Silas." I pat my thigh. "You don't have to swim if you don't want to, mate."

Em shakes her head. "Chickens, both of you."

She wades out, cooing to Silas. He's not buying any of it, preferring to stay on the dry sand and rub against my leg. A freak wave rushes in, and before I can yell a warning to Em, she's swamped and disappears. Shit. My pulse skyrockets. I rush in to help. Cold water swirls around my ankles and seeps into my joggers. Em surfaces, coughing and spluttering.

She swipes hair from her eyes. "Crap. What happened?"

Thank Christ she's all right. My heart lifts at the bedraggled sight in front of me. "You got dumped."

Her long-sleeve T-shirt clings to her skin, the nipples poking out and looking far too suckable. If I was a gentleman, I wouldn't stare. But I'm not, so I do. She's like a tiny water nymph, and when she realises what I'm staring at, she becomes a fiery one—eyes blazing, red hair shining in the sunlight.

She folds her arms across her chest and glares. "I need my backpack."

I do my best to appear contrite, even though I'm not, because the outline of Em's breasts is seared in my brain. We return to our picnic spot, and Em pulls out a towel.

All moisture disappears from my mouth as she rubs it over her body. The wet fabric of her T-shirt hugs every curve and while I'm enjoying the show, I don't like the goosebumps peppering her arms.

"You won't get dry that way. How about you take your shirt off and put the jacket on?"

Em hugs the towel to her chest. "Good try, Greg."

"I promise I won't peek." I point at Em's fingers, which are turning a disturbing tinge of blue. "Come on. You're freezing."

She huffs. "Okay. But no peeking."

What sort of man does she think I am? I don't need to perve on a woman to get my jollies.

She turns her back and peels the T-shirt over her head. I look away, but not before I'm greeted with toned trapezius muscles and a smattering of freckles. I wonder if she's ever sunbaked topless and has freckles on her breasts as well. I swallow, suddenly feeling like a gawky teenager with his first half-naked woman. Not an experienced man who's had countless women in his bed. Maybe I'm not as adult as I thought I was.

Further up the beach, the emptiness is filling with surfers and walkers, but they're still far enough away to be nothing but blobs in the distance.

"I'm decent now," says Em.

I turn around. The fresh air and cold water only make her more beautiful. She positively glows. "Warmer?"

"Yeah." She glances down at her jeans. "At least my top half is."

While part of me imagines soaping her up in a hot shower when we get home, another, more protective part of me just wants to see her dry so she doesn't catch a chill. Yet another first for me.

I hold out my hand. "Shall we go back to the car?"

Em shivers. "Yes, please."

Chapter Fourteen

Emily

The bathroom steams up as I linger under the largest rainwater showerhead I've ever seen. Greg all but carried me in here and ordered me to warm up. It was deliciously caveman-like and yet respectful. My fingers and toes prickle, the hot water slowly washing away the ocean's chill.

Greg's scent consumes me, infusing heat into my skin that has nothing to do with the shower. It's all thanks to the sandalwood body wash, shampoo and conditioner. I'm surprised he has conditioner and try not to think about it being here for all the random women he brings home rather than for himself. It's a win regardless since my hair would rival the knotted mess of a cat's furball without it.

I shut off the shower and grab a huge white fluffy towel. Even it smells like Greg. I dry off and slip on a football jersey he left for me. It's very modest, skimming the tops of my knees, which is just as well because the boxer shorts he put with them are twice my size. I leave them behind. No way they'll stay up.

Threading my fingers through my hair brings some semblance of order to my curls. There's no sound from outside. I have no idea what Greg and Silas are doing. At least

Silas wasn't wet, but his coat was full of sand. Greg can pretend all he likes that Silas is a nuisance, but I've seen the adoring glances he sends the dog's way. The gentle caresses of Silas' head. Soft murmurs of "good boy". Greg's a softy under his blunt exterior.

My hand rests on the doorknob. Am I really going out there with no underwear? I glance down. I'm more decently covered than most women on a night out, yet I've never felt more vulnerable. It's like the layers of protection I've hidden behind to avoid being hurt are being peeled away one by one.

I pad down the hallway, the floorboards cool beneath my feet. The air is warmer than I expected. Greg must have turned on the ducted heating. Splashes of colour masquerading as art hang on the walls. Greg doesn't strike me as an art enthusiast, so my guess is he engaged an interior designer to fit the house out with a modern look.

I round the corner to the kitchen. Light bounces off the shiny appliances, but there are no signs of life.

A soft murmur draws my attention to the back door and the garden outside. Silas crouches between Greg's legs, head resting on Greg's thigh, his one eye closed. Greg passes a brush through Silas' hair. It slides through like butter, telling me the bristles are either wide apart or he's been brushing Silas the entire time I've been in the shower. It does fluttery things to my chest.

I slide the door open, shyness overcoming me. "Hi."

Greg's gaze snaps to my legs, making me even more ultra-aware of my lack of underwear. He strokes Silas' ears and stands.

"Do you want me to give Silas a bath?" I ask.

"Nah. He's good. I've brushed out most of the sand. One of those mobile dog wash guys is coming around next week.

It can wait until then. Lucky he didn't go in the water." His gaze drifts to my damp hair. "Unlike some people."

Awareness zips between us. It would be so easy to fall into Greg's arms. Let him carry me to his bedroom, but I'm not sure I'm ready yet, even though we'll inevitably end up there. "I guess I should be going."

Greg's eyebrow lifts. "You'd leave in my T-shirt?"

I tug at the fabric as if that will make it longer. "Everything else is wet."

A sexy smile lights up Greg's face, leaving me in no doubt what he's thinking.

I take a step back. "Ah, ah. Don't you say anything naughty, Sergeant Anderson."

"I wouldn't dare." He chuckles. "I've thrown your jeans and shirt in the washer. I'll put them in the dryer next, and you'll be free to escape by lunchtime."

"Oh." That's thoughtful. This man keeps surprising me. "Thank you."

He shoves his hands into his pockets and rocks on the balls of his feet. "We can always watch a movie while we wait."

Mmm. Is that code for sex? The smart thing would be to leave, but returning home to my tiny unit and listening to my neighbours argue doesn't appeal. I can see why Greg bought a house. He has too much presence to be confined to four walls, even if those walls belonged to a penthouse apartment. "That sounds good, but I get to pick since this is still officially our second date."

Greg's brown eyes sparkle as his gaze rakes over me. "You always go on dates without underwear?"

He's impossible. The T-shirt reaches my knees, so everything is covered, but I pull at it anyway. I glare at him, although the heat in my cheeks gives me away. "You don't know that."

He looks pointedly at my crotch. "There'd be a wet patch if you'd put your soaked knickers back on."

The way he says wet patch, all low and growly, sends a flood of moisture to my lady parts. Damn him. At least he can't see my pointy nipples, the jersey fabric thick enough to keep everything hidden.

"You left boxer shorts for me."

Greg grins. "That was to show I was sensitive. You've got a curvy arse, but you're still tiny compared to me. No way they'd fit."

I laugh. He's hard not to like when he's playful. "You're impossible."

Silas barrels towards me and nudges my leg. I rub his ears, so soft and velvety. Perfect timing.

Greg mumbles, "Cock blocker," and steps away. "I'm guessing you'd like a hot cup of tea?"

"Yes, please."

"Alright. I'll sort out a snack and drinks. You scroll through Netflix and see what takes your fancy."

I slap my chest with my palm. "You're going to trust me with the TV remote?"

"Don't let it go to your head, Red." He chuckles and strides into the house.

I take a moment to enjoy the view. Greg's hot in a suit, but that bum was made for jeans. Silas nuzzles my leg and looks up at me with one round puppy dog eye, not unlike Greg when he wants something. "Don't worry, sweetie. I'll keep my hands to myself."

Then again, you don't date a man like Greg without expecting intimacy. Or wanting it. And I so want it. I'm just not sure if I want it today. Plus, I need to keep reminding myself that this is a no-strings-attached fling. Nothing more. Men like Greg don't change their ways overnight, and I won't risk my career or my heart for any man.

Chapter Fifteen

Greg

My chest tightens as I watch Em settle onto the couch, feet and all, and work the remote. She looks good in my clothes. In my house. Silas trots in her direction. Nope. No way, buddy. You're not blocking me this time.

"Silas," I whisper. His ears prick up.

"Come. I've got a big treat for you." I open the fridge door, and any thoughts the sneaky mutt had of joining Em disappear. He lurches towards me and sits on his haunches, barely missing my feet. "Good boy."

Silas' one eye pops from his skull when he sees the massive bone. The same one he'd enjoyed at the beach. This will keep him busy for a few hours. I peel off the plastic wrapping. The pungent odour of fat and raw meat hits my nostrils. Gross. I still can't believe Em had this in her backpack or that I allowed it into my fridge.

Silas follows me into the garden, more obedient and subdued than I've ever seen him. Drool slides down one side of his mouth. Lovely.

"Okay, boy, here you go." I offer the revolting piece of dead animal to him. He grabs it and races to the other end of the lawn without a second glance. Ungrateful dog.

I return to the kitchen and wash my hands twice to get the smell off. And a third time, just to be sure.

With a teapot in one hand and a cheese platter in the other, I stroll into the living room. Em drops her feet onto the floor and smooths the jumper down her thighs. It sits a few inches above her knees. My throat constricts. It's going to be torture sitting next to her, knowing she isn't wearing anything underneath it.

Em shuffles along the lounge, making space for me. She grabs a piece of brie and pops it in her mouth. "Yum." She rolls her eyes and half sucks, half chews the cheese. The rolling motion of her throat has my dick stirring. Shit. Down, boy. Not yet.

"I have to be honest, Greg, I'm still getting used to this domesticated side of you. I'd never have guessed you were such a whiz in the kitchen." She shoves a large strawberry between those luscious lips.

It makes me even more hungry to strip her naked. Devour her. Then let her feast on me. "And you call me sexist."

She opens her mouth to respond. Juice spills onto her chin.

I place a finger on her lips. "No talking while you're eating, Miss Saunders."

She moves her head before I give in to the urge to slide my finger between those enticing lips and risk having her race out the door. I return to the kitchen, grab a teacup and saucer for Em and prepare a coffee for myself. When I return to the living area, there's a chick flick on the screen.

The Princess Diaries? She's got to be kidding me.

Em looks up, all wide eyes and innocence. "I found my favourite movie."

"Great." Just great. I lower myself onto the lounge and tell myself she could have made a worse choice, although I'm not sure what.

Em bursts out laughing. "You should see your face."

"Yeah, real funny."

"You said I could choose."

"Yes, I did." Even if she wanted to fool around, my dick wouldn't be up for it after this torture. Em grabs the remote off the table, the jumper riding higher on her leg. My pants tighten. And so does my chest. Okay, I guess my dick can handle any abuse Em dishes out. She looks perfect in my jersey. Like she belongs on the lounge. In my house. My life.

Those thoughts would have had me hurrying any other woman out the door. Instead, I kiss the top of Em's head. "As long as I'm sitting next to you, Red, I don't care what we watch."

Em pats my thigh, and I freeze. "You're a good guy, Greg." She hits a button on the remote and *Die Hard* bursts onto the screen. "Gotcha." She lifts her hand from my leg and bounces her arse on the lounge, clapping her hands.

I tweak her nose. "You're playing with fire, little girl."

She pours herself a cup of tea, all ladylike. Adds a dash of milk. "And you're too easy to tease."

Warmth surges through me. Em's playfulness is addictive. I'm not sure I could ever get enough of her. "You really want to watch *Die Hard*? Because I meant it, Em. It's your choice."

"Absolutely. It's my favourite movie, after *The Matrix*." She does karate chops with both arms. "Because Keanu Reeves has all the moves."

Has he now? Wait 'till she sees my moves. "Bloodthirsty much?"

She shrugs. "They're just movies."

It's like Em has two personalities—the quiet, conscientious one at the station and then this rock climbing, action movie afficionado, dog whispering dynamite. Why would she hide her real self at work? Has someone hurt her? Not that Em can't look after herself. The more I learn about her, the more it's obvious how capable she is.

I press a kiss to the inside of her wrist. "As long as you're not a karate black belt and able to kick my arse, we're good. My ego would never recover."

She gives a shaky laugh, curls wisping across her face and covering her eyes. "Surely, you don't mean that?"

"Yeah, I do." Her smile wavers. I know I sound like a chauvinistic pig, but this is a sore point for me. I clasp her hand and kiss her fingertips. "We had a trainer at the academy who was a martial arts expert." And a stunner who rebuffed my advances, but I keep that titbit to myself. "She took a little too much delight in whipping my arse in front of the rest of the recruits. Even broke two of my ribs. I swore no one, woman or man, would ever beat me again."

"Oh, Greg, that's awful. Did anyone report it?"

"Nope. Everyone laughed, including our superiors. She was about your height. They thought it was hilarious."

She opens her mouth as if to say something, then closes it. The sparkle in her blue eyes fades. "Well, you're safe with me."

Her earnest reassurance makes me want to pick her up and never let her go. Instead, I sink further into the lounge, one eye on the TV, the other on Em. My fingers itch to run through the curls on her head. Instead, I drape my arm across the back of the seat. It's an obvious move, but what's a guy to do? Em gives me a side eye but doesn't push me away.

"Where's Silas?" she asks.

"He's out in the yard demolishing that half a cow you brought with you."

"Good." She nods. "He'll like that."

It's been years since I last watched *Die Hard*, and I soon lose myself in it, even if the plot is far-fetched. Cops who break the rules get their arses handed to them in real life. At some point, Em shuffles closer so our sides are touching and my arm rests across her shoulders. It seems wrong to interrupt the action on screen with a different kind of action in the living room, so I enjoy the warmth of Em's body and the sense of companionship I've only experienced with Jake. Not that hanging out with Jake has ever, and I mean *ever*, given me a semi in my pants.

Em leaps from the seat. "Yes! Die, you bastard."

Whoa. I did say bloodthirsty. She turns to me with a huge smile and holds out her palm. I slap her hand for a high five and before I can overthink it, I pull her onto my lap. She touches her forehead to mine, her blue eyes hazy with desire. If it was any other woman, I'd already have my tongue down their throat and my hand between their legs, but Em's different.

"Are you going to kiss me, Detective?"

"Only if you want me to, Miss Saunders."

Her gaze drops to my mouth. "I do."

Finally. I lower my head and suck on her bottom lip. It releases with a pop, and I cover her mouth with mine. Her tongue slips between my lips, bringing with it a hint of strawberry and lavender. She runs her tongue across my teeth and the roof of my mouth. Tangles with mine. It's a slow exploration, one that has my dick flying at full mast.

I adjust my position to relieve the pressure. Em wriggles closer, pressing her full breasts against my chest while her bare arse grazes my dick. It takes all my willpower to keep my thoughts and actions above the waist. The soft, braless globes feel like heaven. My fingers itch to cup them. I ease my hands under her jumper until they're sitting below the curve of her soft flesh. No sudden movements. I don't want to scare her off. I stroke the underside of one breast. Em's breath hitches. My fingers freeze.

She releases my mouth. "Don't stop," she whispers and resumes kissing me.

That's all the permission I need. My tongue thrusts into her mouth, taking control, while I inch my hands up and cup her breasts. Fuuuck. The nipples are hard little buds begging to be sucked. I flick them with my thumbs. Em whimpers and shoves them against me.

An annoying knock pierces my consciousness, demanding to be heard over Em's soft moans and heavy pants. Wait. The panting is me.

Em wrenches her mouth from mine. "Greg, is that someone at the door?"

"Nope." I pull her against me.

"Yes, it is."

I stop tweaking her nipples and drop my hands to her waist. No one ever calls on me announced. I'll rip Jake a new one if it's him and Claire with another surprise visit. Or he'll rip me one when he sees who I'm with.

Em's face is flushed, her pupils dilated. Goddammit. She's a woman ready to be fucked.

The knocking starts again. An insidious thought slips into my head. What if it's that random I picked up at the club two weeks ago? She was pissed when I sent her packing. Would she come back claiming she left something behind just to mess with me?

Em climbs off my lap, pulling at the jumper to avoid flashing me. "You'd better get it."

"Yeah." I stand, my dick catching on my zipper. Fuck. I adjust myself.

The colour in Em's cheeks deepens. I ruffle her hair. "You did that to me, Red."

She looks away. The moment's ruined. I can see the wheels turning in that brain of hers. There'll be no sex now. Not today. Unless the world is on fire, the arsehole at my front door is toast. And if it's that random, Julia, burnt toast.

I run my hands down my shirt. It covers my crotch. Which, in my current state, is a good thing.

Bruce Willis has nothing on me and my blue balls as I stride down the hallway, primed for battle. There's more knocking. For Christ's sake. I'm coming.

I swing open the door, ready to tell whoever it is to fuck off. Standing there is the last person I expected to see.

※

"Hey, Greg." Troy gives me a short nod, then shoves his hands in his pockets, and stares at my feet. He's wearing cream pants and an Argyle sweater, making him look like he came from the golf club. However, his slumped shoulders and dishevelled appearance are more akin to pacing the streets.

"What are you doing here?"

His gaze lifts to mine, shadows dulling the sheen of his royal blue eyes. He sweeps his fingers through his hair. It's blonder than the last time I saw him. "I was hoping we could talk."

"About what?"

Troy's opposite to me in every way. He's a successful politician with a model wife and two kids. Boy and girl, of course. The only thing we have in common is our love of quality clothes. For this reason, we rarely see each other. He's certainly never just shown up at my house unannounced.

Troy glances behind him. "Do you mind if I come in?"

"Oh, sure." I mind a fucking lot, but it must be serious for him to seek me out. Then I remember never responding to the text he sent me.

Troy strolls through the door. "I tried to call, but you didn't answer."

No. My phone is turned to silent. For a reason. A five-foot, redheaded, luscious curves reason.

Em stands by the lounge, her hand raised in an awkward wave. "Hi."

Troy swallows. "I'm sorry. I didn't know you had company." He turns to leave.

"It's okay," says Em. "I need to be going, anyway." She

glances down at the jersey she's wearing. Troy's gaze drops to her bare legs. Fucker. "Um … my clothes, Greg?"

She looks adorable, with her face matching the colour of her hair. "They're in the laundry. They should be dry. I'll get them for you."

"That's okay. I'll find them."

She hightails it up the hallway.

Troy takes in the blanket on the couch and the food on the coffee table. "I can still go."

"Nah. Too late now." I pick up the plates on the small table and walk into the kitchen. "You want a coffee?"

"You got anything stronger?"

The world might not be on fire, but something big's obviously going down in my brother's life. "Whiskey, it is."

Em returns five minutes later in her jeans and puffer jacket. No one would know she's not sporting any underwear. Which is just as well, because I don't want my brother ogling her. Married or not, he's got eyes and, no doubt, has already made conclusions seeing Em wearing my jersey and nothing else.

I can't let Em leave with that look of shame in her eyes. I curl my arm around her waist. She stiffens but doesn't pull away. I take it as a positive sign. "Em, this is my brother, Troy. Troy, this is … Emily."

"Nice to meet you," says Troy, all impeccable manners as he nurses his whiskey glass.

"You too." Em gives him an awkward smile.

Em stiffened even more when I hesitated. I nearly said girlfriend, but I didn't want to presume. Is that what I call her after two dates? Troy most likely assumes she's one of many, and I fear Em will think the same. Normally, I don't give a shit, but with Em, I do. She's special. I don't want to just bang and forget her. It's a foreign feeling that's doing my head in.

Em grabs her backpack. "I'd better go."

"I'll walk you out."

Em rushes through the door. I grab her arm and pull her back. "Hey. I had a really nice time today."

"Me too," she tells the ground.

"Em." I lift her chin with my fingers. "I'm sorry about the interruption."

"That's okay."

"It's not." I smooth a strand of hair from her forehead. "I promise I'll make it up to you. Troy and I aren't close, so it must be important for him to call on me like this."

She puffs her cheeks out and sighs. "I'm embarrassed."

I chuckle, which earns me a death stare. "You shouldn't be. What Troy walked in on is none of his business."

"He probably thinks I'm one of your fuck buddies."

"Enough." I kiss the top of her head. "I've never gone on morning beach or rock-climbing dates before. And I've never watched a movie with a woman."

She looks up at me. "A movie? Really?"

Fuck it. I might as well be honest. It's not like she doesn't know the sort of guy I am. Or was. "It's usually dinner, then sex. Or just sex. But you're different."

Her lips form a big 'Oh'.

I swoop in and kiss her, plundering her mouth with my tongue. She kisses me back. I lose myself in her taste, her scent. God, this woman. What's happening to me? I wrench away before I start dry humping her, my breath ragged. Em clings to my biceps, panting.

"Can I see you again?" I ask.

"You'll see me at the station on Monday."

"That's not what I meant." I rub my stiff groin against her so she's in no doubt about what I'm asking.

She gives me a coy smile. "There's a good chance I'll say yes if you ask me out on another date.

She sashays to her car. I love seeing the confidence in her step, which has me wondering again, why does she hide this ballsy side of herself at work?

Chapter Sixteen

Greg

"You have a dog?"

"Yes, Troy. I have a dog." This is becoming tedious. Why are people always surprised by Silas?

Troy nurses his empty glass and stares out the door that leads to the garden. "It's ugly."

"And temporary." I pour myself a drink and Troy a second one. "I'll be rid of him once his owner is out of hospital." A sharp pain lances through my chest. Blasted mutt is growing on me.

I grab a jacket, open the sliding door, and step outside. Silas glances at me, then returns to his bone. He's been at that thing for hours. It's half the size now.

Troy joins me, and we sit on the outdoor sofa overlooking the harbour. Boats bob on the water as people take advantage of the sunny day.

Troy picks up Silas' hairbrush, then must realise what it is because he drops it and pulls out a sanitiser bottle. "Emily's not what I imagined."

What the fuck? "You only just met her."

Troy rubs the sanitiser into his hands like his life depends on killing all germs that might have been on the brush. "I mean, she doesn't look like a typical one-night stand."

I clench my fists. I swear, if he disrespects Em, I'm decking him. "That's because she isn't one."

"I did wonder. Can't imagine you dressing your flings in a football jersey." Troy inspects his hands, no doubt looking for any specks of dirt or grime he missed. "Unless you've got a fetish for that sort of thing."

I cross my arms. "She's the woman I'm dating, and you should watch your mouth before you get shown the door."

Troy regards me with steadfast eyes. "Interesting."

If I wasn't used to dealing with lowlifes in the interrogation room, it might unnerve me, but all it does is piss me off. Fucking politicians think they're better than cops. "What the hell does that mean?"

"I never thought you'd settle down."

"Hold on there." I raise my hand. "I'm dating her, not putting a ring on her finger."

"If you say so."

I pinch my brow. Troy likes to play mind games. That's what makes him such a successful politician. I don't have the patience for that shit. "Forget about Em. Why are you here?"

Troy gulps his whiskey. Jesus. It's top shelf. The least he could do is savour it. He raises his glass. "Any chance of another one?"

"Depends on how you got here?"

"Don't worry, *Mum*. I caught a taxi."

I let his snarkiness slide and retrieve the bottle of Glenfiddich from the kitchen.

"Since when do you confide in me?"

"Since I need a favour."

"Ah." That explains it. "And here I thought we'd hug and say how much we loved each other."

"You're such a prick. I'm sorry I came." Troy lurches off the chair.

"Sit back down." My voice comes out sterner than I mean to. It's the tone I use on crims. Troy surprises me by obeying and dropping into his seat. I top up his glass.

He twirls the whiskey, the amber liquid sparkling in the sun. "I'd like you to do a background check on someone."

Not what I expected. "Who?"

"A woman called Sophie Dubois."

"And who is she to you?"

Troy drops his glass on the table and hangs his head. "The woman I had a one-night stand with."

What the hell? "You cheated on Felicity?"

His head snaps up. "Jesus, Greg. Yell louder. I don't think they heard you in Tasmania."

"But you have the perfect marriage." Or so my father tells me every time I'm unfortunate enough to cross his path.

Troy plucks at his jumper. "Not everything is what it seems. We've had our challenges."

I sip my whiskey, needing the warm burn to ground me. "Why do you want me to investigate this woman?"

"She's blackmailing me."

"Shit."

"Exactly." He scrubs his hands over his face. "She wants one million dollars deposited into her bank account, or she's sending photos to Felicity."

I lean forward and drop my voice so I'm not accused of telling the entire country. "Photos?"

Troy's face turns a deep crimson. "I let her take a few pictures on her phone. I thought she erased them."

What the fuck? I'm surprised he let his guard down like that. "Were you out of your mind?"

"No. Just thinking with my cock."

I burst out laughing. "You sure were."

Troy pours himself yet another whiskey. We nurse our glasses. A horrible feeling settles in my gut. Looks like my brother and I are getting trashed this afternoon. We haven't done that since ... ever.

I stand and pace to the door and back again. Despite our differences, I never thought Troy would do something like this. "Why'd you cheat?"

Troy lurches out of his chair and stumbles towards the rear fence. I follow. Silas hunches over his bone, giving us the evil eye. I nod my head at him. Don't worry, mate. Your skanky side of cow is safe from us.

"Felicity hasn't been the same since Melanie was born. I figured it was post-natal depression, but it's been twelve months. We haven't slept together in all that time."

Jesus. A year without sex is a fucking long time. It's been over two months for me, and I'm climbing the walls. Or, more accurately, becoming way too acquainted with my right hand. But then I'm not married—has he forgotten those vows about better or worse?

Getting judgemental won't help, so I prop myself against the fence and keep my voice neutral. "How did you meet?"

"At a conference a month ago. We hit it off. One thing led to another." He shifts uncomfortably. "You know."

No, I don't. I've never cheated. It's always one woman at a time. We enjoy each other for a night, or a week tops, then move on. Until Em.

"I messed up, Greg. She had this sexy French accent and perfect curves, and ..." He looks away from my scowl and sculls his glass. Another piece of me dies watching top-shelf whiskey squandered.

"You could have her arrested for blackmail."

"True." He leans against the wooden palings, looking older than his thirty-five years. "But then she'd release the photos and my marriage would be over. Not to mention my career."

This is why I've never done relationships. Good old dad couldn't keep it in his pants. Now it seems Troy can't either. It must run in our blood. Which is why this thing with Em can only be short term. I'd cut my balls off if I ever hurt her that way. "Why not hire a private investigator?"

"I can't risk it leaking to the media. Dad would kill me. Besides, I figured you might find out more in the police system."

My stomach drops. God forbid Troy screws up his career, but he thinks it's fine for me to take the risk? "It's against regulations to access a person's details unless it's part of an investigation. So, unless you press charges ..." I shrug.

"I know. I was a lawyer once."

"And yet you're asking me to break the law, anyway."

Pink tinges his cheeks. "Yeah."

"Jesus, Troy. Every action in the system is tracked. I'd need a good reason to look this woman's name up; otherwise, my career would be cactus."

"You can't bypass it?"

"I'm not an IT guru."

Troy squats in front of Silas. "Hey there, boy. Want to trade places?"

Silas growls and bares his teeth. I don't blame him. My brother's breath reeks of alcohol.

"Okay, maybe not." Troy backs up and trips.

I grab his shoulders and steady him. "You don't want to be Silas. He's got no balls, so your screwing days would be well and truly over."

Troy winces and covers his groin. "Ouch."

I whistle. "Come on, Silas. It's getting cold out here."

He ignores me, totally focused on gnawing his bone.

"Fine. But don't blame me if you freeze what's left of your privates off when the cold front sweeps through."

It's toasty warm inside the house, and I shed my jacket. "How about I make us some dinner?"

"You don't have to do that."

"Yes, I do. I'm not sending you home with a belly full of whiskey and nothing more."

The half-empty bottle dangles from Troy's fingers. I grab it before it can meet an unhappy ending. It's bad enough Troy's guzzling the twenty-year-old single malt. I don't think I could survive seeing the remains puddled on the floor.

Troy holds out his glass. "Another one?"

No doubt Felicity will blame me for leading her husband astray. I give Troy one finger, hoping he's too drunk to notice. He crashes on the lounge, and I wince as the whiskey sloshes around the inside of the glass, but nothing spills.

Luckily, there's a vegetarian lasagne in the fridge. When I made it, I'd imagined serving it to Emily, together with a bottle of Penfolds Bin 404 Cabernet Sauvignon, after an afternoon of sex in every room of my house. So much for that plan.

My brother burps. If he vomits on my new lounge or the rug, I'm charging him. It's tempting to snap a photo. Our father would have a stroke if he saw his favourite son drunk and slovenly. But photos are what got Troy into this mess in the first place. That, and dropping his pants.

I check my phone. Two texts.

Emily: Thanks for a lovely day. Hope your brother's ok.

Emily: Please give Silas a kiss. I forgot to say goodbye to him. xx

I imagine one of those kisses is for me. Although I'm not giving Silas any, so I'll take them both. I shove the phone away. When did I get so sappy?

There's a bang at the sliding door. Silas' face is pressed against it, his tongue like a grotesque leech on the glass. Stupid dog. I slide it open. "I told you it was getting cold."

He ignores me and traipses in, a trail of dirt behind him. He must have buried what was left of the bone. "Silas, stop."

He surprises me by obeying. I grab a tea towel and wet it. "Come here." He tilts his head as if to say, *make me.* "Bloody mutt."

I go to him and wipe and dry his paws. It's impressive the way he sits and lets me do it. Jake's got no hope with his dog, Ruby. She'll do anything for Claire, but when Jake opens his mouth, it's like she goes deaf. I snigger. Maybe I should try that trick myself next time Jake's barking at me.

Two hours later, Troy and I have chased the whiskey down with food. And then finished off with a couple more whiskeys. Troy's passed out on my couch. Pouring him into a taxi is going to be fun. Not.

His phone rings. I see the caller ID. Bugger. I'd better answer. "Hi, Felicity."

"Greg?" She stumbles over my name. I'm impressed she even recognised my voice.

"Yeah. Troy's at my house."

"Can I speak with him?"

A soft snore drifts from the couch. "He's sleeping."

"Sleeping?" Her voice rises an octave.

"He had too much to drink."

"What? We're supposed to go out with his father and Elise tonight." Ah, Elise. The stepmother who's closer to my age than my old man's.

There's a shuffling of the receiver. "Greg?" My father's deep, gravelly voice barrels down the line.

Perfect. Just perfect. "Hey, Dad."

"What have you done to Troy?"

I grit my teeth. I've kept him from being a total wipe-out. Troy's head would be in the toilet if I hadn't slowed down his drinking. Fed and hydrated him. You're welcome.

"We've been catching up."

"Are you in trouble?"

"No!" Of course, he'd think that.

"Put him on."

Silas sniffs at Troy, turns his nose up, and flops onto the rug as far away from him as he can get. Good call.

"I can't. He's passed out on my sofa." The phone goes quiet. "Dad?"

"We're meeting with a developer tonight." His tone is clipped like he's biting the words through his teeth.

"You'll have to do it without Troy. He's in no fit state to see anyone."

"Trust you to ruin an important event." He pauses, and I hear voices in the background. "Alright. I'll send a car to collect him in the morning. Eight am. Make sure he's ready."

The phone goes dead.

"Bye to you too, Dad."

I pull a blanket out of the cupboard and drape it over Troy. I should be angry with him, but for all his faults, I know he loves his wife. This Sophie woman must have been bloody smooth with her seduction moves.

The room spins. I may not be as drunk as my brother, but I'm still going to sport a nasty headache in the morning. I pull up Em's texts and reply.

Greg: Troy's passed out on the lounge. Silas says he'll wait until he sees you again for his kiss xx

I stumble to my bedroom and strip off. It's been twelve hours since breakfast on the beach and the day certainly didn't pan out as I'd envisaged. Still, Em and I kissed, and she tasted as good as I remembered from our botched hook-up. Sweet. Too sweet.

Once I'm in the shower, I soap up and place one hand on the wall, the other one on my aching erection. It's hard as fucking nails, to the point of pain. All those hours with Em and no relief means I won't last long. I curl my fingers around the shaft and rub from root to tip. Tip to root. Precum beads on the end. I adjust my stance and squeeze. Rub faster. Harder. A tingling warmth spreads low, and my balls tighten. I remember the soft fullness of Em's breasts, the hard nubs begging to be sucked. Fuuuck. That's all it takes to set me off. My dick swells, and my hips buck as cum shoots all over the walls. I keep squeezing and pulling, panting and groaning until there's nothing left.

My heart races as I lean against the tiles and catch my breath. Hot water washes the mess down the drain. I've come with my hand more times in the last two months than in the previous twenty years. It's a poor substitute for the real thing and needs to stop. Time to pull out all the guns and entice Emily Saunders into my bed once and for all.

Chapter Seventeen

Emily

I scroll through the intel reports from the weekend. It was unusually quiet. No bashings or thefts. Not even one overdose. Whereas, twenty kilometres east, I'd drugged myself silly on Greg's kisses. They still linger on my lips. The man sure knows how to use his mouth. And his tongue. His hands and fingers.

I'm playing with fire. I know that. The date would have been perfect if Greg hadn't made that comment about his ego never recovering if I was a black belt. It's awful that he was humiliated by an instructor at the academy, but it was a reminder that, deep down, men aren't attracted to women who are too strong and capable.

"Emily?"

Greg's warm chocolate rumble tickles my ear. His arm brushes against me. Not that I can feel much since I'm still wearing my long black cardigan. The office was like an icebox when I arrived. But just knowing it's Greg is enough to send a flurry of goose pimples across my skin.

"Hi." My voice comes out squeaky. *Way to sound cool, Emily.* I clear my throat. "I mean, good morning, Sergeant Anderson."

His eyes are dull, like he hasn't slept, and the surrounding lines are etched deep. They crinkle as he sends me a cheeky grin. "How was your weekend?"

I shrug. "Oh, you know. The usual."

"Really?"

"Yep. I fell into the ocean, watched a movie." My gaze drops to his mouth. "Gorged on yummy things that aren't good for me."

He rests a hand on my desk. "Is that so?"

My nipples harden. Has Greg's voice always been this deep? Sexy. Burrowing directly between my legs? "What about you?"

"Similar, without the swim." His gaze lingers on my breasts, his jaw tightening. My nipples automatically harden.

He leans closer. "Although I missed out on dessert."

This is so dangerous. We shouldn't be flirting at the station. Now I'm hot. Like burning up, going to burst into flames, hot. The beady eyes of Sergeant Seymour rest on me and douse the flames faster than any fire hose.

A shadow forms in my periphery. "Sergeant Anderson, Ms Saunders."

What the hell? Where did Inspector Matthews come from? By some miracle, I nod and smile instead of jumping like a scared rabbit.

Greg is equally cool, straightening to face the inspector. "Morning."

"You look like shit."

"Gee, thanks." Greg scrubs a hand across his face. "My brother surprised me with a visit on Saturday."

Inspector Matthews looks him up and down. "I'm guessing, one that involved copious amounts of alcohol?"

"Yep. I'm getting too old for it. Took me all Sunday to recover." Greg points at the computer screen. "Send me those stats, will you, Em?"

Stats? What stats?

He bends and grabs a pen from my desk, winking as he straightens.

Oh. I could slap my forehead. He's covering to draw away any suspicions Inspector Matthews might have. "Sure. I'll have them to you in an hour."

Greg slips the pen into the top pocket of his shirt. "How about a coffee, Jake?"

"I think you might need two of them." The inspector turns his shrewd gaze onto me. "Emily, can you join us in my office in ten minutes?" He doesn't wait for an answer, pivoting and striding down the corridor.

I widen my eyes at Greg and mouth, "What?"

He shrugs, but the lines between his eyebrows deepen. He turns and ambles after the inspector. We're not busted already, are we?

After nine minutes and thirty seconds—not that I'm counting—it's time to find out what the inspector wants. The station is warmer than when I first arrived, and I'm burning up since Greg said hello, so I take off my long black cardigan. The last thing I need is to start sweating in Inspector Matthews' office. That would be a dead giveaway.

My new ankle boots with three-inch sturdy heels, purchased yesterday in a fit of unfulfilled lust, tap along the tiles. The light buzz in the office falls silent as all heads turn as one in my direction. Bugger. I didn't think this through. In the same lust-fuelled shopping expedition, I bought a red woollen dress that hugs my curves and finishes two inches above the knee. It seemed modest in the dressing room. So, why are all eyes on my legs? I mean, I'm wearing thick black tights. It's not like they can see anything.

I hold my head up and continue down the corridor. The inspector's door is open. He sees me hovering and waves me in. Greg swallows several times, his eyes widening as they travel up and down my body. "That's a lovely dress, Em."

My cheeks burn, and I smooth my hands down the soft

fabric as I glance at Inspector Matthews. His face is unreadable. "I hope it meets the dress code. I saw it yesterday and fell in love with it." And I wanted Greg to see me in it. But that little confession won't be leaving my lips. It's taken me a year to get used to wearing dresses, and while I still loathe the stiff corporate outfits, this dress is more my style, giving me freedom to move and teaming perfectly with boots that don't cut off circulation to my toes.

"It's perfectly acceptable. Claire has a similar one in black." The inspector's face softens at the mention of his fiancé's name, and for a fleeting moment, he looks less intimidating. He clears his throat. "Let's begin, shall we?"

I sit on a chair next to Greg and cross my legs.

Greg's shoulders and jaw stiffen, and both men stare at each other like two duelling noblemen. Does that mean Inspector Matthews knows and is about to go all kung fu on us for hooking up together? Although that doesn't make sense. Even though he's made it clear he disapproves of workplace relationships, he's also admitted it's none of his business what happens outside work hours.

Inspector Matthews clears his throat. "I have an unusual request for you, Emily."

Oh. Not what I expected. "Okay."

Maybe we're not in trouble. So why is there a tic pulsing in Greg's jaw like he's not happy?

Inspector Matthews leans back in his chair and steeples his fingers under his chin. "You know the homeless man, Jimmy Sharmon, is still in hospital."

"Yes, sir."

"He's confused and frightened and not responding well to our attempts to interview him. I want to try a different approach."

Oh wow. My pulse quickens, and a rush of adrenaline sweeps through my body. Is he asking me to help on the front line? "What do you need from me?"

The inspector pushes forward and rests his elbows on the desk. I squirm at the intensity in his blue eyes. "Mr Sharmon is wily enough to realise Sergeant Anderson knows bugger all about dogs. He was desperate when he begged him to take Silas."

Greg grunts. "Thanks a lot, Jake."

"You know it's true. Get over it." He waves his hand. "The point is, if Jimmy sees how safe Silas is, he might open up. And by safe, I mean, knows someone competent is helping care for his dog."

"You're such a dick," Greg mutters under his breath.

"What did you say?"

I jump at the low growl in Inspector Matthews' voice.

Greg juts his chin and stares down the inspector. "Nothing, *sir*."

Inspector Matthews lets it go, as he should. He's the one out of line. Greg's amazing with Silas. "Jimmy knows more than he's telling us, Emily. But he's too scared to say it."

I glance down at my dress. I'll never get dog hair out of it.

"Don't worry, Em. Jake's not suggesting we go today." Greg pats his trouser leg. "Besides, this is pure wool. Cost me a bomb. No way I'm letting Silas drool over me in this suit."

The inspector smiles. Like really smiles, all the way to his eyes, and for a moment, I see why Claire fell in love with him. He's attractive when he's not snarling, although he's got nothing on the brooding powerhouse sitting next to me. "The hospital has asked us to wait a few days. Give Mr Sharmon more time to heal. If he's up to it, you and Greg will go on Friday, and there'll be two uniformed police to accompany you as well."

Why would we need backup? Does he think I'm a liability? It better not be because I'm a woman. I cross my arms. "Is that necessary?"

"Just a precaution." He holds up his hand. "And before you ask, I've already cleared it with your boss."

Sergeant Jacobs won't be pleased about me spending time with Greg. She's made her disdain for him very clear. But it's an excellent opportunity to prove myself in a policing situation. I press my hands on my thighs to stop them from bouncing. "Thanks, sir. I'll do my best."

❧

"Oh, my, that's horrendous."

I slam the door shut and gulp in mouthfuls of fresh air, tainted with exhaust fumes, to cleanse my nostrils of the gas Silas emitted in Greg's car on the way to the hospital. Even with the windows wound down, the interior was a biohazard. Nothing short of an apocalyptic event would have me climbing back into the confines of the sleek Audi right now. Thank God we made it here alive.

Greg fans his face. "Told ya."

Silas sniffs at the asphalt, oblivious to the fuss.

"He never smelt like that when we took him to the beach. Did you feed him something different last night?"

"Nope." He shrugs. "Sometimes he just starts smelling."

"Well, something's wrong with his diet. We need to change it. Pronto."

"We?"

"Yes, we. You heard Inspector Matthews." I point towards my chest. "I'm half responsible for Silas."

Greg wiggles his eyebrows at me. "You could be fully responsible for him if you wanted."

"Ha! Nice try, but I told you, I'm not allowed to have a dog."

Greg catches my hand. "Thanks for doing this, Em."

His grip is firm, warmth radiating through his palm. He brings my fingers to his mouth and kisses them. "I didn't get a chance to tell you on Monday, but you looked hot as fuck in that red dress."

Heat rushes through me. "I seem to remember getting a text along those lines."

"Yeah, but it's not the same as saying it in person." He glances down at my jeans. "Although you look good in anything. Or"—he winks—"nothing at all."

He's impossible. "You haven't seen me in nothing."

"Not yet."

A horn honks and we jump apart. What are we doing? It's a public place, and this is work. Not a date. Even if we are casually dressed.

A silver Lamborghini barrels through the car park at three times the speed limit.

"Entitled prick," mutters Greg.

I couldn't agree more. Which brings me to the conundrum that is Greg. The man I've lusted from afar has a reputation for being a cocky, entitled womaniser. The man I'm getting to know still has elements of a playboy, but a thoughtful one. Caring and sweet. It's a dangerous combination.

Silas and I enter a small garden area while Greg goes inside the hospital to collect Jimmy. The perfume from a bed of roses is a welcome relief after being locked in the car with Silas. He also seems to appreciate a small hedge, marking out his territory on at least ten different bushes. Two uniformed police officers stand nearby. Inspector Matthews was vague about the need for backup. Initially, I thought it was because of my presence, but I'm not so sure now. There's more going on here than the inspector and Greg are letting on.

Ten minutes later, Greg walks towards me, one arm around an elderly gentleman, his other hand wheeling a stand with a bag of fluids attached. Jimmy is dressed in long grey pants and a cream woollen pullover. Not clothes I'd expect someone living on the streets would own. *A gift from Greg?* A familiar fluttery feeling fills my chest. What sort of person goes out of their way like this for a homeless man? Someone I could fall in love with, which would be foolish.

I'm not looking for a long-term relationship, and I'm certain Greg isn't either.

Jimmy lifts his gaze, tears filling his eyes when he sees Silas. The dog's tail swishes faster than a butterfly's wings, and he pulls at the lead. I hold him back. Jimmy's much more fragile than I was expecting.

Greg helps Jimmy sit on a bench seat. Tears stream down Jimmy's cheeks, and Silas whines. My eyes moisten at the emotional reunion, and even Greg looks a little weepy. I move closer. Silas makes no attempt to jump on Jimmy. Instead, he sits at his feet and looks up at him with one adorable puppy dog eye.

Jimmy buries his head in Silas' fur. "Thank you, Sergeant Anderson. Thank you."

Greg and I share a look over the top of Jimmy's head, and I cling to Silas' leash, keeping myself grounded. Greg's macho exterior cracks and pain leaks into his irises. His features become softer. More vulnerable. Now that I know more about his family, particularly his father, I realise how much he keeps hidden from everyone.

Silas whimpers and the moment is lost, Greg's attention returning to Jimmy. "As you can see, Silas is well." There's a catch to his voice.

"He smells nice." Jimmy strokes Silas' ears. "And such a pretty collar."

Warmth fills my chest, and I shoot a 'told you so' at Greg. "Yes, it is."

Jimmy's gaze roams over me, but not in a creepy way. "Who are you?"

"This is Emily, a friend of mine," says Greg. "She's been helping me out with Silas."

Laughter dances behind Jimmy's eyes. "You can't handle one small dog, Sergeant?"

"If he didn't shed hair standing still or fart like he was trying to gas me to death, he'd be fine."

Jimmy chuckles and then coughs. Bloody spittle dribbles at the corner of his mouth. *That's not normal.* I glance at Greg. His jaw is rigid. He's seen it too.

Silas plants his butt on Greg's feet and rests his head on Jimmy's lap. It's so adorable I want to cry. It's like he's saying, *I belong to both of you.*

"I don't feel right sitting here while a lady stands." Jimmy gestures to the space next to him. "Please, sit, Emily."

"Okay." I perch on the seat.

His gnarled fingers glide across Silas' back. Greg slides his feet from under Silas and parks himself on Jimmy's other side, his hands clasped in front of him. The dark blue jeans and check shirt do nothing to hide the strength beneath the fabric. If Greg's trying to make himself appear less intimidating, it isn't working. The man behind the badge is a formidable beast in his own right.

"So, Jimmy …" Greg spreads his hands on his thighs. "We had an ulterior motive for bringing Silas to visit."

"Really?" Jimmy snorts. "I'd never have guessed."

I place my hand on Jimmy's arm. It's so thin I could wrap my fingers around it and then some. "Greg worries. It's who he is."

"I know. Otherwise, he wouldn't look out for the likes of me." Jimmy pats Silas' head. The action seems to calm him. "There were two guys."

"You sure they were men?" asks Greg.

Jimmy snarls. "I'm not that far gone that I can't tell the difference."

"Okay, okay. Can you describe them?"

"It was dark, and they were wearing hoodies." Jimmy shivers beneath my palm, but he continues, his voice shaky. "There was a ring. Very flashy. Had a huge sapphire in the middle of it."

Greg's knuckles go white. Interesting. The ring must mean

something. I stroke Jimmy's arm, like he's doing to Silas. "Do you remember anything else?"

"You're a sweet girl."

"You're avoiding the question."

"Yep." He swallows, his Adam's apple bobbing. His hand stills on Silas' head. "I'm sure they meant to kill me, but something scared them off." His fingers shake, and I want nothing more than to hug him, but I don't know how he'd react to such a display from a stranger.

I feel rather than hear Greg's intake of breath.

Greg squats, ruffles Silas' fur, then looks up at Jimmy. "Why do you think that?"

"One of them was muttering about leaving no evidence behind. He had a stutter."

It doesn't mean the attackers intended to kill Jimmy. It's possible they were referring to items that might have traces of DNA that could link them to him.

Greg scrubs his fingers through his hair, the only sign he's agitated. "Was dope really what you were buying, or something stronger?"

"I swear that's all it was. I wouldn't take that chemical shit." Jimmy looks at me. "Sorry for the language."

I wave him away. "It's fine. I've heard a lot worse." And said it. Which proves what a gentleman this enigma of a man is.

"I've got Silas depending on me, Sarge. Pot takes the edge off. I'm still in control when I smoke it."

That's what all drug addicts believe, but to his credit, Greg doesn't lecture Jimmy.

"So, why do you think they'd want to kill you?" Greg presses.

"You wouldn't have a smoke on you, would you?" Jimmy gives me big puppy dog eyes.

I smother a laugh. "No." I wave my finger at him. "And

the way you were coughing earlier, I don't think you should have one, anyway."

He smiles. "You can't blame an old man for trying." He sighs and resumes patting Silas. "They were both strangers, but one looked familiar. Like maybe I've seen him around. That's all I remember."

Jimmy breaks into another round of coughing. Greg springs up from the bench and pats him on the shoulder. "You've done well."

Jimmy strokes Silas' muzzle. Silas presses into his hand. "Thanks again for looking after my mate. He looks happy."

"He should be." Greg grunts. "Crazy mutt's taken over my house."

Silas cocks his head at Greg, his face breaking into that smile only dogs have, like he's understood what Greg said and couldn't agree more.

Jimmy shivers. The clouds have darkened further, dropping the temperature.

I stand. "We'd better get Jimmy inside."

"Wait." Jimmy stretches a bony hand out to Greg. "What about Silas?"

"He'll be fine. I told you I'd take care of him." Greg glances at Silas, his gaze softening. "Not sure I'll be okay, though."

Jimmy sneezes, and then those deep, bone-chilling coughs return. I pat his back, which only seems to make it worse.

Silas rubs against Jimmy's trousers and looks at Greg as if begging him to make it stop.

I grab some tissues from my handbag and give them to Jimmy.

He wipes his mouth. "Sorry." His voice is hoarse like his throat is filled with shards of glass.

"Don't be sorry. You concentrate on getting better. Greg will look after Silas, and I'll keep an eye on both of them for you." I give him a wink.

Jimmy nodes his head at Greg. "You'd be a fool to let this one go, Sarge."

One of the uniformed police nearby turns his head. Oh, no. Can they hear from over there?

Greg shoves his hands into his pockets. "Em's a friend. That's all."

It shouldn't bother me, but hearing Greg say I'm nothing more than a friend leaves a tiny cut on my heart.

"Sure." Jimmy beckons me closer and whispers in my ear, his breath raspy and a little on the nose. "The sergeant's a good bloke underneath that gruff exterior. Just needs a strong woman to tame him."

A strong woman to tame Greg? I'm not sure Jimmy's got that right or that I could be that woman.

Jimmy says one last goodbye to Silas, kisses the top of his head, and then shuffles to the hospital entrance with Greg's arm secured around his waist. There's intelligence behind Jimmy's tired eyes. I itch to know what his life was like before he became homeless. What caused him to be alone on the streets.

Silas whines but stays by my side. I drop to my haunches and run my fingers through his fur as I watch how Greg gently escorts Jimmy through the hospital doors. This thing between Greg and me is supposed to be a bit of fun. Nothing serious. But the more time I spend with him, the more I like him. Respect him. And the more I realise I could fall in love with him if I don't guard my heart.

Chapter Eighteen

Greg

Eyebrows climb busybody foreheads as Em and I stroll into the station, Silas trotting between us. Dylan pushes away from the front desk where it appears he's been chatting up a female constable, his dog nowhere in sight. He's lucky it's me walking in and not Jake.

The door between the foyer and the central part of the station opens, and the boss himself strides through. "Good, you're back." His gaze drifts to Em, then returns to me. "You took your time."

Jesus Christ. Does he think we had a quickie while we were out? "Jimmy's still not in the best of health. We couldn't hurry him."

Jake grunts, giving me a nod that's as close to an apology as I'll get. He points at Silas. "Why didn't you take *that* home first?" I feel Em bristle beside me, but she's smart enough to keep her mouth shut.

"I wanted to brief you as soon as possible."

Jake's eyes light up. "Alright then. In my office. You too, Emily."

Jake would stroke out if we took a dog into his sacred

space, so I give Silas over to Dylan and promise to rearrange his internal organs if any harm comes to him.

Once we're settled in Jake's office, I bring him up to speed on our meeting with Jimmy. His irises all but glow when I tell him about the sapphire.

"What's so special about the ring?" asks Em.

I glance at Jake, uncertain how much information Em is allowed to know.

Jake answers. "It's Terence Leadbetter's signature ring."

Em's eyes gleam with intelligence. "Ah. The big drug dealer you arrested last year."

I continue on from Jake. "Yep. If it's the same ring, then whoever bashed Jimmy may well be the new boss while Leadbetter's in jail." And that begs the question, why would a man of his position go after Jimmy himself? And what is the blonde's connection?

"Which means Jimmy's lucky to be alive," says Jake. "They're a ruthless mob."

Emily sucks in a breath. "That's why you wanted uniformed police with us?"

Jake nods. "We didn't know about the link to Leadbetter, but something's off about the attack on Jimmy. We're not taking any chances."

Em rubs her hands together. "So, what do we do now?"

My gut folds in on itself. The hospital was relatively safe, and Em made a difference, calming Jimmy the way she calms Silas. But we're not letting my woman get any more involved. It's too dangerous. We need to shut this down fast. Jake had better be on the same page as me on this one.

Holy shit. Since when did Em become my woman?

Jake adjusts his tie. "We've already stretched protocol asking you to help today."

"But Jimmy ..." Em lifts her chin like they're fighting words. She holds Jake's gaze for a couple of seconds, her blue eyes fierce, then drops her head. "Of course. I'm sorry. I got carried away. It was fun to escape from the computer for a while and see what happens in the real world."

"Investigating an attempted murder isn't fun, Emily." Jake pinches the bridge of his nose. "It's dangerous."

Her cheeks turn pink. "I didn't mean …"

I get it. Pushing paper, or more like scrolling through emails and analysing data, must get boring at times. And, while she might be a ninja climbing fake rock walls, that's a world away from coming face-to-face with thugs carrying knives and guns. Crims would eat her alive.

"Emily, you're trained as a civilian intelligence analyst, not a cop." Jake sighs. "You're a crucial member of the team. We'd be lost without your expertise."

Em preens at the praise, as she should. Jake can be pretty miserly handing it out. But I don't miss the stiffness in her posture or the extra rosiness in her cheeks telling me she's embarrassed. "Thanks, sir. I do my best."

"Would you mind checking Silas hasn't destroyed the station?"

Em smiles, but it's the kind that doesn't reach her eyes. She knows it's a dismissal. "Sure."

Em bolts out of the office, and Jake nods at the door.

I get up and close it. "What's up?"

He crosses his arms, expression grim. "There are whispers the Professional Standards Command has launched an investigation into our unit."

Internal affairs? I freeze midway back to my chair. "What the fuck?"

"My thoughts exactly."

"Why?" Blood rushes to my head, sending a loud roar to my ears. No one wants internal affairs up in their business. They're a bunch of ball-busting, power-hungry freaks. I slump into my seat.

"I think you know why, Greg." Jake's expression is as

blank as it gets, which means he's a seething cauldron of fire underneath. "We've both questioned why two of the last three raids were off the mark. It's not a long bow to assume someone on the inside is feeding information back to the drug cartel."

He's right. But the thought of one of our own being crooked feels like losing a kidney and one nut. "So, what do we do?"

"Nothing. Just make sure you do everything by the book. No shortcuts."

I smooth the creases on my trouser leg. "I don't know what you mean, Inspector."

"This is no joke, Greg." Jake slaps both palms on the desk. "These guys don't mess around. You could lose your job."

I swallow the bile creeping up my throat. "Do you think they're already talking to people?"

He doesn't answer right away. His hypnotic blue eyes bore into me. No blinking. No movement at all. "Yep. I reckon they'd go after the weak links."

I cross one leg over the other. "They could target Dylan, I guess. But he'd end up blurting it out to me."

"What about Emily?" Jake whispers the words softly, his gaze firmly on mine as if gauging my reaction.

"No way." I fold my arms to hide the white bolt of anger that lights up inside me.

Jake lifts an eyebrow. Bastard. "Emily's such a quiet thing. Yet, the moment we asked her to help with Jimmy, it was like a switch flipped."

I hug my arms closer to my chest. He doesn't know her like I do. "She hasn't got a deceptive bone in her body, Jake. If internal affairs approached her, she'd tell me."

The creases between his eyes deepen, and his fingers curl into fists. "Why would she go to you and not me? She's Claire's friend."

Shit. I need to put him off track.

I wave my hands at him. "You're the scary, uptight inspector in charge of this unit. Trust me. You'd be the last person she'd confide in."

His expression relaxes. "Fine. Just be alert." He picks up a pen and points at the door. "Don't you have a report to write, Sergeant?"

I salute him. "On it now, *sir*."

I close Jake's door behind me. While I'm pissed about internal affairs getting involved, I understand. Another botched drug raid, and Jake and I would call them ourselves. It doesn't mean we like them. Pompous pricks. But despite Jake's warning, there's one thing I still haven't done that can't wait.

My cop antenna is screaming there's more to the woman blackmailing Troy than fast cash. And while I can't risk my badge using the police system to investigate her, there are other ways of getting to the truth. I slip into the car park and pull up the number of the private investigating firm I'd saved on my mobile. They have a reputation for obtaining information when no one else can.

"Redlight Investigations."

I glance around to make sure I'm alone. "Hi, I'd like your help identifying someone who's threatening my family."

There's silence for a few seconds and then a tapping sound. "We have an opening that's come up Monday morning. Can you come then?"

"Yep." I'll make it work. I exchange particulars, then hang up.

Jake's warning rings in my ears, but as little as Troy and I have to do with each other, I can't ignore his plea for help.

I saunter back into the station to find Emily at her desk and Silas curled up next to her. Warmth seeps into my chest. She was so good with Jimmy today. Jake's right; there's much more to Em than meets the eye. Like passionate kisses, a sexy body and an even sexier mind. She's agreed to stay over tonight. We both know what that means, and I can't wait. Jake can scratch his head all he likes about the conundrum that is Emily Saunders, while I'll test all the different ways I can make her come undone.

Chapter Nineteen

Greg

Last night didn't go as planned. Not even close. I knew the conversation with Jake had upset Em, but I hadn't realised just how much. By the time I convinced her that Jake didn't think less of her, she'd passed out on me. It gives me yet another first—sharing a bed with no sex. My morning wood, which is evening wood, only harder and more painful, urges me to wake her up. Explore her body. But it would be a violation when we're not lovers yet.

So, I do another first and lie on my side watching Em sleep, a soft, barely there snore, breaking the quiet of the bedroom. I count the freckles on her nose. Across her cheeks. Then kiss the tiny frown mark in the middle of her forehead. Her eyelashes flutter, but she doesn't stir. Having Em lying next to me feels right. Like she's meant to be here. Forever. Instead of sending shivers down my spine, the thought warms the cold organ in my chest.

I roll out of bed, my groin throbbing, throw on a dressing gown and slippers and head into the living area. Silas pants and thumps his tail. I let him out of the crate and slide open the back door. He charges outside. His first stop is the fence where he once spotted a possum. He does it every morning without fail, but I'm not sure if he's ever seen the possum again. Still, he lives in hope.

A faint tinge of pink glistens on the horizon. I inhale the brisk air and blow out a stream of fog. Something about first light calls to me: a new day, a chance to start over. And with a beautiful woman lying in my bed, it's starting off nicely.

Silas returns, and I slide the door shut. I pop a pod into the espresso machine, pour my coffee and take a sip. The hot liquid hits the spot, warming my insides and sending a buzz through my body.

I prepare a pot of tea and toast. Em loves her food, so as long as she doesn't have a major hangover, she'll be hungry. I linger at my bedroom door. Do I let her sleep? Wake her? The semi I've been sporting all morning answers the question. I adjust myself and turn the knob.

Em's fiery mane fans across the white pillow. She looks like a pint-sized angel in the king-size bed. The door clicks behind me, and I'm rewarded with a flicker of blue and a shy smile. "Hi."

"Hi, yourself." I stroll to the bed, trying not to look too eager. "How are you feeling?"

"Not too bad." She shuffles upright, eyeing the food. "Breakfast in bed?"

"Figured you'd be hungry."

She pulls at the T-shirt I changed her into last night, her smile fading. "You undressed me?"

I don't like the way she's looking at me. Like I'd take advantage of her drunken state. "Em, I didn't touch your bra or knickers or anything in their vicinity. I just wanted you to sleep in comfort."

"Of course." Her smile returns brighter, those blue eyes shining. "Thanks. This T-shirt is softer than my pyjamas."

"What would be softer is wearing nothing at all." I wink.

She wraps her arms around her middle. "That'd be a bit cold."

"I'd keep you warm."

She rewards me with a soft blush. I'm tempted to forget feeding her and go straight to dessert, but her stomach rumbles. I hand her the tea and toast.

That sense of rightness I experienced when I woke up beside Em hits me again. My brain yells, run! Run fast. This woman could destroy me. My dick says get over it and fuck her already. But it's the niggle in my chest that screams the loudest. Would it be so bad if she never left?

Em sips her tea and launches into the toast, devouring it with quick precision. Even hungover, her appetite is a force to be reckoned with.

I brush stray curls from her face. Any excuse to touch her. "Feeling more human now?"

"Yeah. Thanks."

I take the plate and cup from her, my dressing gown shifting to reveal the tent in my pants. Em's gaze darts to my groin and her breath hitches. My dick twitches and her pupils dilate at the movement.

Well, well, well. I think we're on the same page here. "Are you up for some morning exercise?"

She bursts out laughing. Snorts. Covers her face. What the hell?

"Sorry." Em hiccups and curls warm fingers around my wrist. "Really, I am. I just … is that one of your standard lines?"

My boner softens, and I squirm at the reminder of my tomcatting ways. This woman, there's no bullshit about her. "No. It's not a line. I just didn't want to come outright and ask if you wanted sex. I was trying to be a gentleman."

Em rocks back and forth, holding her ribcage, her shoulders shaking. She's done it again. Reduced me to a gauche teenager. What the hell do I do now?

"I'm sorry, Greg." Em wipes her eyes. "My defence mechanism is laughter or sarcasm."

"Lucky me. I get both."

"I'm nervous." She squeezes my arm and lifts those shimmering blue eyes to mine. "Because, yes, of course I want to have sex with you. That's why I stayed over."

"You're sure?"

I could kick myself. What am I doing?

"Yes." She traces her fingers along my chest and slips them under the robe. Pinches a nipple.

I grunt as blood surges south. This is the demanding rocket that climbed all over me at Jake and Claire's engagement party—the complete opposite of straight-laced Em at the station. My brain's right. I'm in so much trouble.

"You've got too many clothes on, Greg."

There's no way I'm saying no. "Easily fixed." I push away from the bed, ditch my slippers and slide off the dressing gown. Make quick work of my pyjama top. Em watches my every move, her tongue darting out to wet her lips. My dick swells. Before the morning's over, I want those lips wrapped around it. I slide my thumbs into the front of my waistband and stop.

"Why are you still dressed, Red?"

She bats her eyelashes provocatively. "I'm waiting for you."

Okay then. I shuck my pants in record time and crawl onto the bed. Em's gaze drops to my crotch and widens. "I knew you were packing some heat, Detective." She giggles. "I'm not sure how it will fit."

I pull the covers down and pin her to the mattress, careful not to put too much weight on her. She's so tiny. My tongue darts out to lick the shell of her ear. Remnants of her floral perfume tickle my nostrils. "I'll have you so wet you could fit two of me inside your hot little body."

Em's hips buck against me. "You're such a dirty talker."

"I'm just getting started."

I peel the T-shirt over Em's head, revealing the soft swell

of her breasts, held in place by a lacy black bra. She settles into the mattress with the sweetest of sighs. Sweat beads across my forehead. I've dreamed of this moment for months. There'd better not be any unexpected callers because nothing and no one will stop me from getting inside Em now.

I slip my hands behind her back, unclip the bra and slide it off. Em's breasts are a good handful, and my mouth waters as two dusky nipples appear. I palm the soft flesh and latch on with zero finesse, sucking and nipping at the tight beads. Em grabs my head and pulls me closer to her chest, so I must be doing something right. My dick pulses with every pull on her nipples. Her whimpers tell me she's fine with me making a meal of her.

"Greg." Em pulls at my hair. "Wait."

Dammit. Am I going too fast? I drag my mouth away from her breasts. "What's wrong, sweetheart?"

She shakes her head and glances to the side of the bed.

Jesus Christ. Silas, head tilted, stares at us like we're deviants. I push away from Em. "Out!"

He whimpers.

"Out." I point at the door. "You know you're not allowed in here." I was a pushover when Silas arrived, allowing him to sleep in the bedroom after Em washed him. When I woke to him spooning me, I was at the shops that same day buying a crate for the stupid mutt.

Em giggles. "He doesn't know what's going on."

"Silas." I lower my voice to a deep growl.

He looks to Em.

"It's okay, sweetie. Off you go. We'll play later."

Silas trots away. Glances back and gives me a stink eye, then keeps walking. Unbelievable. Traitorous dog. I jump out of bed and shut the door. He's not disturbing us again.

Em shoves the sheets to her feet, her gaze planted on my groin. I stalk towards her, drinking in the tiny black panties and creamy flesh of her breasts. Not a freckle in sight. Good to know she doesn't bare those perfect globes in public.

I crawl onto the bed and suck each nipple into my mouth. Lave them with my tongue. Then start the delicious journey towards nirvana. Em quivers as I lick down her ribs to her belly button. I swirl my tongue around the indent and continue over tight lower abs. She's firm all over except where it counts. I lick along the top of her knickers. Her hips buck. I bite the fabric and pull it down, revealing soaked underwear and soft, trimmed fiery curls. My mouth waters as her feminine salty essence consumes me. It's been years since I was with a woman who wasn't bare. I'd forgotten how intoxicating the scent of an unwaxed pussy could be. I press a kiss to her mound and continue tugging her underwear down her legs with my teeth until I'm on my knees at the end of the bed. I lift the knickers to my nose and breathe in the delectable moisture left behind.

Em rises on her elbows, eyes wide. She's my every wet dream—heaving breasts and glistening pussy—telling me she's ready and aching for me. As I am for her. I stroke my dick, shuddering as precum seeps from the tip.

She whimpers. "What are you doing?"

"Getting ready to eat you."

I glide trembling hands along the inside of her toned legs, stopping an inch away from Em's dewy entrance. I'd pinch myself to prove this is real and not a dream, but that would mean taking my hands off Em, and there's no way I'm doing that. Nuzzling the damp curls, I slide my tongue along the seam. Em's fingers tangle in my hair, pulling me closer to where I want to be. My nose rests on her mound as I peer up at her face. Her cheeks are flushed, eyes wild and dilated. I sit back, pull her lips apart, and dip my tongue between her folds. The taste is exquisite—a warm, salty cream with a hint of musk. I lick the crevices while Em tears at my hair. I'm not sure she's even aware she's doing it. I rim her opening, and her arousal floods my tongue.

My erection pulses like a bitch. As much as I want to gorge on Em, I'm going to blow my load if I don't get inside her soon. I flick my tongue across her clit. Her hips jerk, and I press my hands against the insides of her thighs. I promised she'd be wet when I entered her, and I always keep my promises.

"Naughty girl. You lie there and accept my tongue lashing."

"Greg," she moans. "Please."

"Please what?" I smile against her pussy, my tongue lightly tapping the bundle of nerves.

"I need to come."

So do I. I suck her clit into my mouth and curl a finger inside her. It's all it takes for her to let go, ramming her pussy against my mouth hard enough to make me see stars. Fuuuck. I maintain suction on her clit, her walls pulsing around my finger. Jesus. My dick is going to be in torturous heaven.

"No more." Em writhes on the bed. "Please, Greg. No more."

I remove my finger and lap at the cream spilling from her pussy—the sweetest I've ever eaten. I can't imagine ever tiring of the taste. Of Em.

Chapter Twenty

Emily

Greg prowls up the mattress, precum dripping from his cock. And what a beautiful cock—long, thick and ready to do battle. I wasn't kidding about his size. I've never had a man that big before. What if he doesn't fit?

My body pulses with the aftershocks of my orgasm. I feel ravaged in the best possible way. Propped on his forearms, Greg hovers over me, his mouth inches from mine. His irises are molten swirls of the darkest chocolate—passion, warmth, possessiveness.

"Ready?"

I nod. More than ready.

He reaches into the drawer of the bedside table, pulls out a condom and rolls it on while holding his body in a plank position with one arm. Impressive. A tiny green part of me wants to rip out the hair of those who came before me and enjoyed these washboard abs, firm pecs, and bulging biceps. I close my eyes, hiding from the intensity of the moment.

"Em, you okay?" Greg brushes my forehead with butterfly kisses.

What the hell? I blink my eyes open. Any other man this

close to my entrance would be worried about screwing me, not whether I was having second thoughts.

"Yeah. It's just … been a while."

He kisses the tip of my nose. "I'll go as slow as you need me to."

His cock nudges my opening. I spread my legs further, and he surges forward. There's so much lubrication; I'd be embarrassed if I wasn't so horny. My walls expand with ease, and he slides into place.

He groans. "Fuuuck. So tight."

I smile, my face pressed against his chest, the coarse hairs tickling my nose. The fullness is overwhelming, my clit throbbing.

"You good?"

"Yeah." His pecs muffle my voice.

Greg pulls out, and my inner muscles contract, trying to suck him back in. He thrusts forward again, and we both groan at the delicious pressure.

"I'm squashing you, Em." And with that, Greg rolls onto his back, taking me with him. I straddle his hips, our bodies still connected. Greg's hooded gaze latches onto my breasts. He thumbs the nipples, and I arch into his hands. "Ride me, Red."

I lower my head and nip his ear lobe. "You're going to let me have control?"

"I'm letting you think you have control." He tweaks my nipples. "Now, get to work."

"Ouch." I'll show him. I rest my palms on his pecs and rock.

Only seconds pass before Greg's iron control breaks and he's thrusting to meet me. His face screws up as if in agony. My breasts bounce, and he alternates between groping the soft flesh and kneading my bum. I've never felt more powerful seeing this gorgeous man at my mercy.

Our grunts and groans, and the musky scent of sex, fill the

room. I won't last long, tension building between my legs as Greg's cock bumps my clit over and over again.

"Are you close?" Greg's voice is raspy, his face red.

"Yes," I whisper. "So good."

"Thank Christ. I'm about to burst."

Greg slides his hand between my legs and swipes a finger across my clit. I shudder as tension unfurls through my body in wave after wave of pulsating magic. His hips snap against mine in a flurry of thrusts. Eyes wild, he holds my gaze as he unravels. It's the most beautiful thing I've ever seen.

I slump onto Greg's sweaty chest, my pussy fluttering with the remnants of my orgasm. Greg's cock twitches as if it's in its final death throes. We lie spent, our ragged breaths louder than an ocean's roar in my ears, the slippery stickiness of sweat and cum a sweet delight filling my nostrils and promising more carnal decadence. Greg threads his fingers through my hair and brushes my cheek. I could lie like this forever. But forever isn't real and eventually, he softens and slips out. Removes the condom, climbs off the bed and disappears into the ensuite.

I roll onto my back and bounce on the mattress. What a workout. It's melted away all the tension from yesterday. Admittedly, the alcohol last night alleviated some of the stress, but it's the sex that's reduced me to a boneless heap.

Greg returns and kneels on the mattress. "You look good lying on my bed freshly fucked, Em."

I pull at the covers, embarrassment setting in now the euphoria is fading. Greg grabs my hand. "Please. Don't cover yourself. Let me drink you in."

I'm not used to such attention after sex. The guys I've known usually want to roll over and sleep afterwards, or in the case of the douchebag at uni, brag to his mates. Greg looks ready to go again. My skin breaks out in goosebumps.

"You're cold." Greg climbs into bed, pulls the cover over us and wraps his arms around me.

I snuggle into his side. "That was amazing. Thank you."

Greg chuckles. "I'm the one who should thank you, Em."

I peer at him through my lashes. "Shall we thank each other, then?"

He presses a chaste kiss on my forehead. "Let's agree we're both awesome in bed."

I nuzzle his ear. I knew sex with Greg would be off the charts, but I never expected this softer side. I can't fall for him. That would be a huge mistake. But it's easy to imagine waking up like this every morning. Too easy. I need to protect my heart if it's not too late.

I push against his chest. "I guess I should get going soon."

Greg rolls on top of me. "You don't think I'm finished with you, do you?" His forehead wrinkles. I resist the urge to smooth the lines away.

"Um. I figure you must have plans."

His voice lowers to a wickedly sensuous baritone. "Yes, I do." He kisses me, his tongue plunging into mine, stealing my breath. My heart. He wrenches his mouth away and pins me with a knee-buckling stare. "My plans today involve fucking you in every room of the house."

Chapter Twenty-One

Emily

I scurry into the station, my long woollen coat swinging behind me. I slept through the alarm this morning. That never happens, but Greg and his countless orgasms rendered me into a bowl of jelly. My body aches in all the right places, and while showering, I couldn't miss the lovebite on my breast. So what if I'm thirty minutes late? I'll make up the time. A weekend of wild sex was totally worth it.

Inspector Matthews and Sergeant Jacobs huddle near my desk, deep in conversation. I slow down to a dawdle, my muscles tensing. They're making it impossible for me to slip into my chair without being noticed. And while Greg's orgasms may have anaesthetised me, I'm still very conscious that I stuffed up on Friday by downplaying the danger with Jimmy. Sometimes I wonder if I'm only good enough to be an intel analyst, not a cop. That the police academy was right in rejecting me.

Sergeant Jacobs makes a show of looking at her watch. "Bad traffic?"

I make my own show of wincing. "Migraine. It's that time … you know."

Her stern expression softens. She takes every fourth

Monday off without fail, so mentioning a period gives me a plausible excuse she can empathise with.

"Well, take it easy." She looks me up and down. I fight the urge to squirm. Can she tell I'm still reeling from a sex-filled weekend? "That's a lovely outfit. It suits you."

Oh. That was unexpected. "Thanks." The stretchy black pant suit is super-comfortable and one of several new outfits. It's a compromise between the stiff corporate suits that were suffocating the life out of me and casual wear.

Inspector Matthews nods his head as if in agreement with my boss. "Emily, I'm glad you're here. I need your expertise." There's no censure in the inspector's voice for my late appearance, and the tightness in my shoulders eases.

"What can I do for you, sir?"

"Sergeant Anderson will be in at lunchtime. Can you be ready to take us through the maps of the drug busts when he arrives?"

"Sure."

It's not like Greg to be tardy. "Is he okay, sir?"

Sergeant Jacobs purses her lips. "He's probably still crawling out of bed after …" She stops midsentence, her gaze flicking to Inspector Matthews. She fiddles with her glasses and bows her head.

The inspector seems to have grown taller, his steel-grey eyes like tiny daggers. A bitter taste coats the back of my tongue at the reminder of Greg's past. Luckily, Sergeant Jacobs doesn't know I was the woman in Greg's bed this time. If I was a boneless heap last night, I can't imagine how he felt. We had quite a workout over the weekend. I've never seen a man with so much stamina.

The inspector glares at Sergeant Jacobs for a few more seconds before returning his attention to me, his expression softening. "Sergeant Anderson is fine. He had some personal things to take care of."

Personal things? Greg never mentioned anything when I was tearing myself away from his kisses yesterday afternoon.

Inspector Matthews leans over my desk. "Are you sure you're okay, Emily? You seem a little flushed."

"I'm fine." I wave him off. "Really. A cup of tea will sort me out."

He wouldn't look so kindly at me if he knew what Greg and I had been up to. And neither would my boss.

The morning drags on like a bad ping-pong match as I consolidate my analysis and the reality of the real world sets in. Did I read too much into the weekend? Is it over now Greg's been inside my pants? Am I okay with that? It's doing my head in.

Sergeant Jacobs drops two pain tablets on my desk. It makes me feel like an even bigger fraud than I already am. I square my shoulders. Stop pretending I'm working and stomp into the kitchen for my fourth cup of tea.

A familiar muscular frame lounges in a chair at the round table. Butterflies take flight in my stomach, and my fingers itch to slip beneath the rich fabric of his suit. Having licked every inch of Greg's buffed body, I'm now addicted. But doubt creeps in about where we go from here, so I give him a small smile.

"Hey, Em." Greg's eyes sparkle as if he's just seen his favourite treat, and just like that, warmth fills my chest and my smile widens.

The butterflies settle down, and heat spreads through my lower body. "Hi."

Greg gestures for me to sit, so I slide into a chair next to him. He leans closer. "I've missed you."

"Then why didn't you reply to my text this morning?"

"Ouch. The lady's got claws."

I cross my arms. My body might be falling under his spell, but I won't be disrespected. "You better believe it."

"I'm not great with the texting thing." He holds his hand up. "My fingers are too big."

My thighs clench. They didn't seem too big to me on the weekend. Not at all. And he's sent me plenty of texts before now. He's giving out mixed messages.

Greg huddles closer, and I swear he enjoys watching me squirm. "You've got a dirty mind, Red."

I glance at the door. We're alone in here, but anyone could walk in. "Behave."

He slouches in his chair, those hooded eyes revealing stark lust laced with affection. My body responds, the station ceasing to exist as I remember what we did in Greg's bedroom. On the kitchen bench. In the shower.

"My phone was flat." Greg's voice drops to that bedroom tone I know all too well. "Otherwise, I would have replied with something guaranteed to wet your knickers."

"Oh." I squeeze my thighs together. It doesn't seem like he's finished with me yet. And I'm definitely not finished with him.

Greg scratches his jaw. "So many firsts."

What an odd thing to say.

He props his head on his elbows, his gaze dipping to my breasts. "How are you today? Not too sore?"

"You still in pain, Emily?" Inspector Matthews strides into the room. "Do you need to go home?"

Oh my God. He has the worst timing. I grip the handle of my cup so hard it's a wonder it doesn't snap off. "No. I'm fine, Inspector Matthews."

"You sure?"

"Yes, sir, I'm sure."

"Good. That's good." He hurries to the coffee machine, obviously not keen to continue the conversation. A giggle bubbles up my throat, but I hold it in.

Greg's forehead crinkles. "What's wrong?" he whispers.

"I was late, so I said I had a headache," I whisper back. No way I'm getting into my period lie with him.

Greg straightens his jacket, his expression as smug as I've ever seen it. Cocky bastard. He winks, then glances at the inspector. "You ready to talk about the next drug bust, Jake?"

Inspector Matthews goes still, his piercing gaze zeroed in on Greg.

"For Christ's sake." Greg shakes his head. "*Inspector.*"

Inspector Matthews continues to glare at Greg, a slight twitch of his lips the only indication he's pulling Greg's leg.

Greg mutters a word that sounds suspiciously like *fucker.* The inspector lifts his chin, grins, and turns back to the coffee machine.

Over the last twelve months, I've been privy to a few unexpected exchanges between these two men. One minute they're all business, and the next, they're behaving like silly teens. It's endearing. But despite witnessing this more human side of the inspector, and being friends with his fiancé, he still makes me nervous. I cross my legs, uncross them, then cross them again. Greg drums the table with his fingers.

Inspector Matthews slides into a chair opposite. "I had a call from Commander Gordon. He's *not* happy."

Greg chuckles. "The commander's never happy."

Inspector Matthews massages his temples. "True. But he has a right to be pissed off."

He glances at me apologetically. Such a gentleman. So opposite to Greg in many ways, but I'd take Greg and his earthiness over the inspector's icy exterior. That's for Claire to thaw.

Inspector Matthews takes a slow sip of coffee, swirling it around his mouth before swallowing. He lowers his voice. "We need to ensure nothing goes wrong with this next operation."

Greg stops tapping the table. "We'll limit the number of people who have the details."

The inspector and Greg share a look. It makes sense they wouldn't say anything in front of me. I'm surprised at how much they've already said.

Inspector Matthew straightens, all businesslike. "Meet me in my office when you finish your coffee, Greg. You come too, please, Emily. Bring all your analysis." He strides out the door.

My spine lengthens at the thought of being included in their inner circle. Maybe I didn't botch things with the inspector after I visited Jimmy?

Greg nudges my hand with his. It's dangerous and sends a gush of moisture to my panties. I glare at him. He winks.

Sergeant Seymour struts in. I pull my hand off the table, but not before he gives me a creepy sneer that strips me naked.

Greg stiffens beside me, then stands. He saunters across to Seymour, crowding him against the coffee machine. "Locked up any innocent people lately?"

"Sod off, Anderson." Seymour's a foot shorter than Greg, his paunch all the more evident alongside Greg's muscled figure, but he holds his ground.

Greg scowls. "One day, Seymour. One day."

Seymour nods his head at me. "You threatening me in front of this pretty young lady?"

Oh no. I don't want Greg getting in trouble because of this loser.

Greg props his hands on his hips, making him appear even bigger. "That's not an appropriate way to speak about a colleague. Do you need a refresher training session on discrimination and harassment?"

Seymour's Adam's apple bobs up and down. It's obvious he wants to give Greg an earful, but he backs away. "As if you're Mr Perfect." He ambles out of the room with his coffee, but not before he gives me another once-over. Prick. Unbelievable.

Greg slides next to me. "Does that creep ever give you trouble?"

"I can handle him."

Greg cups my chin. "That's not an answer, Em."

I lower my eyes so he can't see all the emotions tumbling inside. "He's done nothing that warrants a complaint."

"Shame. I'd love to bust his balls." Greg places a palm on my thigh.

I jump and glance at the door. "What are you doing?"

He moves his hand away. "Sorry. It's hard to keep myself from touching you." My insides melt at his admission. He tugs at his tie. "Jake and I are worried, Em. You're smart enough to read between the lines. If we don't find answers to the failed drug busts soon, Commander Gordon's going to be out for blood. And he'd love nothing more than to see me go down."

I've heard Greg grumble about the commander before, but I had no idea of the extent of their animosity. I cover his hand with mine. "Why's that?"

He kisses my forehead. A reckless, dangerous move. When he pulls away, his eyes are brimming with disappointment. I want to climb into his lap and soothe away the pain.

"I'm not perfect. I've bent the rules. Nothing illegal, but Commander Gordon is a 'by the book' kind of guy."

That makes sense. Greg's all about getting the job done and helping people. As much as I believe in our laws and processes, they can be illogical at times. And slow.

"Then we'll just have to find the missing link," I say.

He cups my jaw, his gaze warm and oh-so dangerous for my heart. "We will."

❧

By lunchtime, Inspector Matthews' office reeks of failure and we're no closer to identifying a connection between the failed

drug raids. I stroll the short distance to the park near Para-
matta River to clear my head. My three-inch boots limit my
stride. They match the pant suit, and they're roomy enough
that they don't destroy my feet, but they're a little higher than
I'm used to.

Mottled sunlight filters through the gum trees, and
magpies and parrots try their best to entertain me. A couple
stop at the edge of the tree line and kiss. It's not overtly
sexual, but it's intimate enough to tell anyone watching that
they've got each other's backs. Naturally, my thoughts turn to
Greg and the weekend we shared. I don't know what
happens next, and I'm not sure he does either. But for the first
time, I wonder if we can make it work.

A sudden longing for home hits me, and I call up Ethan's
number.

"Hey, sis." I can barely hear his voice over a loud roar in
the background.

"Are you on the tractor?"

"Yeah. Wait a moment." A few seconds later, the noise
disappears. "What's up?"

I hover near the banks of the river. "Nothing."

"Em, let's not play this game. What's going on? Do I need
to come to Sydney and beat someone up for you?"

I bite back a laugh. "No. And as I've told you before, I can
fight my own battles. Thank you very much."

He sniggers. "That you can."

I envy my brother. He's already found the love of his life
and is so happy. He just has to figure out how to break it to
Mum and Dad. "How did you know Simon was the one?"

There's silence except for Ethan's heavy breathing.
"You've met someone?"

I scuff my boots in the grass. "Yeah. I like him. A lot. And
it scares me."

He sighs, and I can imagine him propping his elbows on
the tractor's steering wheel and gazing across the field. "I

don't know, Em. It's lots of little things. But I guess the main one is that I just feel comfortable with Simon. Like I can be myself, no pretence, and that's enough."

Tears prick my eyes. I'm more relaxed with Greg than with any man I've ever known. Any person. But I haven't been completely truthful with him about my kickboxing skills. Or about my attempts to get into the police force. I want to trust Greg with my failures. With the parts of me that have been ridiculed. But can I?

A beeping tone tells me there's another call coming through. I grab it like a lifetime, suddenly not so eager to discuss my feelings for Greg with Ethan.

"Sorry. I have to take this call. Thanks for the chat. Say hello to Simon for me. And Mum and Dad." I hang up and answer the other line. "Hello."

"Good afternoon, Ms Saunders."

I don't recognise the gravelly voice. It must be a scammer or telemarketer. Now I regret hanging up on Ethan. "I'm not interested."

"This is Senior Sergeant Dixon from the Professional Standards Command."

My stomach flips. Why are they calling me? "Sorry. I thought you were a crank call. How can I help?"

"I'd like to have an informal chat. Can you meet me at a café in the city later this afternoon?"

What the hell? That doesn't sound suspicious. At. All. It must be a scammer. "As I said before, I'm not interested."

"Ms Saunders," he replies, his voice full of authority, "I really am from the Professional Standards Command."

The hair on the back of my neck prickles. I've never heard of scam calls like this. Maybe he is legit.

I glance around self-consciously. "Why can't we meet at the station?"

"Because what we need to talk about is highly confidential. The fewer people who know we're meeting, the better. I'll have appropriate identification. The assistant commissioner will also be with me. You can google him on the internet."

Assistant commissioner? My mind goes to how I could possibly help them. But there's nothing. I'm an analyst. I just do what I'm told.

He takes my silence for acquiescence. "Shall we say five o'clock?" His voice becomes muffled. It sounds like he's talking to someone else. "One more thing, Ms Saunders, you are not to speak to anyone about this phone call or our meeting. Not your commanding officer or Detective Inspector Matthews or anyone else at the station. Do I make myself clear?"

My knees wobble, and I stumble to a nearby park bench. "Yes, sir."

Senior Sergeant Dixon ends the call. My heart races like I've just done a few laps around the park. What could internal affairs possibly want with me?

Chapter Twenty-Two

Emily

The café in the city is nondescript. No one would suspect a clandestine meeting was about to occur within the innocuous coffee-coloured walls. It's larger on the inside than it looked outside. I adjust my eyes to the gloom, and a server greets me with a warm smile.

"Can I get you a table?"

I peer over her shoulder. "Ah, I'm here to meet someone."

Two men lounge in the corner, their dark suits making them appear like ordinary businessmen, but the set of their shoulders tells me they're police. Not to mention they're both staring at me, and all the tables nearby are empty. Thank God I went home before coming and changed into one of my stiff corporate skirt suits, complete with stockings and toe-pinching court shoes. I blend right in. I point in their direction. "Over there."

"No problem. I'll bring you a menu."

I walk towards the two officers, my head held high, fingers clenched around the handle of my handbag.

The men stand and gesture for me to sit. I slide next to the assistant commissioner. His face is easily recognisable from my googling. He's also so high up in the police world that, again, I ask myself, what do internal affairs want with a little intel analyst like me?

"Thanks for coming, Ms Saunders."

I clasp my hands in my lap. "I didn't think I had a choice."

"We appreciate this is daunting for you," says the man who must be Senior Sergeant Dixon.

Understatement. Even though I can't think of anything I've done wrong, it's scary as fuck. I was always a straight-A student and never got into trouble, so I never saw the inside of the principal's office. This is a new and not very pleasant experience. Another understatement.

The assistant commissioner passes me a glass of water. "There's no need to look scared, Ms Saunders. You're not here to be reprimanded."

"Thanks." The word comes out scratchy. I take a sip. Sit taller, or try to, because the two men dwarf me. "What do you want?"

Senior Sergeant Dixon turns his striking whiskey-coloured eyes on me. Reminds me of a tiger. Or a lion. "As I explained on the phone, Ms Saunders, what we're about to discuss is highly confidential. It's not to leave this table."

My shoulders and the sides of my neck tighten. I don't miss the warning beneath his tone. "I understand, sir."

"I'll get right to it. Complaints have been made against the drug squad based at Parramatta Station." He taps a folder in front of him. "Combine this with too many instances of targets evading arrest, as if they knew they were about to be busted, and we can't discount the possibility that we have one or more crooked police officers on the team."

My empty stomach caves in on itself. My appetite fled after the phone call earlier. If I'd had lunch, I would be in danger of bringing it back up. Greg said things were heating up with management but never mentioned internal affairs. Is he aware they're involved? "What does that mean, sir?"

The assistant commissioner leans in his chair. "We're

saying that all drug squad members, including Detective Inspector Matthews, are under investigation."

My chest aches and my stomach growls in protest. Inspector Matthews leads the team, and Greg is his right-hand man. Nothing happens without those two knowing about it. There must be some mistake.

"Why are you telling me this?"

Senior Sergeant Dixon sips his coffee. "We understand you and Detective Sergeant Anderson have become ... how shall I say it? Close."

What the hell does that mean? I focus on the dark brown timber of the table. The swirling wood grain pattern. "I've just been helping him with his dog."

"And that requires you to spend all weekend at his home?"

My head snaps up. Despite Dixon's intense expression, I maintain eye contact, refusing to admit to the fear toying with my internal organs. "How ...?"

"There's nothing we don't know."

I clench my hands until I feel the nails biting into my palms. "What do you want from me?"

"We want you to observe Sergeant Anderson. Make a note of anything unusual when you're with him. Anything that could suggest he's on the take."

My stomach is stretched with knots on knots as I try to digest what I'm being told. It's wrong. I can't spy on Greg. Not after everything we've shared.

I cross my arms. "No." The word drift across the table like a pungent odour, the gloom of the café taking on a sinister appearance.

The assistant commissioner looks down at me like I'm a recalcitrant child. "Given the references you received from your previous job, you were fortunate to be assigned to the drug squad at Parramatta."

Those knots in my stomach tighten further. *Is he threat-*

ening me? I shouldn't be surprised they know what happened at my last posting. The sergeant in charge was an arsehole who didn't like it when I beat him in a throwing competition at a team building event soon after I joined. He seemed determined to ruin me after that. Not only did he have disparaging things to say about my wardrobe, but he would often go around my immediate boss and give me ridiculous assignments to watch me fail. Misogynistic prick. But these guys don't know that. They only know what's written in the reports.

Senior Sergeant Dixon regards me over the rim of his coffee cup. "Your cooperation in this confidential and delicate investigation would go a long way towards helping you with another application to join the police force, if that's what you still want."

My mouth goes dry. "How do you know …?"

Dixon points to the folder on the table. "We have intel on everyone involved with the drug squad at Parramatta, including you, Ms Saunders."

Sweat slides down my spine. That's creepy. No wonder cops are wary of internal affairs.

"But if I'm in a relationship with Greg, surely you can't expect me to spy on him?"

"On the contrary, it's perfect. With the exception of Inspector Matthews, Sergeant Anderson keeps people at arm's length. Besides, whatever *relationship*"—Dixon draws quotation marks in the air—"you think you have with Sergeant Anderson won't last. The man is a confirmed bachelor."

The reminder of Greg's horndog ways leaves a bitter taste in my mouth, but I won't let this man sully what we've shared.

"And if you don't cooperate," says the assistant commissioner, his eyes all glittery like a predator preparing to pounce, "then we'll have to assume you're mixed up in whatever illegal activities are going on."

I clasp my hands in my lap and lower my head. He's bluffing. They wouldn't be having this conversation with me if I was under suspicion. But I have no choice. They've made that clear. Besides, I can't believe Greg is guilty of anything except giving mind-blowing orgasms. And it's ridiculous to imagine the straitlaced Inspector Matthews as crooked.

"I guess I have to."

"Not the most enthusiastic answer, but it'll do." Senior Sergeant Dixon gestures towards the door. "You may go now."

His sudden dismissal surprises me, but I don't argue. The sooner I'm away from these men, the better. I push the chair back, my legs a little rubbery as I stand.

"One more thing." Dixon's voice drops an octave. "As we said at the beginning, this is highly confidential. There will be severe repercussions if you speak to anyone about it. I'll be in touch by phone."

"Yes, sir."

I slip out the café door, my head spinning and my legs still shaky as a light drizzle hits my face. *Severe repercussions?*

My heart thumps like I've run up and down several flights of stairs. There's no way I can spy on Greg, but Senior Sergeant Dixon's warning was clear. If I defy him, he'll squash me. Ruin my career so that I'll never work with law enforcement again.

I jab a trembling finger at the pedestrian lights. I need to get as far away from the café as possible. The lights turn green, and I race across the road, weaving between the other pedestrians and cursing my ugly court shoes as the sting of a blister brings tears to my eyes.

I don't stop running until I reach the station platform. A couple of women glance up from their mobile phones and do a double take. I'm guessing I look wild. I certainly feel it. I lean against a pole and rip off one shoe to ease the pain on my heel. Do I tell Greg what happened? I can trust him to keep it a secret. Or can I? He's likely to go in all guns blazing and confront them head-on, ruining both our careers. No. I can't tell him. It's too risky. To him and to me.

What do I do?

I press my hands to my chest as if that will stop my heart from racing. Take a deep breath. And another one. Allow logic to filter through the panic. The answer is obvious. I tell internal affairs nothing because there'll be nothing to tell, and in the meantime, I find out who the crooked cop is. Then Greg will be in the clear.

Chapter Twenty-Three

Greg

The last two weeks have been a blur of sex, work, and thinking about sex. Every single breathy moan and scream from Em's mouth is forever imprinted in my mind. I'd spend every waking moment with her if I could, but I have crooks to lock up and a blackmailer to find. Which is why I'm in the heart of Sydney's business district after hours and not feasting on Em's luscious body.

Redlight Investigations takes up half the sixth floor of a pristine office building. With floor-to-ceiling windows, light mauve-coloured walls and potted plants in every corner, it's clean, inviting and tasteful. And nothing like you might expect a private investigator's digs to look like.

My initial consultation was held in a nearby park on a bitterly cold day due to a fire emergency, the building off limits for several hours. So, this is the first time I've stepped inside the office. Good to see they invest some of the exorbitant fees back into the business.

Even though it's late, a receptionist ushers me into the office of Devlin Becker, PI. His suit is expensive, and his smile is warm, but it's his eyes that grabbed my attention the first time we met. They're a piercing grey, full of knowing, like there's nothing he hasn't seen or heard. I liked him immediately.

I sit across from his large cedar desk. "I was surprised to get your call. You've moved quickly."

"We aim to please." He points to a whiskey bottle. "Want some?"

"No, thanks."

He nods and pours himself a drink. "I'll cut to the chase. We believe we've identified the person of interest." He pushes a file across the desk. "You'll find two photos and a dossier. I've also emailed them to you. I'm ninety-nine percent certain she's the woman who blackmailed your brother. He'll be able to confirm once he sees the pictures."

"Thanks." I pick up the manilla folder and glance inside. I don't dare ask Becker how he obtained the information. As a cop, I may not like the answers.

Becker nurses his whiskey, a slight tic pulsing beneath his eye. "This chick is bad news, Sergeant Anderson. I'd tread very carefully if I were you."

Becker's report is disturbing, raising possibilities I'd never considered. After a night of tossing and turning, I wake up in a cold sweat and set out for the local cemetery.

The smell of freshly cut grass is out of place alongside the century-old headstones. There are no flowers. No trinkets lying on the graves in memory of the dead. No signs that anyone remembers. But the grandeur of the tombstones, the loving words etched into stone, are proof the people they memorialise were once loved. Missed.

I shove my hands in my pockets, ignoring the emptiness gnawing at my soul. Will I be missed when I'm gone? My brother would make sure I had an expensive as fuck tombstone, but would he cry? Would he regret the years spent apart?

And what about Em? She'd shed tears. But should she? Her soul is pure. Mine … a murky mess. If Em was any other woman, I'd be cutting ties after sating myself with her delectable body, but I'm only hungrier. I can't imagine ever getting enough of her. Am I setting myself up for heartache? Loving someone has only ended in misery in the past. I don't know if I can risk it again.

"Are you gonna stand there all day staring at the graves, or what?"

The crackly voice catches me by surprise. Shit. I'd been lost in my own world. Not a smart thing to do in my line of work.

It's Ian, the homeless man I asked to meet me here. Away from prying eyes. I have a hunch about Troy's blackmailer, and I want to test it out before I tell Jake. Which is why I'm here without his knowledge or approval.

"Cemeteries creep you out, Sergeant?"

"Nope. Just thinking about something else."

"Sure, you were." He takes a drag on a cigarette. "Nothin' like a grave to remind you of your mortality."

"And yet here you are, inhaling that cancer stick as if you can't wait to have your own headstone." I shake my head. "I thought you'd given up? Do you want to get sick again?"

"It's the first one I've had in years." He scuffs his feet on the ground, the frayed shoelaces flipping across the worn leather. "I needed a hit, and refuse to cave into anything harder."

I glance around the cemetery. Not a soul in sight. Still, we can't be too careful. A bottlebrush tree drapes over a couple of graves in the distance. I guide Ian to the bench seat under it and we sit.

He rubs his knees. "Bloody arthritis."

"Paracetamol would be better for the pain than cigarettes."

I sound like a nagging parent, but I'm concerned for Ian. He's been clean of drugs for years. Why fall back to smoking now?

"Yeah. But not as much fun." He pulls at his shirt. It's the same one he wore when I last saw him, but dirtier. He sucks in more toxic smoke, then stubs out the cigarette. I say nothing about the butt he drops to the ground. "So, what did you want to talk about, Sarge?"

"Tell me more about the sexy blonde you mentioned. The one giving out new clothes."

Ian's gaze shift sideways like he's expecting someone to lunge at him. "Is this off the record?"

"You have my word."

He scratches his face, drawing attention to dirty, ragged fingernails. "She wasn't doing it out of the goodness of her heart, that's for sure."

No surprises there. "What did she want?"

"Pain killers."

I nod. "Go on." Although, I already suspect where this is going.

"She came after me and Jimmy and some of the older blokes. Offered us money if we'd get scripts filled."

My hands press into the seat. I knew Jimmy had lied to us. "And what were they for?"

"Oxycodone."

"That's heavy stuff."

"No kidding. I was on it when I had cancer."

Oxycodone fetches a high price on the black market. It's been under our radar, illicit drugs taking all our focus. "How long have you been doing it?"

Ian shifts on the seat and looks away. "About six months. A new script every couple of weeks. Alternating between pharmacies."

"How much did she give you?"

"Fifty bucks for each one."

Not bad money for a homeless person. But it doesn't explain why Jimmy was attacked. "Do you think Jimmy's bashing is related?"

"I know it is. He asked her for more money. Made a stupid threat to go to the cops if she didn't."

Silly old fool. He could have been killed. But something's not making sense. Leadbetter's into coke and meth. Not prescription fraud. Or is it a coincidence that the ring on the guy who assaulted Jimmy looked like the one Leadbetter owns? It seems unlikely.

"Why did he say that to her?" I shake my head. "No, don't tell me. He was drunk."

"Yeah. The look on her face went from sweet as pie to pure evil, and she started screeching in French and waving her hands like a madwoman."

I knew it! "French, you say?"

He nods. "She had this sexy accent and killer body. We were putty in her hands."

Just like my brother.

I pull out my mobile and scroll through the photos. Hiring that private investigator was worth every cent.

I hold the phone so Ian can see the screen. "Is this the woman?"

"What the hell?" He jumps backwards and looks around like I'm trying to trap him. "How did you know?"

"I didn't." I take a deep breath. Fight the tendril of fear curling around my gut. Sometimes being right sucks. What the hell has Troy gotten himself into? "She's wanted for a separate investigation."

My fingers tremble ever so slightly as I slip the phone back into my trouser pocket. Now that I've confirmed Sophie Dubois is the same woman Ian and Jimmy told me about, I have to wonder if Troy was targeted because he's a politician or because of my position in the drug squad. "Are you still doing the scripts for her?"

Ian hesitates, and I know he's about to lie. I hold up my hand. "The truth."

He hangs his head and talks to the dirt. "Yeah. I don't dare stop. Not after what happened to Jimmy." He straightens, his fingers twisting on his lap. "Are you gonna arrest me now?"

"Nope." I've got bigger fish to fry, and Ian's going to help me. "I promised this was off the record. But I want you to ring me after she makes contact again."

Ian lifts his hands and shrugs. "I have no phone."

"Nice try." I chuckle. "I'm not giving you a mobile. You can call from the shelter."

"You're a hard man, Sergeant."

"If that was the case, I'd be hauling your sorry arse down to the station."

We're still alone in the cemetery, only the birds and the odd bee to witness our conversation. I pull out my wallet and hand Ian a one hundred dollar supermarket gift card. "Thanks for meeting with me."

His eyes light up, and he snatches the card.

Jake wouldn't be happy if he got wind of this chat. He'd be even less pleased about the voucher. But it's not like it's cash. Ian can only use it to buy grocery items. Not cigarettes or alcohol. And I paid for it myself.

He pushes to his feet. "I'm off to do some shopping. Nice doing business with you, Sarge." He gives me a silly wave and lurches off.

A lorikeet hangs off the bottlebrush, stabbing at one of the remaining flowers. I watch for a while, impressed with the bird's determination to suck every last drop of nectar from the centre. Reminds me of the woman who set Troy up. Sophie Dubois' days of seducing men for her own gain are drawing to a close.

Chapter Twenty-Four

Emily

My brain is a haze of numbers from all the mapping I've completed as I search for trends that Inspector Matthews can use in his investigation, no matter how obscure. I'd also hoped to find clues to help me identify the crooked cop and escape the wrath of internal affairs, but no such luck. Greg's been in the field a lot, which is just as well. When he's at the station, I feel like a giant neon sign hangs over our heads telling everyone we've had sex.

I tear my gaze away from the computer screen and roll my shoulders back. Sergeant Seymour chooses that moment to saunter past and leer at my breasts. Prick. There's something off about him. Even Greg thinks so. As Seymour continues into the bathroom, I realise the office area is empty. The general duties team has a homicide briefing and the drug squad detectives are at the shooting range for practice.

This might be my one chance to snoop. Grabbing my handbag as if heading to the ladies, I slide off my chair and cross the room to where the drug squad sits. Detective Bryan's desk is closest. It's hard to imagine him being crooked, but maybe his quiet, unassuming persona is a front?

His desk is devoid of any clutter. No notebook, no sticky notes. Not even a stray pen or pot plant. Nothing.

The office is eerily quiet, but it won't be for long, so I can't afford to linger. I amble past the cubicles looking for anything untoward. I hadn't realised how tidy the detectives are. All their desks resemble Bryan's—spotless. Except for Detective Laura's desk. My pulse kicks up as I take in the stack of files.

A quick glance tells me I'm still alone, so I step inside her cubicle and flick through the folders. A scrap of paper flutters out. It has handwritten dates and addresses of the last three drug raids, as well as names and phone numbers. What the hell? This information belongs under lock and key, not left out where anyone can see it. I grab my mobile and snap a pic. She keeps to herself, but I haven't missed the covert looks she gives Greg and even Inspector Matthews when she thinks no one is watching. I figured she's got a crush, but what if she has a more sinister motive for keeping tabs on them?

My heart thumps louder than an out-of-control jack-hammer as I return the paper to its position inside a yellow folder. A quick scan of the room tells me I'm still alone. My gaze returns to Seymour's desk. He's not part of the drug squad, so he's not under suspicion, but my gut tells me he can't be trusted. Whether it's more than him being a creepy male, I don't know. Still, there's no harm in taking a little peek.

My palms are hot and sweaty by the time I take the dozen steps to Seymour's workstation. It's the polar opposite of the drug detectives' desks. Food crumbs and something sticky coat what surface isn't taken up by several car magazines.

I'm in luck. Seymour's mobile is on the desk. I look around to check I'm still alone because there's no way I could talk myself out of trouble if I'm caught holding his phone. I prod the screen with my finger. It's locked. Bugger. Then again, what did I expect? I punch in 000000. It doesn't work.

Then I try 123456. Then 654321. Still nothing. What other numbers would make sense to his simple brain?

I keep my eye on the corridor. So far there's no sign of anyone returning, but if I hang around Seymour's desk much longer, I'll get caught. Hang on, he makes no secret sixty-nine is his *favourite* number. What if that's part of his pin? I've got nothing to lose. I punch in 696969 and cross my fingers. The mobile unlocks. Yay! What a sleazebag!

I pull up the recent call list. Then snap a photo of the screen with my phone. I close it and check messages. His mother is at the top of the list ... never expected that. The only other name is Dee, and when I click on it, the first thing I see is a photo of a woman's breasts. Ew. That's definitely not what I'm looking for. There are no other texts saved. The sounds of laughter carry through from the lunchroom, and they're getting louder. Shit. I return his phone to the table and back away.

My hands shake as I near my desk. I'm two steps away from my chair when Seymour returns, his hand on his junk. His eyes narrow and his gaze flits to his desk as if he's got something to hide. Interesting.

Somehow, I trip, stumble and end up on the floor with the contents of my handbag scattered around me. My hands and knees smack against the hard floor. Ouch. That's it, I'm ditching these boots! No more high heels for me.

My mobile lands near Seymour's feet. Thankfully, it's inside a cover and has the screen lock activated, so all that comes up is a picture of canola fields in full bloom. The last thing I need is the photo I snapped appearing and him recognising it.

He laughs and kicks a box of tampons towards me. "Stick to baby heels, Emily. You're not impressing anyone." He saunters to his desk.

I mentally count to ten to stop myself from responding. You can't win with arrogant arses like him.

My nerves are shot after my less-than-impressive attempt at spying, so I slip on a pair of flat shoes that I keep under my desk and go out for lunch. I grab a pie from the bakery and stroll along the concrete path near Parramatta River. Inhale a deep breath and rid my lungs of the stale air-conditioned air. Dirty grey paints the sky, casting a dull sheen on the water's surface. There's not another person in sight, the weather too bitter for any but the most determined walkers.

My phone rings. "D" for Dixon. My stomach clenches. It's the third time he's called in as many days. He seems to be running out of patience.

"Ms Saunders. Are you alone?" Senior Sergeant Dixon's voice is deep. Sombre.

"Yes. I'm by the river."

"Any news to report?"

I haven't had time to digest what I found earlier, but there's no time like the present. Besides, I have to try. For Greg's sake. And mine. For us. "I came across a couple of pieces of information that might be helpful."

"Go on."

I clear my throat and take a deep breath. "I found an unusual list of contacts on Detective Nielson's desk and—"

"Ms Saunders, you're supposed to be observing Detective Sergeant Anderson, not rummaging through the personal effects of other officers."

His censure cuts through my bravado. I didn't think this through. "Yes, I know, sir, but—"

"There are no buts, Ms Saunders." His tone is like a slap to my face. "What information do you have on Sergeant Anderson?"

I hate being stuck in this position of spying on Greg. My stomach turns on itself, and I have a sudden urge to go to the toilet. I stare at the river. It's as murky and unwelcoming as the man on the other end of the phone. "I've hardly seen him this week."

"Did you know he was observed giving a bribe to a member of the public yesterday?"

Dread pools in the bottom of my stomach. It can't be what it looks like. There must be a reason that doesn't make Greg a bent cop. "Maybe he was checking out a lead?"

"We don't deal in maybes. Only facts."

"Of course." The wind picks up, and I pull my coat tighter around my body.

"Ms Saunders, we need you to observe, not draw conclusions. Can you do that?"

No. I can't. But saying so would be career suicide. "Yes, sir."

I rub my temples. Lies. I'm full of lies. After what Greg and I have shared, we're more than attached. We're entwined. I feel like he knows me better than anyone ever has, even Ethan. He just gets me. No judgement. No expectations.

"Good. While I don't condone your actions, Ms Saunders, send through the details of what you found with your amateur sleuthing. We'll review it. In the meantime, I suggest you focus on Sergeant Anderson and leave the other officers to us."

Dixon ends the call. Amateur? Condescending prick. But at least he's agreed to look at the information. I can't ask for more than that.

A few spots of rain splash on the dirt in front of me. I push away from the tree and retrace my steps. My head spins. Greg alluded to bending the rules to get the job done, but he's not making it easy for himself. He's already got Commander Gordon watching him. Would he be more careful if he knew internal affairs also had him in their sights?

The few drops of rain become a constant drizzle. I quicken my steps.

Gah! I hate all the lies.

Chapter Twenty-Five

Emily

My hamstrings scream at me to stop, but I give one last kick and step away from the punching bag. I rip off my boxing gloves and gulp down water.

Scott saunters towards me, his expression fierce, belying the casual sway of his body. "What the hell was that?"

I shrug and wince as my neck muscles let me know they're not happy, either. "I needed a workout."

He stabs a finger at the punching bag. "*That* wasn't a workout. It was a bloodbath. Thank God you didn't have a sparring partner. You'd have killed them."

I laugh, and even that slight movement sends a shiver of pain through my body. "You're exaggerating. I was simply blowing off some steam."

He looks me up and down. I'm a mess, sweat dripping down my face and chest, lungs heaving as I suck in much-needed oxygen, ribs stinging with every breath. His expression softens. "Did the detective give you the flick?"

"What?"

"It's okay, Emily. Greg's not known for staying with the same woman for very long."

My cheeks burn even hotter, if that's possible. "Greg hasn't broken up with me."

"You broke up with him?"

"No." I shake my head, a spray of sweat flying in the air. Scott jumps back. "I had a shitty day at work. That's all."

He crosses his arms, his expression suggesting he doesn't believe me. I shift under the weight of his gaze. I'm telling the truth. I have had a bad day, one in which I found myself increasingly trapped by internal affairs and lies.

But that's not the worst of it. I've done what I told myself not to do … I've fallen in love with Greg. It's the only explanation for the fluttery sensation in my stomach, the way my body tingles whenever he's near, the sense of belonging I have when I'm with him. I feel like I can do anything, be anything, when we're together. Except be completely honest.

Or can I? I ignore the searching look in Scott's eyes and take another swig of water. I don't need women's intuition to know that the longer I keep the truth from Greg, the harder it will be for him to understand, or forgive me, if he ever finds out. What if I disobey the internal affairs' command and tell Greg what they've asked me to do? Am I willing to risk my career for a man? One who's known as a womaniser? Except, he's not like that with me. Or am I fooling myself?

It's all just so confusing! Why, oh why, did internal affairs put me in this position?

Scott takes hold of my hands. "At least your gloves protected you from serious damage." He runs his fingers across the swollen knuckles. "I suggest you have a nice long soak in a bath of Epsom salts and pop some ibuprofen when you get home. It's gonna hurt like a bitch in the morning."

❧

My body aches as if a truck has hit it. Forearms, back, hips. Glutes, quads, calves, hamstrings. There's no muscle that doesn't scream blue murder. Sunlight peers through the cracks in the curtain, teasing my eyelids open. I glance at the clock, pain shooting down my neck. Dammit. It's eight am. I should have been at the station two hours ago.

I reach for my mobile, wincing as my muscles protest. Scott wasn't exaggerating when he said I'd be sore today. Three missed calls from Greg, a missed call from Sergeant Jacobs, and even a call from Inspector Matthews. That can't be good.

My doorbell buzzes. I ignore it. Since I should be at work, it's unlikely to be anyone important. No way I can crawl out of bed yet. I guess I overdid it yesterday. Thumping against my door starts up. "Emily, are you in there?"

Greg? What's he doing here?

I roll to my side and perch on the edge of the mattress. Next time I'm stressed, I'll do what normal women do. Eat a bucket of ice cream. Or a box of chocolates. Down a bottle of wine or two.

I shuffle into the living room. The ivory silk nightie my mum gave me as a birthday present for my twenty-first offers little protection against the chilly morning, but it was the only material that didn't scratch like barbed wire against my sensitive skin when I collapsed into bed last night.

The door swings open. Greg storms in, hand inside his jacket where he keeps his gun. He rakes his gaze up and down my body. His pupils are tiny laser points, missing nothing. He clasps his hands around my arms, squeezing the overused muscles.

"Ahhh …" I yelp. Ouch, that hurts.

He lets go but hovers over me, his breaths uneven. "Are you okay, Em?"

"Yeah." But confused by the sudden intrusion.

Dylan strides in, hand at his holster, Milo by his side. Man and dog regard me with large, round eyes. I wrap my arms around my waist, conscious of how thin my nightie is.

Greg must realise too, because he shields me from Dylan's view. "Where's your dressing gown?"

"In the bathroom."

"Dylan, get Em's robe for her?"

A few moments later, Greg helps me into my plush black bathrobe and onto the couch.

Milo sits at my side and licks my fingers. "Hey, boy." I stroke the soft fur on his head, avoiding the questioning gazes of the two men. This isn't awkward. At, all.

Greg kneels at my feet and lifts my hands, his gaze alternating between the bruised knuckles and purplish shadow on my right knee which peeks out from between the folds of the gown. "Do you need a doctor?" The words are shaky, as are his fingers.

"I'm fine." And I'll be a whole lot better when I'm alone again.

"If someone hurt you, we'll …" Greg clears his throat and tugs at his tie.

Oh my God. He thinks I've been assaulted. "No. No one hurt me. I overdid it in the gym yesterday. That's all."

"These knuckles look like you've been punching somebody." His voice lowers to the smooth chocolate baritone I've heard him use to soothe Silas. "You don't need to be scared … or ashamed."

"No, really. I was kickboxing. I got carried away."

Greg's shoulders loosen, and he cups my chin. His irises are swirls of the finest, darkest chocolate. I could lose myself in those swirls if my body didn't ache so badly. "Kickboxing?"

"Yeah." I glance at Dylan, who's doing a terrible job pretending not to listen. "It's a great way to keep fit and learn self-defence."

"Jesus." Greg rakes his fingers through his hair and flops onto the couch next to me. "You had us worried."

Dylan steps forward and pats Milo. "Sergeant Anderson

broke every traffic rule to get here."

"I didn't break any rules," growls Greg.

"If you say so."

Greg glares at Dylan. "Why don't you make Em a cup of tea? White, no sugar."

"Yes, sir." Dylan backs away and into the nearby kitchen area. Although, it's open plan, so he can still see us.

"I'm sorry." I place a hand on Greg's arm. "I slept through my alarm again. I've never been so sore after a workout."

"Kickboxing's a tough sport, Em." He shakes his head. "A little thing like you needs to be careful."

What the hell? I withdraw my hand and fold my arms, wincing as my ribs remind me they're not happy. "What did you just say?"

"You heard me, and I'm not apologising. You scared the shit out of me when you didn't turn up to work. Or answer your phone." His expression is as severe as I've ever seen it.

Warmth seeps into my bruises at his concern. "Sergeant Jacobs and Inspector Matthews won't be happy with me."

Greg glances at Dylan who's looking at the teapot like he's never seen one before. It shouldn't be that foreign to him. I use a teapot at the station. Most people prefer tea bags, but I love the flavour of a properly brewed tea.

Greg lowers his voice. "Use the same excuse as yesterday."

"A headache?"

"No. The other one. Jake mentioned it." He touches the tip of his finger to my nose. It's endearing but dangerous, given Dylan's only a few metres away. "Since you're usually an early bird and live alone, he was worried you might have had some female emergency when you didn't turn up this morning and we couldn't get hold of you. It happens. In case you haven't noticed, he's a little overprotective of the women in his life."

Oh God. Kill me now.

No woman wants to talk about periods with a man she's only been dating for a month or have a big boss at the office discussing her bodily functions.

Greg pats my thigh, the warmth from his palm comforting. If I had my period, I could imagine curling up on his lap while he massaged my lower back. Fed me chocolates and hot tea.

"You can say you sent a text, but it didn't go through. It's just a white lie, Em. Perfectly harmless. And I'll make sure Dylan keeps his trap shut."

Greg's suggestion that I lie should have warning bells ringing in my ears. But, despite what Dixon at internal standards thinks, my intuition says Greg isn't a crook. The dirty cop has to be someone else.

❧

An hour after Greg and Dylan leave, my doorbell buzzes again. Who could it be this time? I'm still in my nightie and dressing gown, snuggled on the sofa under the blanket Greg wrapped me in before leaving. I heave myself off the couch, tighten the belt on my robe, and stumble the few steps to the door.

Claire's face comes into view as I peer through the peephole. What's she doing here? I open the door and stand back as she bustles in.

"Hi. Sorry to barge in on you, but Jake said you weren't feeling well. I thought I'd swing by after dropping Oscar at school and see if you needed anything."

"Shouldn't you be at work?"

Claire shrugs. "Monica's pretty chill about hours. It's what we do that counts. Not how long we spend in the office."

She looks me up and down. I'm thankful for the robe covering the bruise on my knee and the woollen gloves I donned earlier to protect my hands.

She hugs me, and I grit my teeth as sharp blades poke my ribcage. "Periods suck. I didn't realise you got them so bad."

"I don't usually." Truth. "I'm not sure why it hurts so much this month." Lie.

"Jake said Greg and Dylan checked in on you, but he was still worried. He figured you might need another woman."

I'm simultaneously touched by the inspector's concern and mortified he's talking to others about my fictitious period. First Greg. Now Claire.

"Besides breaking into my flat, they were most helpful." I point to the sofa. "They made me tea and filled a hot water bottle."

"Wow. I'm impressed."

She and I both. Greg's caring side continues to seduce me even more than the orgasms. "Would you like a cup of tea?"

"I don't want to impose."

"You're not. I could do with some company. I'm feeling like a bit of a fraud." Not a lie.

"Period pain is a valid excuse for sick leave, Emily. Don't downplay it."

I couldn't agree more, which makes me a terrible person for faking it. If only she knew. I walk into the kitchen and switch on the jug. It's then I realise my mistake. It'll look odd if I don't remove my gloves.

Claire solves the problem for me. "Hey, let me make it. You sit down and relax."

"Thanks."

I perch myself on a chair, making sure the gown covers my legs, and watch while Claire fills the pot.

She nibbles her lip. "I have a confession."

What could Claire possibly confess to me? I glance at her stomach.

Her gaze follows mine and her cheeks bloom. "Oh, no, I'm not pregnant."

"Sorry. That was rude."

"Don't apologise." Her eyes sparkle. "It's not for lack of practice."

La, la, la. Too much information. Inspector Matthews is a big boss at the station. I refuse to think of him as a man. A man with needs.

Claire chews her nails. Sips her tea. "I really came here to ask if you and Greg are seeing each other."

My vision narrows, the edges blurring. *How could she know?* This is one of those moments when years of schooling myself to keep a blank expression should have kicked in. But the question catches me by surprise. From the look on Claire's face, the truth is plastered all over mine.

"I'm sorry, Emily. I shouldn't have asked. That wasn't fair of me."

"I … I …" I stutter. "Why would you think that?"

"Jake mentioned how happy Greg's been lately, and when he said Greg had checked on you, I just knew. He wouldn't have done that for anyone else. Mention female things like periods and babies and Greg's scrambling for the exit." She gives me a wry smile. "Besides, the few times I've seen you and Greg together, sparks have flown."

Great. So much for keeping things on the down low. "Does Inspector Matthews know?" It would explain the little chat he had with me.

"He's suspicious but believes Greg's promise that nothing's going on." Claire shakes her head. "And don't worry. I won't say anything. That's for Greg to tell when he's ready to admit he's in a relationship."

"Greg doesn't do relationships."

Claire's eyebrow lifts. "How long have you been seeing each other?"

"A month."

"Has he taken you on more than one date?"

"A couple." Rock climbing, lunch, a picnic. Sex all over his house, but I'm not sure that counts as a date.

She nods. "You're in a relationship."

"No. We're having fun. It isn't serious." And it's complicated. I don't want to get my hopes up.

Claire grabs my gloved hand, and it takes all my willpower not to wince from the pain. "What are you afraid of?"

"Nothing. But Greg … well, you know. He's had a lot of women. And I knew that going in. I don't expect him to change for me."

"But you'd like him to?"

"Claire, please. I'm keeping my expectations low. And we're keeping this quiet because Inspector Matthews—"

She shakes her head. "Jake."

I laugh. "He'll always be Inspector to me. He doesn't like staff fraternising. And neither does my boss."

"Mmm … There's no law against it."

"No. But it can create an uncomfortable environment when relationships don't work out."

"Greg's a wonderful friend to Jake." Claire traces the rim of her cup. "He puts on this gruff cop persona, but there's a caring guy behind the badge. All he needs is the right woman to make him realise there's more to life than a new floozie each week."

Claire's words are similar to what old Jimmy said. Could they be right? "I'm not sure if I'm that woman, Claire. I like Greg." Love him, but I'm not ready to admit that to her when I can barely admit it to myself. "But I don't kid myself that he wants anything more than a fun time."

Except in my dreams. Then, I allow myself to fantasise about a world where I don't have to pretend to be someone different to get ahead. A world where I'm not asked to spy on the man I love. A world where I can have a relationship *and* a career without fear of being judged by colleagues and superiors.

Chapter Twenty-Six

Greg

E m's as cute as a button. It's the only way I can describe her as she fusses at the lunchroom sink, spooning tea leaves into a teapot.

Dylan hovers next to her. "You sure I can't help?"

Em waves him away. "I'm fine."

He looks unconvinced, which he should because it's a bald-faced lie. Em's fingers are twice the size they were yesterday. Although, she's wearing gloves to hide the swollen digits. She didn't argue when I told her I'd give her a lift to work this morning. Proof, as if I needed it, that she's still in a lot of pain. When I broke into her apartment and saw the marks on her hands and knee, fear like I've never experienced consumed me. I was ready to commit murder on her behalf. In fact, I still might. Her trainer has a lot to answer for. No student should come away from a lesson as bruised and battered as Em. It reminds me of the sadistic instructor at the academy and the gleam in her eyes when she cracked my ribs.

The instantaneous hot water system isn't working, so we have a temporary jug for the tea drinkers. It boils, and I bound out of my chair and grab it. Em's told me before that the water must be boiling when she adds it to the pot. One hundred degrees Celsius. Not ninety-nine degrees. Not ninety-nine point five, but one hundred. She glares at me. I respond with a grin. "You can scowl all you want, but the swelling will go down faster if you don't exert yourself. Let me help."

Her chin lifts and, for a moment, it looks like she's going to fight me. *Bring it on, little lady.* But she steps away. I pour the water, careful not to splash. The last thing Em needs is third-degree burns to accompany her bruises and swelling. I grab the teapot, and Dylan brings the milk. That leaves Em with her cup and saucer. It rattles precariously, but she deposits it on the table in one piece and sits.

I itch to hold her hand, but I can't. Not with Dylan watching. "See? That wasn't so hard?"

She screws up her nose. "What do you mean?"

"Accepting help."

"Very funny."

Jake strides in, raking his fingers across his head. He halts and shifts on his feet. "Emily. It's nice to see you. Are you feeling better today?"

Em's face switches from white to red in milliseconds. "Yeah. Thanks."

A crimson stain spreads across Jake's cheeks as well. He glances at her hands, no doubt curious about why she's wearing gloves, but he says nothing. Instead, he turns to me, his face a mask. The hairs on the back of my neck stand at attention. Something's up. I've worked with Jake long enough to recognise the signs. "Can I see you in my office?"

It's a command dressed up as a question. "Sure."

He pivots and retraces his steps. I dawdle behind. He couldn't know about my meeting with Ian, could he?

"What the fuck were you thinking?"

Okay, then. Jake knows about my meeting with Ian. "Let me explain."

"Not yet." Jake jabs a finger at the chair across from his desk. "Sit."

His voice carries a tone I've rarely heard directed at me, even when I've pissed him off. It doesn't bode well.

He slumps in his seat, shoulders sagging. Papers are strewn over the desk and the floor like he scattered a pile with his arm. Lost his cool. That's not like Jake. "I've just got off the phone with Commander Gordon."

Interesting. Maybe it's not about Ian. The politics higher up are toxic. Jake's much better at smoothing ruffled feathers than I am, which is why I'm more than happy to remain a sergeant. "What crawled up his arse today?"

Jake bangs the table, his fingers balled into tight fists. "This isn't a joke, Greg."

Shit. The last time Jake was this worked up was when he reprimanded me for roughing up a suspect. I cross my legs at the ankles, trying to appear nonchalant. "What's going on?"

"You were seen meeting with a homeless man in the cemetery." Jake scrubs his face. "And handing him something, which he quickly shoved in his pocket."

I uncross my legs and straighten. "Is someone following me?"

Jake plants his hands on the table. "So, you don't deny it?"

"No." Christ. I didn't want to tell Jake about Troy's problem, but it looks like I don't have a choice. "I wasn't doing anything wrong." I cross my fingers. Much.

Jake gives me a look that says he thinks I'm full of shit. "Then why did I have to hear it from the commander and not you?"

I grip my thighs. This is my boss talking now. Not my friend. "How does he know? Am I under surveillance?"

Jake's lips press into a thin line. I'm not answering his question, but hell, surely he's wondering the same thing.

"He wouldn't say, but I have my suspicions."

"And?"

He holds his right hand up. "First, what were you doing?"

"Fine." I scrape back my chair and pace. Will he believe me? It's not like I have much to do with my family. "Troy had a one-night stand."

"Your brother?"

"Yeah. The woman has photos. She's blackmailing him for one million dollars."

"Jesus." The tension in Jake's face softens. "But what's that got to do with what went down at the cemetery?"

"I know it's wrong to use police resources for a private matter." See, I understand the rules. When I want to. "I hired a PI to track her down. Found out she's tied to Leadbetter."

The muscle at Jake's jaw pulses. Despite putting Leadbetter behind bars last year, the bastard's syndicate is still a thorn in our sides.

"Troy's description of her sounded similar to the one Dylan and I were given when we visited the homeless after the attack on Jimmy."

"That's a long bow."

"Yep. But I trusted my gut. It's rarely wrong." Never wrong.

Jake leans forward. "So, what were you giving Ian?"

I look away from the steel in Jake's eyes. "A one hundred dollar grocery card."

"In other words, you bribed him."

"I prefer to think of it as a thank you. I promised our conversation was off the record."

He bangs the table less forcefully this time. "You should have told me."

Jake's right. I've gone against protocol. "What are you going to do?" I stop pacing and shove my hands into my pockets to hide the slight tremble. I can't afford another mark on my record.

Jake drums his fingers. "I told Commander Gordon your visit to the cemetery was all part of our investigation."

"Jesus, Jake, thank you." I sink onto my chair, humbled by Jake's protection. He could lose his badge if the commander caught him lying.

Jake throws me a bottle of water. "Here, have a drink. You look like you're about to faint."

I take a sip, grateful for the cool fluid sliding down my dry throat. Jake drums his fingers on the table again. It's annoying as fuck, but I keep my mouth shut. He's already shown me slack I don't deserve.

Jake stands, walks to the door, and flicks the lock. I take another sip of water. *What's going on?*

He returns to his desk, propping himself on the edge. Deep furrows crawl across his forehead. Between his eyes. At the edges of his mouth. "It's possible internal affairs has surveillance on us. They may even be monitoring our phones."

A slither of fear crawls up my spine. "You think it's that serious?"

He nods. "I've got a feeling."

And that itch a cop gets at the back of his neck is sometimes all we have to go on. "Fuck."

"My thoughts exactly." Jake returns to his chair. "I'm pissed, but I don't blame the hierarchy. Everything's pointing to an inside job. But, like I told you two weeks ago, it's even more imperative we do everything by the book." He jabs a finger at me. "No. Going. Rogue."

I sip my water. Wish I could promise I won't bend the rules. Break them. Jake knows me better than to demand it. He does what he always does. Warns me. Guards my back. But only so far. If I cross the line completely, he'd be the first one to bury my arse, no matter how much it gutted him.

Jake taps on his keyboard. "Let's start from the beginning. Bring me up to speed with *everything* you've been doing off the record. We'll find the rat, shut Leadbetter's operation down for good and prove to the commander, the commissioner, and internal affairs that we're worthy of this task force."

Chapter Twenty-Seven

Emily

Greg's quiet as he drives me home from the station. Clouds roll in, and a few spots of rain splash onto the windscreen. My fingers throb. The small amount of typing I did today has inflamed the swollen joints.

He misses the turn to my apartment building and continues straight, running an amber light. "Hey, what are you doing?"

"I'm taking you to my house. You need someone to look after you tonight."

"You can't just decide that."

"I'm the one driving." He pats the steering wheel. "So, yes, I can."

This is ridiculous but also a little hot. It does things to my insides, even though I should be annoyed at his domineering attitude. "I don't have any clothes."

His gaze dips to my breasts and back to the road. "You won't need any."

"I'm serious. I'll need a change for tomorrow."

"Then we'll swing past your place in the morning."

I huff and sink into the seat. All my life, I've been determined to prove I don't need anyone to help me, especially a man. So, why do I find Greg's behaviour comforting rather than annoying? I close my eyes, the pain in my hands mingling with the one in my heart. How caring would he be if he learnt I've been told to spy on him?

I must doze off because before I know it, we've reached Greg's home. Silas is all wiggly bum and sloppy kisses. I pat his head. "Hey, boy, it's good to see you too."

Greg guides me to the sofa. "Relax. I'll get you some painkillers. You're too pale."

I don't have the energy to argue. Besides, I hurt. Everywhere. Silas jumps up beside me and snuggles. Greg returns with two paracetamol. I gulp them down with water. He drapes a throw rug over me and turns on the heating. Five minutes later, I'm nursing a cup of tea and a biscuit. A girl could get used to this sort of attention.

Greg slides next to me on the couch. Silas raises his head briefly, then settles down. I stroke the soft velvet of his ears. "I'm surprised Silas isn't begging you for a walk?"

"Don't be fooled. I usually have a beer first. Give him another half hour and he'll be bouncing off the walls demanding to go out."

I sip my tea. The scene is so domestic. I'm not sure what to say. "How was your day?" I close my eyes for a moment. What an inane question.

"It was the usual." Greg picks at his trousers. He's lying. But why? He and Inspector Matthews were closeted away for hours this morning.

I let it go. If I ask too many questions, it would look odd. It's none of my business. And I've already decided that I'm not telling Internal Affairs anything Greg confides in me. "Well, mine was excruciating." I flex my fingers and immediately regret it. "I should have taken the day off."

"Yes, you should have." He kisses my nose. "Kickboxing is a dangerous sport. You can do a lot of damage if you don't do it right."

Blood surges to my cheeks. I don't appreciate the underlying suggestion that I'm weak. "Are you saying I'm not good enough to do it?"

"Not at all. The way you scaled the rock climbing wall, I have no doubt you'd kick arse. But martial arts is a whole other ball game."

"How do you know I'm not a black belt?"

He looks pointedly at my hands. "If you were, you wouldn't have made such a mess of yourself."

I should tell Greg the truth, but what he's not saying is he wouldn't like it. He's already told me his ego wouldn't recover if I had a black belt in karate. Especially after what happened to him at the academy. My martial arts skills have always intimidated men like it's an affront to their masculinity. One of my ex-boyfriends had the gall to say it made me less sexy. Even though he was a spineless prick, his barb stuck.

"Are you hungry?" Greg asks.

I'm grateful for the change of subject. "Starving." I didn't dare attempt to eat a sandwich today. Sergeant Jacobs thought I was odd for wearing gloves, but I told her I feel the cold more when my periods are heavy. It's the lamest excuse ever, but she seemed satisfied with it.

"I'll take Silas for a quick walk. Will you be okay?"

"Of course. I'm not that injured."

Greg clasps my gloved hands and kisses my fingers. "With all due respect, Miss Saunders, I disagree." He kisses the woollen fabric and gives me his signature grin. "What you need is a warm Epsom salt bath. And I'm happy to volunteer my services as your bathing attendant."

A giggle bubbles up my throat. He's so deliciously naughty. Does it really matter that he doesn't know I'm a black belt? Despite my growing feelings for him, our relationship can't go anywhere, and I don't want to see the desire fade from his eyes. Not yet. "That's very generous of you. And selfless."

"Be careful, Red." He taps my nose. "When you've recovered, I might have to punish you for your insolence."

Heat floods my body. Greg's given hints of a kinkier side, but so far, I've not seen it.

૪

A floor-to-ceiling stained-glass window dominates the spacious ensuite, revealing breathtaking water views. In front of it is a two-person spa bath where Greg introduced me to the power of water jets the last time I stayed over. My face warms at the memories. His bedroom, or in this case bathroom skills, were impressive.

Greg drops a fluffy grey bathmat onto the floor, turns on the taps and throws a handful of salts into the bath. The relaxing lavender fragrance drifts on the steam. His gaze darts to my hands, still covered by the gloves. "Do you need help to undress?"

There's no sexual innuendo in the question, only warmth and concern. It undoes me more than any sophisticated seduction. I shouldn't be surprised after he hand-fed me bite-sized pieces of frittata for dinner. "I'm good."

I ease the gloves off, flinching at the friction. The bruising to my knuckles is for amateurs, not a seasoned kickboxer like me. It's proof, as if I need it, that the pressure of the internal affairs investigation is getting to me. Next is my dress—a simple pullover that catches on my head. I tug at the stupid thing, sending a streak of pain through my fingers.

A growl reverberates against the walls, and Greg peels the fabric away. "Don't be stubborn, Em. Let me help." I surrender to his capable ministration, and I'm soon stripped naked while he's fully dressed. I won't lie. It's incredibly erotic. I like being vulnerable with him because I'm no longer worried I'm another conquest. I trust that whatever is happening between us, while temporary, is special for him, too.

Greg takes my arm and helps me into the tub. I sink into the water, bubbles tickling my skin.

"How's that feel? Not too hot?"

"No. My fingers burn a little, but my muscles love it."

Greg grabs two washcloths and soaks them in cold water. "Here. Put your hands along the sides of the tub, and I'll wrap them up."

I do as he asks, the coolness soothing against the swollen joints. "Thanks."

Greg's throat bobs up and down, his eyes glued to my chest. With my arms extended, my breasts thrust out and the bubbles tease my nipples. "Jesus, Em, you're making it hard for me to be a gentleman."

I give him what I hope is a coy smile. "Who said I wanted you to be a gentleman?"

He shakes his head. "Behave. You're too injured to be fooling around. That bruise above your knee is twice the size it was yesterday. And you've got a new one forming on your thigh."

I pout. "You're no fun."

"Don't worry. There's plenty of time for fun. When you've finished soaking, I'm going to lay you on the bed and lick you dry, paying special attention to every single crevice. Make sure you're thoroughly clean."

Oh my.

Greg proceeds to wash me, sliding a cake of soap down my arms and legs, then back up my stomach and breasts. It's an odd mix of sensual and reverent, leaving me feeling cherished yet panting for more. His shirt is saturated by the time he finishes. He rips it off and throws it in the direction of the clothes bin. My mouth waters at the sprinkling of hair across his powerful pecs and the goody trail disappearing into his waistband. I'd reach out and touch, but the washcloths wrapped around my hands are like cuffs, pinning me in place. Greg's jeans and boxers follow, and then he's sliding into the tub with me.

Greg's gaze catches on the ugly bruise on my knee, and his eyes darken. I drop it under the water, uncomfortable with the scrutiny.

He traces one nipple with his finger and then the other. Goosebumps prickle across my skin, and my breath hitches. "I think you're incredible for learning new skills and wanting to be stronger, but I'm still furious your trainer didn't take better care of you. It'd be different if you were experienced."

My heart flips at the concern in Greg's voice. I should tell him the truth, but as much as I appreciate his concern, I sense a dash of chauvinism, and it pisses me off. "If Dylan turned up to the office bruised from kickboxing or karate, would you be all up in his face telling him he shouldn't have done it?"

Greg laughs, splashing water out of the tub. "That would never happen. Dylan's too much of a wimp to go anywhere near hand-to-hand combat. Luckily, he's got a gun to defend himself. And even then, I worry he'll shoot himself in the foot."

I flick water in his direction. "That's cruel."

Greg smirks. "It's the truth."

He cups one breast and massages. My annoyance melts into the water. "You never cease to amaze me, Em. After your magical powers with Silas and our rock climbing date, I've learnt to expect the unexpected when it comes to you."

I arch into his palm, ignoring my aching muscles. Ignoring the warning bells, to tell him the truth about kickboxing. About internal affairs. That I've fallen in love with him. "It's my fault. I should have stopped."

"Why did you keep going when you were hurting yourself?"

"I don't know. I guess I was trying to prove I was as good

as the other guys." It's not the real reason I'm a bruised mess, but it's one reason I became a black belt. So, it's not a complete lie.

Greg tweaks my nipple and relaxes into the bubbles. While his eyes are warm and possessive, there's a lingering question in the slight uplift of his eyebrow. Time to deflect before he asks more questions.

I drop my arms, and Greg rushes to hold my hands out of the water. "What are you doing?"

"They're getting tired."

"Say no more." Greg stands, water sloshing off his body, and steps out of the bath. Droplets trickle down his pecs, biceps and muscular thighs. The thick patch of dark hair at his groin glistens with moisture, leaving my mouth devoid of it. His balls are heavy sacs guarding the perfectly formed appendage between his legs. It's semihard and growing with every second I gawk.

He strokes himself, hastening the swelling, and groans. "You're killing me, Em." Greg slips one arm under my waist and the other behind my knees and lifts me like I weigh nothing. Then he sets me on my feet and rubs a fluffy towel gently over my body. As with the soap, his attention is more nurturing than sexual despite his obvious erection. He unwinds the washcloths from my hands, kissing each finger.

"Time for bed."

$\approx$

The mattress is soft and welcoming. I feel weightless as I lay sprawled on it, Greg standing naked at my feet. I might come from his heated gaze alone.

"Spread your legs wider, Red." Greg's voice is husky, his eyes black holes beckoning me to fall into them.

I've always resented men taking control in the bedroom, but with Greg, I don't mind. I revel in the seductive power of my body. He might be calling the shots, but he's as mesmerised as I am.

Greg strokes himself a few times. "I'd tell you to put your arms above your head, but I know they're tired. So, I want you to keep them by your sides. Can you do that?"

I nod, heat pulsing through my core at the command.

"You don't move those arms unless I say so, or there'll be no orgasms. Understand?"

He wouldn't dare? Would he? "Yes, Detective."

His eyes harden. "That's yes, *sir*, to you."

My breath catches in my throat. "Yes, sir."

He rewards me with a lascivious grin, kneels and clasps my foot. He strokes the arch with his thumb. "Such tiny feet." Then sucks my big toe into his mouth. Holy shit. His breath is hot and wet as he twirls his tongue around the digit. I never understood why anyone would think feet are erotic, but with each pull of his mouth, my pussy quivers.

He licks along the other toes, slips his tongue between them and drops kisses across the top of my foot. "Delicious."

I close my eyes and moan.

"Keep looking at me."

My eyelids snap open at the command.

He takes my other foot in his hand. "I want you to see every wicked thing I do to you."

"Yes, sir."

"Good, girl."

My insides clench. With anyone else, I'd be kicking their face and getting the hell out of here. I won't ever be disrespected again. But this is Greg. He's not belittling me. It's all part of the game of pleasure. One that I've never allowed myself to play. One I could get addicted to.

Greg lavishes the other foot with his tongue, then licks the sides of each calf. He halts at my knees and presses soft kisses around the bruises.

He continues up my body, skipping my desperate pussy

and kissing my hip bones and tummy, licking at my belly button. The stubble on his jaw scratches the delicate skin, heightening the pleasure. I itch to drag his head between my legs, but I dare not move my arms. Disobey. From the gleam in his eyes, I have no doubt Greg would carry through on his threat of orgasm denial if I did.

Each breast is treated to the warm, wet haven of Greg's mouth. He sucks on the nipples, nipping them into tight buds.

"Jesus, Em, you have the sweetest body." His eyes are a whirlpool of lust and possessiveness, but I mustn't confuse his attentiveness for love.

"Come closer," I beg.

"Ah, ah." He nips the side of my breast. "You're not calling the shots here."

I lick my lips. "I know ... *sir*." I smile at how his eyes dilate when I say 'sir'. "But I need to taste you. Please."

His Adam's apple bobs. "Since you asked so nicely ..." He crawls onto his knees and straddles my face. His cock is swollen and glistening. Leaning on the iron bed head, he angles it towards my mouth. "Ready?"

"Yes, please."

I open up, and he feeds his cock in. Without the use of my hands, I'm at his mercy, but he stops when I start to gag and pulls back. I curl my tongue around his tip, revelling in the salty, musky taste, and hum.

He fists my hair and grunts. "Fuck."

He pushes in again, and I hollow my cheeks and suck. His eyes close and his jaw tightens. I might be in the submissive position, but I wield all the power. His cock swells and his hips thrust. I know it won't be long before he comes, so I increase the suction and am punished when Greg pulls out.

"No!"

"Yes." He shuffles down my body and tweaks my nipple. "I want to come inside your pussy."

"You could do both?"

"Nope. Don't think I haven't felt you wincing. We're keeping this short ..." He slides his tongue across my lips. "But very sweet."

I sigh. He's right. Even though most of his weight is off me, my body aches. The bruising above my knee pulses like it has its own life support system. And my hands ... they're bearable thanks to Greg binding them with wet cloths.

Greg licks back down my tummy and over my hip bones until he reaches the apex of my thighs. He grabs my butt, inhales and groans. The warmth of his breath has me bucking my hips, seeking his mouth. He glides his tongue between the folds, parting them. Circles the bundle of nerves in the centre, then rims my opening. The vision of his head between my legs is as erotic as his wet, warm tongue on my heated nether regions. He returns to my clit, alternating between sucking and flicking. I surrender to the fire building in my core, hotter and hotter, faster and faster, stronger and stronger, until a ripple of pleasure explodes outwards and inwards.

Greg laps my pussy, easing me down with gentle strokes. He looks up at me, his chin shiny from my juices. "Perfect."

My thighs clench, remnants of my orgasm sending a delicious flutter of pleasure through my body. Greg opens the bedside drawer, pulls out a condom and rolls it on. He enters me in one smooth motion, keeping his weight on his elbows. We stay like that for a few moments, my walls adjusting to his size. He presses soft kisses to my eyelids, forehead, nose. Then sucks my bottom lip into his mouth. His eyes are dark pools of lust sprinkled with a softness that makes my heart ache for something I can't have. Something I didn't know I wanted. He releases my lip and begins to pump. His movements are slow and steady, a gentle rocking motion that stimulates my clit and my G-spot.

"You feel so good, Em." He nuzzles my cheek. "I never want to leave."

My heart thumps. I know he means he never wants to leave my body, but the hopeful organ in my chest interprets it as something different. But what's the point? The only happy ending Greg and I can have is in the here and now. I rock my hips, urging him to speed up, to stop making love, because that's what he's doing. He ignores me, maintaining a steady rhythm. Tears fill my eyes. A girl could get used to this.

My tongue darts out to lick the beads of sweat from Greg's chest. He pumps faster, his grunts becoming louder. The friction on my sensitive walls is too much. They contract around Greg's cock with the ferocity of an explosion, my entire body convulsing. Greg yells out my name and shudders as he finds his release.

He immediately lifts himself off me, his face contorted like he's been through the worst torture. He winks and disappears into the bathroom. I stare at the stucco ceiling and focus on returning my breathing back to normal. My heart back into my chest.

When Greg returns, he pulls one of his T-shirts over me, and we spoon under the covers. "You okay, Em. I didn't hurt you?"

"Yeah. I'm good. More than good."

He kisses my head and pulls me in tighter against him, his softening cock nestling between my butt cheeks. "Sleep well."

My brain is wired. That was intense. I don't want to read anything into it, but it's hard not to when someone makes you feel like you're the centre of their world. And that's exactly what Greg just did. There are so many things I want to say, but his soft snores fill the room a few minutes later.

I lie awake for much longer. I'm head over heels for this man, which means I'm screwed. Because even if he was prepared to change his ways for me, there's no escaping the fact I'm lying to him.

Chapter Twenty-Eight

Greg

The waterside mansion, my home for the first fourteen years of my life, has been transformed into a fairy garden with statue replicas from across the ages, including Michelangelo's David, ice sculptures and enough solar lights to power the east coast for a year. There's even a rainbow display with a pot of gold under the Japanese maple tree I used to climb as a kid. It's hard to say if the scene is romantic or creepy as fuck, but it sums up my stepmother's taste. Dramatic and expensive.

I squeeze Em's hand, grateful for her presence. I warned her the party would be about as much fun as a root canal, but she wasn't deterred. Sucking in a deep breath, I let the salty air soothe the beast inside. I'd sooner trawl through month-old garbage looking for evidence than smile and pretend I give a shit about my father. But here I am, dressed in a monkey suit, smiling at his wife, Elise, like she's the most loving woman in the world and not a marriage-breaking gold-digger with daddy issues. Everything about her grates on me, from the obvious fillers in her lips and cheeks to the ridiculous five-inch heels on her feet.

As her cloying perfume threatens to overpower me, I'm

struck with the realisation that she embodies the type of woman I've typically fucked until Em came into my life. My knees buckle. Jesus. Is that what I've become—my old man?

"I'm so glad you could make it, Greg." Elise air kisses my cheeks, the crinkling of her nose telling me she's as happy to see me as I am to see her.

"I wouldn't miss it for anything," I lie. "It's not every day my old man turns sixty-five."

She purses her lips. "I must say, your father and I were surprised when you said you were coming." She glances at Em. "With a plus one."

In other words, they hoped I wouldn't turn up at all. By choosing the police force instead of politics, I'm an embarrassment my father would rather forget. I wouldn't be here at all, except for Jake nagging and saying family matters, and that I'll regret it later when the old man carks it. I'm not sure he's right, but here I am.

Elise opens her arms to Em. "Who is this darling creature?"

Em sticks her hand out, avoiding the fake kisses. "Emily Saunders, ma'am. I've heard a lot about you."

Elise stares at Em's fingers, encased in black lace gloves to hide the faded bruises, as if flames might burst from them at any moment. She touches Em's hand briefly in the limpest of handshakes and takes a step back. "Greg's told us nothing about you."

I tense. Why does she need to make a dig at someone she's only just met? But Em simply shrugs. "You know Greg."

Elise's hawk-like gaze rakes over Em, taking in her youthful glow, glossy natural curls, and delectable cleavage that I plan on worshipping later tonight. Em's dressed for comfort in a black velvet dress that cinches at the waist and falls midthigh, lace tights and long suede boots, out-classing Elise in every way.

"Yes." Elise's gaze returns to me, her eyes narrowing.

"That's why it was a surprise when Greg said he was bringing a ... *friend*."

The sooner I get Em away from this viper and amongst more pleasant company, the better, but that's no easy feat when the guest list reflects the hosts—shallow, pretentious and mercenary. It leaves my brother and the catering staff. Troy's probably the only politician here who hasn't completely lost his soul to the dark side. Yet.

"We'd better keep circulating." I pluck two glasses of champagne from a passing server and steer Em through the crowd, waving at the few people I recognise.

As soon as we're out of earshot, I say, "Sorry about that."

"It's fine. You did warn me." Em's head swivels from side to side, taking in the opulence, the women who must be freezing in their tiny gowns and stilettos. Totally inappropriate clothing for a garden party in June, but it's all the fashion, and that's all that matters. "Your father's very wealthy."

"Yep. Politicians make good money." I shake my head at the seven-piece orchestral band set up by the pool, the soft strains of Mozart drifting across the yard. The old man doesn't even like classical music.

"Dad inherited the house from my pop. Pop was an honest man. Saw through my father's greed and left me and Troy sizeable trust funds."

"Wow. Is that how you bought your home?" Em's face blooms and she squeezes my hand. "I'm sorry. That was rude."

"No, it's not. It's a fair question. And yes, I used some of it to buy my house. Our trust funds are complex beasts. You'd have to dig deep to discover I'm the recipient. I'd challenge those arseholes in internal affairs to unravel the details, all designed to avoid tax, of course."

Em's face whitens like she's seen a ghost.

"Don't worry." I tuck her under my arm. "It's legal, even if it is morally dubious. And it lets me help the homeless, which pisses my old man off. It's a win-win."

She gives me a wobbly smile. "I had no doubt it would be above board."

We stroll deeper into the backyard, down a flight of steps and along a narrow wooded path, until the noise is behind us and the harbour beckons in front. This small alcove remains unsullied by the ostentatious trappings of wealth on the rest of the estate. It's the one spot that still feels like the home I grew up in before it all went south.

Em drops my hand and leans against the wooden fence. "What's the point of coming to the party if we're going to hide out?"

Trust Em not to mince words. "We're not hiding."

"Mmm …"

I itch to slide my fingers through her curls. Kiss the knowing look off her face. Bend her over the palings and lose myself inside her. With any other woman, I wouldn't hesitate. Sex is a powerful anaesthetic for coping with fucked up families. I should know. But there's no way I'd risk Em being seen in a compromising position. Or being embarrassed.

Em adjusts her jacket, but not before I drink in more of her lush, creamy cleavage. My honourable intentions slip away on the breeze, and I draw her into my chest. One kiss. Where's the harm in that?

I nuzzle the shell of her ear. "You cold?"

"A bit." She wraps her arms around my waist and rubs against me. The little vixen knows exactly what she's doing as my erection prods her stomach.

"Em," I warn.

She peers up at me, her blue eyes wide and innocent. "Yes, Detective."

Where are my handcuffs when I need them? "We can't do this here."

"Cuddle?"

I slap her arse. "You know what I mean."

She giggles. "Sorry." She rubs against me again. "Not sorry."

The scuff of shoes on the sandstone path tells me we're about to have company.

I allow myself a few more seconds to enjoy the feel of Em's softness against my groin. "I'm glad you came tonight."

"Me too. You shouldn't have to suffer alone." She rests her head against my chest. "But you can't count this as a date."

"I won't." I run my fingers through her hair. The curls are unpredictable, just like Em. She feels good in my arms. Too good.

The bushes rustle, and Felicity stumbles from the path, long mahogany hair swinging wildly across her shoulders, flowy silver dress swishing at her hips. "Oh. I'm sorry. I didn't think anyone would be here."

Em pushes away from me, but I clamp my arm around her waist.

"We needed to escape the noise." I kiss the of top of Em's head. "Em, this is my sister-in-law, Felicity. Felicity, this is Emily."

Em gives her a little wave. "Nice to meet you."

Felicity smiles, but it's wobbly. And so are her hands.

I step towards her. "Are you okay?"

"Yeah. Just had one drink too many."

I guide her to a wooden bench seat. It's the only furniture in this cosy haven. She leans heavily on me and collapses onto the seat. Up close, Felicity's distress is more evident. Dilated pupils swallow her hazel irises. I've seen enough alcoholics and druggies to recognise the difference between drunk and high. She's popped a pill of some sort. I'd bet my badge on it.

Em perches next to Felicity. "Champagne goes straight to my head too."

"You're pretty." Felicity giggles and leans her head on

Em's shoulder. Yep, she's definitely flying in the clouds. "Whatever you do, never have kids."

What the fuck? Em and I share a look over Felicity's head.

I haven't spent much time with my brother and his family. Our lives have taken very different paths, but Felicity's always struck me as a dedicated mother.

I crouch in front of her. "Why's that, Felicity?"

She slides her hand down her modest chest and flat stomach. "Because men don't want stretch marks and saggy boobs."

Does she know my brother cheated? "I'm sure Troy doesn't care about that. He loves you." Which is why sticking his dick somewhere else was a colossal fuck-up.

She whisks her head off Em's shoulder. "Then why's he working all the time? And never wants sex?"

Christ. I stab my fingers through my hair. I do not want to be discussing sex with my sister-in-law. Em's eyes widen. She's certainly seeing my family at their worst tonight.

"Politicians have a lot of demands on them." I offer up the lame excuse.

Felicity's head lolls to the side, her mouth drops open, and her eyes flutter shut. I doubt she heard what I said. She's out cold. Em stands, and we lift Felicity's feet so she's lying across the bench.

"Wow." Em shakes her head and looks up at me. "Is your brother cheating on her?"

The tone of Em's voice has my hackles rising. "What makes you say that?"

Em has that pissed-off look I know too well. "Because she's a beautiful woman, despite what she said about herself."

"It's not my business to tell."

"In other words, he's cheating and bro code means you keep his secret."

I clasp Em's upper arms and pull her towards me. "Don't

you go getting all judgy. It means whatever Troy told me in confidence remains between him and me."

Em leans into me. "I'm sorry. You're right."

And yet she judges. I feel it in the stiffness of her body as I hug her close.

A twig snaps and the man we've been talking about strides towards us. He freezes, then spies Felicity on the bench and rushes to her side.

"She's okay, Troy," I say. "She just passed out."

"Damn." He rubs his hands up and down his face. "At least she didn't do it in front of everybody."

Jesus. He's unbelievable. "Is that all you care about? What people think?"

"Of course not. I mean. Yes, I care. But I'm more worried about Felicity drinking too much." He glances at Em.

She pulls away from my embrace. "I could go powder my nose or whatever and give you some privacy."

I grab her hand. "No."

"He's right," says Troy. "You don't want to mingle alone amongst that lot. They'll eat you alive."

Em's hands swing to her hips. "I can take care of myself."

"Down, Red." My chest puffs out at how she doesn't take any shit. She handled Elise like a pro. Maybe she's the one who'd eat Dad's sycophants alive.

"Troy, is it possible Felicity had more than alcohol tonight?"

"Absolutely not." He shakes his head. "She doesn't do drugs. Neither of us would ever do anything illegal."

"I'm not accusing her of breaking the law. Is she on any medication?"

"No." Troy snaps out. "Wait. Yes." He smooths stray hairs from Felicity's face, the adoration for his wife painted all over his face. It makes me want to shake him for being stupid enough to wet his dick elsewhere. "The doctor prescribed her

antidepressants a couple of months ago. About the time ..."
He trails off, shuffling his feet.

Ah. The time he went to the conference and met Sophie Dubois. Did Felicity sense Troy's interest had strayed? Then sought solace from pills and the bottle? She wouldn't be the first person to do that.

"Felicity looks drugged out, Troy. Not just drunk. I'd say alcohol reacts with the meds she's taking."

"Shit."

"Exactly."

"Guys." Em stretches her hand out, palm up. "It's starting to rain."

I smile as a drop splashes on my nose. "Good."

Troy glares at me. "How's that possibly good?"

"It means the party will move inside. We can carry Felicity to your car without anyone seeing us."

"And what do I tell Dad?"

"You don't tell him anything. You drive Felicity home, and I'll tell him you got a call from the babysitter about one of the kids being sick."

Troy's gaze drifts towards the path up to the house, then back to me. He knows his options are limited. His shoulders slump and he nods.

My brother spends too much time behind a desk and eating out and no time in a gym, so I score the task of carrying Felicity up the stairs and across the backyard. Not that it's difficult. She's model thin. I doubt she weighs more than fifty kilos. As predicted, the crowd has dispersed, abandoning the melting ice sculptures and the myriad of lights.

Troy drives off. Em and I huddle under the umbrella she retrieved from my car and saunter to the front door of the house. My father's going to be pissed to see me and not Troy. I'd be lying if I didn't admit I'm going to enjoy his discomfort.

The front door swings open and we come face-to-face with the thunderous expression of my father. The light from the chandelier above his head adds a sinister gleam to his eyes.

"Happy birthday, Dad."

"What the hell are you doing out there?" His voice booms, similar to mine but more cultured.

"Enjoying the rain?"

His jaw ticks. He doesn't look like he's had anywhere near enough alcohol to deal with the black sheep of the family. But good manners trump annoyance and he stands aside and waves us in.

I drop the umbrella into a stand and shrug off my coat. It took the brunt of the rain as I shielded Em.

My father's shrewd gaze rakes over her. She doesn't wait for me to introduce them. "Hi, Mr Anderson. I'm Emily." She sticks her hand out, and he immediately shakes it.

"Hello, Emily." He flexes his hand. "That's quite a grip on you."

"Sorry." Em tilts her head to the right and peers up at him through her lashes. It's a tell I'm starting to recognise. One that calls bullshit on whatever words are coming out of her mouth. Although, I have an urge to throw her over my knee for hurting herself. My father wouldn't notice, but the tightness around her eyes tells me it cost her to shake his hand that hard. She's still not fully recovered from the kickboxing incident.

The clink of glasses and clanging of plates filter into the foyer. The black-and-white theme is simplistic and chic. Unfortunately, it's Elise's inspiration, proving she's not a complete airhead.

"So, how come you're answering the door? I'd have thought you'd have minions taking care of that tonight."

My father ignores the insolent tone in my voice. "I was looking for your brother. He seems to have disappeared."

I keep my expression blank. "We saw him and Felicity

leaving. Troy asked me to apologise. He got a call from the babysitter. One of the kids was sick."

"Mmm ..." Dad's jaw tightens. He hates surprises. No doubt he'll give Troy a reaming tomorrow about good manners and protocol.

"It must have been serious for them to leave the party without telling you," says Em.

My father's razor-sharp gaze returns to Emily. She stares right back at him. I want to high five her. There's no other woman I know, except perhaps Monica, who would have the balls to stand up to him with such confidence. She impresses me, yet again, with her steel.

Dad's expression softens, but he continues to eyeball her. "Are you a police officer as well, Emily?"

"God, no." Em laughs. "I'm an intelligence analyst."

"I see." He glances over his shoulder. Nothing of interest for him here. Em would have to be a lawyer, doctor or CEO for my father to display any genuine enthusiasm.

Dad pats me awkwardly on the upper arm. "Thanks for coming. Feel free to show Emily through the house. Elise has outdone herself with the recent renovations. We'll catch up later." He pivots and strides down the hallway.

Em slips her hand into mine. "Wow. He looks so much like you."

"Jesus, Em. Don't say that. He's a prick."

She squeezes my hand. "He has the same stubborn set to his jaw, same chocolate eyes and same broad shoulders."

I tug her against me. "What do you mean, stubborn?"

"You know exactly what I mean." Her eyes sparkle with mischief, and I've a good mind to kiss her silly. She places a palm on my chest as if she knows what I'm thinking. "Your dad doesn't seem as bad as you described."

"He's worse." I snort. "Don't be fooled by the veneer of civility. My father would tear out your jugular and spit on your corpse if he thought it could win him votes."

Em's face drops. "I'm sure he's not that evil."

"He's allowed developers to destroy sacred bush and caused dozens of vulnerable people to be homeless after turning caravan parks into prestige housing estates."

Em draws circles on my chest with her finger. "He must have done some good things; otherwise, he wouldn't have been elected."

"I guess." I scan the foyer, checking out the latest wall art —black-and-white photographs of Sydney from last century. They're new. No doubt purchased to match the updated decor.

I shouldn't have come. Every time I see this house, and that gold-digging wife of Dad's, I'm reminded of the childhood stolen from me. My father's an expert at justifying his decisions and be damned the consequences for others. Like having an affair with Elise and choosing to leave Mum. Choosing to leave me and Troy. Throwing money at us as if that made up for discarding his family and starting a new one. My mother never recovered from his lies, which is why I always let women know the score. I'll never lie to them like Dad lied to Mum.

"Greg, I'm sorry this is so painful." Em runs her hands up and down my back, soothing me.

I fold my arms around her waist and bury my head in her hair. She smells fresh, like rain. Grounding. Energising. I could hold her all night. For the rest of my life.

Fuck. My lungs stall midbreath. I'm falling in love with her.

Chapter Twenty-Nine

Greg

Sophie Dubois contacted Ian. That's why I'm hiding behind a tree in a cold-as-fuck sports ground, waiting for her to show. She'd better make an appearance, or I'll arrest Ian for being a public nuisance and wasting my time.

Traces of Em's perfume cling to my jacket. It's a distraction I can't afford. My mind's been all over the place since my father's birthday party on Saturday. I'm obsessed with her smile, her tendency to trip over her own feet when she's wearing high heels, the way her nipples pucker when I blow on them. I adjust my trousers. Christ. I need to get a grip. I've never allowed a woman to interfere with my concentration on the job. Another first with Em.

A car pulls into the nearby car park, and a blonde steps out, sparkling stilettos sinking into the grass. Bingo. Ian stumbles towards her, looking like he's still drunk from a heavy night. He missed his calling as an actor. A man exits the driver's side, towering over the woman. He must be the muscle and possibly one of the men who bashed Jimmy.

I nod to two constables positioned next to a dumpster and stroll out from behind the tree, my badge in front of me. "Sophie Dubois, may I have a few words?"

The man pivots and runs straight into the two constables. His hands go up in surrender.

The woman glares at Ian. *"Tu mouchard,"* she says in a slinky French accent.

I'm guessing she's just called him a rat or something similar. I keep my right hand near my gun, but Sophie Dubois doesn't strike me as the violent type. She's got goons for that.

Her eyes widen as she takes me in. "Sergeant Anderson."

Shit. Troy takes after Mum and, unfortunately, as Em pointed out, I'm the spitting image of Dad. If Sophie Dubois recognises me, then it's looking increasingly likely that Troy was targeted because of my position in the drug squad. "You know me?"

She makes a zipping motion across her lips and smirks.

A grey gloom pervades the interview room, but it's not enough to dampen the gaudiness of Sophie Dubois sitting at the small table in a blood-red knee-length dress. She crosses her legs, causing the fabric to slide up one thigh. "Ooh." She fans her face, that stupid smirk still plastered to her lips. "Two hot detectives *pour une seule femme?*"

I lean against the wall while Jake ignores her comment and sits across from her. He introduces himself and goes through the preliminaries, reminding her of her right to remain silent, then slaps the scripts we found when we arrested her on the table.

Sophie squares her shoulders. "I have nothing to say."

"Well, I do." Jake picks up a script. "These prescriptions for Valium and oxycodone look legitimate, but I have no doubt our team will determine they're fake. It'll be easier if you come clean now rather than wasting our time."

"Easier *pour toi.*"

"We have several people ready to testify that you've been

giving them fifty dollars per prescription to get these filled."

"Homeless drunks and addicts?" She shakes her head. "No one will believe them."

"Then how did the scripts end up in your handbag?"

"*Je ne sais pas*." She shrugs. Of course, she doesn't know. "If you do your job properly, I'm confident you won't find my fingerprints or DNA on them."

I clench my fists by my side. Lying bitch. And I'd bet my badge the accent is fake. But what did we expect? She's hardly going to roll over. I'm surprised she's saying anything at all without her lawyer present.

I take two steps and bang my hands on the desk. "And what about Troy Anderson? We know you're blackmailing him."

Jake nudges my thigh in warning. I'm supposed to zip my mouth and let him ask the questions, but it's bloody hard knowing what this woman has done. For the hundredth time, I wonder how Troy fell for her tricks.

She sneers and runs her fingers down her throat and rests her hand between her breasts. "I have no idea what you're talking about. I had a consensual sexual liaison with Troy Anderson. *C'est tout*. He should have kept his pants on if he's worried about his wife finding out."

It's a veiled threat, and for the first time in my life, I feel the urge to wrap my fingers around a woman's throat.

Jake places his hand on my forearm. I back off and return to leaning against the wall, doing my best to appear unaffected even though I'm fuming inside.

Jake throws a piece of paper on the desk. This will be interesting. "How about we start again, Ms Dubois? Or should I say, Ms *Leadbetter?*"

Sophie's smile vanishes, and she crosses her arms. "I've humoured you boys enough." Her Aussie drawl slips through, the French accent forgotten now she's been exposed. "I'm not saying anything more without my lawyer present."

Chapter Thirty

Emily

The station buzzes with excitement on Monday afternoon. A development in Jimmy's case has the drug squad detectives talking in whispers and looking like Christmas and Armageddon have collided. It's a dichotomy I can't figure out. I itch to ask Greg what's happened, but he and Inspector Matthews are locked in the interview room with a suspect.

Detective Laura Nielsen stops at my cubicle, her intimidating frame casting a shadow over my desk. "Hi there, Emily."

I choke on the muesli bar in my mouth. Laura rarely talks to me outside the morning briefings. "Hi," I say, wiping crumbs from my face.

She smiles, and the hairs across my nape all stand on end. "Any idea who Inspector Matthews and Sergeant Anderson are interviewing?"

"No. Sorry."

"Mmm ..." She glances down the corridor. "It's all very hush, hush. Must be big."

"I guess so."

Those grey eyes rake over me. If we weren't in a police

station, I'd worry she was going to put me in a headlock, which makes no sense. My heart doubles its beats. I hold her gaze until she looks away.

"Okay. We'll have to wait until they finish." She hesitates like she wants to say more, then strides off.

Well, that was weird.

Sergeant Seymour scurries down the corridor, looking like a man on a mission. I'd hoped the photo I took of his call log might be incriminating, but Dixon from internal affairs hasn't said anything about it or the list from Laura's desk. After his initial flurry of phone calls, Dixon's only rung twice in the last two weeks. Although his tone has been borderline aggressive, grilling me about Greg's movements and any 'pillow talk' that might be relevant. Basically reminding me I'm a horrible person who's spying on my boyfriend. Not that I'm giving him anything useful, because as I expected, there's nothing to say. Greg's not a dirty cop.

I finish the report I'm working on as the clock flips over to four pm and stretch my neck. It's been a long day, not helped by a lack of sleep. Thoughts of Greg's father's party on Saturday kept me awake for most of the night. I'm so glad he invited me. It gave me an insight into his fear of commitment. While I've had my issues with Mum and Dad, they gave me love and a stable home. Greg wasn't as lucky. I'd have trust issues, too, if I had a father like his.

There's still no sign of Greg or Inspector Matthews, and the rest of the cops are closeted in the main conference room. As much as I want to hang around and find out what's happening, I'm exhausted and had enough for the day. I head to the car park, my mind on a certain sexy detective sergeant. And that's how I crash into Seymour.

"Fuck." He shoves a plastic bag into his pocket, then grabs my wrists, squeezing them hard. There's a flash of grey to my right and the sound of footsteps. "What are you doing out here? I thought everyone was in a meeting." His eyes are wild, almost black, as his gaze flits between me and the door.

"I'm going to my car. Let me go."

His lips curl into his signature creepy grin. "Not so fast." His fingers tighten around my wrists.

I stand my ground. Refuse to wince, even though it hurts like a motherfucker. He won't intimidate me. "I don't know what your problem is, but we're in a police station. Back off, Sergeant Seymour."

He shoves me against the wall and lowers his face to mine. His eyes are more than black; they're vacant. Shit. He's high. "Here's the thing, Emily. There are no cameras in this area. No proof anything untoward is going on. No Sergeant Anderson to run to your rescue."

My expression must give me away because he sniggers. "You think I haven't noticed you preening around him like a cat in heat? All the women pant after him. You're just one of many, little girl."

My jaw clenches. Is that what everyone else thinks too? I glance at a small plastic bag near his feet. It's similar to the one he slipped into his pocket. Did he drop it? He tracks the movement and squats to pick it up. With my wrists released, I take the precious few seconds to slide my hand into my bag and hit what I hope is the number for the station on my phone. Then I adjust my stance. There's no way this overweight desk jockey is going to beat me. Not when I'm wearing culottes and sturdy, one-inch boots.

He retrieves the bag and slips it into his other trouser pocket. The light is dim, but I'm almost certain white powder is inside it.

"Are you buying drugs? Is that why you're skulking around out here?"

"You should mind your own business, Ms Saunders. I imagine Sergeant Jacobs would not be impressed if she found out you're fraternising with a certain detective."

Heat rushes to my face. "Are you threatening me?"

He shakes his head. "I'm just telling you like it is."

Seymour's hand shoots out to grab my neck, but I'm ready for him. I fend him off with my left forearm, then kick my right leg out and sweep him off his feet. He crashes to the concrete.

"You, bitch," he howls.

I jab my finger at him. "Touch me again or say anything to Sergeant Jacobs, and I *will* report you." There's no way I'm letting this slime bag jeopardise my career prospects.

I run to my car, my insides shaking, and my ears pricked for any sound that suggests Seymour is chasing after me. When I climb inside, I see he's still slumped against the wall. I shut the door and engage the locks. A tiny voice nags at me. My phone! I pull it out of my handbag.

"Ms Saunders? Emily?"

I put the mobile to my ear. "Senior Sergeant Dixon?" In normal circumstances, I'd be mortified that I accidentally called him of all people, but after what just happened, I don't care.

"Yes, it's me. Are you okay?"

"I am now. Did you hear that? It was Sergeant Seymour."

"It was muffled, but I got the gist of it. You showed incredible initiative in ringing me."

"Thanks, sir." He doesn't need to know I was trying to call the station, not him.

"Don't worry about Seymour. He's our problem now. Can you keep this incident to yourself?"

"Sure." What's another secret?

"I'll be in touch tomorrow."

He hangs up, and I manoeuvre the car out of the parking area. My heart thumps like a battering ram against my rib cage. While Seymour's a sleaze, I thought he was all talk. I never expected him to get physical. Then again, drugs will make people do extreme things.

I rub my wrists. How will I explain the bruises to Greg? With more half-truths.

I bang my palms on the steering wheel. The impact reverberates up my forearms. Ouch. That wasn't smart. But dammit, I'm so tired of all the lies. I can't keep up this subterfuge much longer. If Greg ever finds out about internal affairs … A shiver runs up my spine. That's not an option. Greg would see it as a betrayal. He'd never forgive me.

Chapter Thirty-One

Greg

I knock on Em's door. I hadn't planned on seeing her tonight, but I need her. I'm still reeling from our interview with Terence Leadbetter's sister. According to our intel, Sophie runs her own side business in black-market prescription drugs. Jake's theory is that her liaison with Troy was innocent, at least as innocent as deliberately seducing a married man can be, until she realised who his brother was. Me. Then she saw an opportunity to fuck with a member of the NSW Drug Squad. I can only assume she hoped to compromise me and get me to do her bidding. In other words, break the law.

We have enough evidence to bury Sophie on the drug charges. But the photos of her with my brother are another story. She could still destroy his reputation. His career. His marriage. And there's not a damn thing I can do about it.

As for the man wearing Leadbetter's ring, he must be the newly appointed head of the syndicate while Leadbetter's in jail. His identity and why he dirtied his hands bashing Jimmy remain a mystery.

Em opens the door and her arms. I walk into them and

hoist her up. She curls her hands around my neck, her ankles around my waist.

I need to forget about drug trafficking, vulnerable people being exploited and liars, and just focus on my woman. "I can't be gentle, Em."

She skims her tongue up my neck. "I don't need gentle, Greg."

A flannelette nightie is all that separates us. It's the least sexy thing I've ever seen. No other woman I've known would be caught dead in the cheap material. But that's Em. There's no pretence with her. No false nails or fake smiles. Or uncomfortable sleepwear.

I cup her arse. No underpants. My dick throbs as I grip her perfect globes and work my belt. The button proves difficult with one hand. I tug, and it goes flying. The sound of my zipper opening has us both groaning.

"Hurry up." Em digs her heels into my lower back.

I grip my erection. Em manoeuvres her hips, and I slide home. My fingers dig into her arse, holding her in place. It's a perfect fit. Our mouths collide, a tangle of tongues, lips, and teeth. A coppery taste floods my mouth. I wrench away. "Did you just bite me?"

She licks her lips and flexes her core, squeezing my dick. "Too much talking, Detective."

"Little tease. You'll pay for that." I thrust into her.

She bounces, sending a bolt of exquisite pain and pleasure through my dick. "Yes. Harder."

I brace my thighs and hammer into her. Sweat trickles under my arms and down my chest. Em's pupils dilate until there's only a hint of blue rimming the edges. I could watch her like this all day, on the edge of coming, lost to everything but me plunging into her. My balls tighten. I knew I wouldn't last long. She's too hot. Too tight. And I'm too jacked up. I slip my hand between us and flick her clit. She goes off, her walls shuddering around me, and I come with a roar.

My breathing is ragged, raspy in my ears. Em's breaths are no quieter. I continue to pulse inside her while her walls contract around me. I nuzzle her hair and breathe in the soft apple fragrance of her shampoo. The musky smell of sex. Of cum.

Shit.

No condom.

What the fuck?

I've never made a mistake like that before. What if she fell pregnant? I wait for my heart rate to skyrocket in panic, but it doesn't. There's no escaping the truth. I love this woman.

Em nestles her face in the crook of my neck. I remain standing, Em's legs still wrapped around me until I feel my cum slipping out. I carry her into the bedroom, our bodies locked together, and lower her onto the mattress. She's got that well-fucked look in her eyes that has my chest puffing out. I did that. Yep, I'm a caveman in a suit. "You okay?"

"Hmm, mm." She wriggles her hips. "Better than okay."

I withdraw, my heart skipping a beat at the loss of connection. "I'm sorry. I forgot to use a condom."

She smiles like it's no big deal. "I'm on the pill. And I got tested for STIs at my last check-up. I'm all good." Her expression wavers. "And you?"

"I never doubted you, Em. And you don't need to worry about me. I've never gone without protection." Until now. "I got myself checked out after Jake and Claire's engagement party."

She quirks an eyebrow. "A bit sure of yourself?"

I tweak her nose. "Just hopeful."

She giggles and pats the mattress, beckoning me to join her.

Her laughter warms the emptiness inside me. She's perfect. And she's mine. I soak a washcloth in warm water in the adjacent bathroom. Em's in the same position when I return. There's something very primal about seeing my cum trickling out of her. Makes me want to tie her up and never let her go. I wipe her pussy and inner thighs. Then kick off my shoes, make quick work of removing my clothes and climb onto the bed beside her.

Em rolls to her side and cuddles into me, an arm across my chest. "You want to talk about it?"

I don't answer straight away. Pillow talk is another first with Em. Another enjoyable activity I didn't realise I'd been missing.

Em doesn't push me. Instead, she runs her fingers through my chest hair.

I trap her hand, enjoying the warmth radiating against my heart. Her eyes snap shut as if in pain.

"Are you okay?"

"Yeah. Just RSI from the keyboard."

I kiss the top of her head. "Can I stay?"

"I'd love that." She nuzzles my neck. "But, what about Silas?"

"Shit. I forgot about him." I have a dog-sitter coming a few days a week to help when I work late. So, I know Silas has been fed and walked. Still, I'm a shitty human being for forgetting him.

I feel Em smile against my shoulder. "How about I pack a small bag and come stay at your place tonight?"

"That'd be great. Thanks."

I look at the cracks in the ceiling, faded curtains on the window, peeling paint on the walls. Em lives in a shit box. Maybe I should ask her to move in with me? We've been dating for less than two months, but we've known each other for a year. So, it's not like we'd be acting too hastily. I'd have to deal with the fallout with Jake, but I've never lived with a woman, so he'd know I was serious about her.

I brush red curls off her cheek. She's so beautiful. "How about you pack a bigger bag and stay with me permanently?"

Em's eyes widen and then her face schools into a mask.

Her body stiffens beside me. What the hell? That wasn't the reaction I expected.

"Oh, Greg."

Fuck. I've been on the giving end of rejection enough times to recognise when I'm receiving it. The hopeful fullness in my heart deflates.

Em's palm presses against my chest. "Don't you think it's a bit soon?"

"Yeah. Sure." Thank Christ I didn't tell her I loved her. I would have looked like a right dick.

"It's not that I don't want to." Em's throat bobs as she swallows. "I think we need more time before taking such a big step."

"Of course. It was just an idea."

I jump out of bed, shaking off Em's attempts to pull me back in. I can't be anywhere near her right now. "I'd better go."

"Okay. Give me a few minutes to pack."

"Don't worry about it, Em. It's getting late. Hardly worth you coming now. I'll see you tomorrow."

Her face drops, but I look away. The last thing I want to see is pity, or worse … lies.

Chapter Thirty-Two

Emily

After a long night of staring at the ceiling, I give up pretending my heart isn't breaking and slip on leggings, an oversized jumper, and boots. It's a little casual for the station and not in keeping with the image I've been trying to project, but they make me feel more like myself. A team player who just wants to do a good job. Not the Emily Saunders smooching up to management or my sexy persona attempting to seduce Greg.

The office is eerily quiet when I arrive, with Greg, Inspector Matthews and Sergeant Seymour conspicuously absent. Sergeant Jacobs conducts the morning briefing as usual, but it's clear no one's paying attention, not even her. I try to bury myself in work but it's impossible to concentrate. I find myself flinching at every sudden noise, no matter how small, hoping it's Greg and then worrying it's Seymour.

By mid morning I can't take the silence anymore. I slip outside and walk briskly down the street to clear my head, stopping every few seconds to check my phone. My calls and texts to Greg remain unanswered. Unread. Fear sticks to the back of my throat. He all but declared he loved me by asking me to move in with him, and what did I do? Pushed him away. Lied. I wanted to say yes, but how could I when internal affairs have me spying on him?

I'm going around in circles, so I ring the one person who can usually settle me down. Ethan.

"Hey, Em, what's up?"

"I just needed a friendly voice."

Ethan responds swiftly, his voice deeper and sharper than before. "Do I need to come to Sydney and beat your boyfriend's arse?"

"No, no. Greg's good." Any other day I'd lecture him about how I don't need him to fight my battles, but I realise it's his way of showing he loves me. I sidestep a dubious mess on the pavement. "It's just … there's some stuff going on at the station that I can't tell Greg, and I wish I could."

"But you work together. Surely, you don't have to keep secrets from him?"

If only it was that simple. "Unfortunately, I do. But it feels wrong."

"That sucks." He grunts. "What's the worst that could happen if you fessed up?"

I'd lose Greg. Then again, I'm already losing him with my lies.

I stop at the pedestrian lights and hug my arms around my waist. Dylan and another uniformed officer are waiting on the other side of the road. It's the same constable I've seen him flirting with at the station. They're eating Maccas and laughing like they haven't got a care in the world. That's when it hits me. My job is safe. It was always safe. Greg would never betray me. I should have told him about internal affairs from the start.

So, why am I still holding back my secrets when Greg trusted me with his?

The lights change, but instead of crossing the road, I pivot and head back to the station. "You're a genius, Ethan."

"You're only figuring that out now?"

"Ha!"

As I hang up, the weight that's been crushing my shoulders lifts. It's time to tell Greg the truth. Way past time. The truth about internal affairs. My kickboxing skills. And most importantly, how much I love him.

❧

Sergeant Jacobs greets me at the station door. "There you are." She pushes her glasses up her nose. She only does that when she's nervous. "Inspector Matthews wants you to join him in the meeting room, please."

"Okay." I follow her inside. "Do you know what it's about?"

"No." She lowers her head and whispers, "But Commander Gordon and someone from the Professional Standard Command are with him." Her voice is barely audible as she utters the last three words.

My stomach freefalls. I drop my handbag at my desk and pick up my notebook and pen, keeping my movements unhurried while my mind jumps all over the place like a jack-in-the-box. Is it about Seymour? *Please don't let internal affairs say anything about me working with them.*

I enter the meeting room and am greeted by the stony expression of Inspector Matthews, Commander Gordon's poker face and the tiger-like eyes of Senior Sergeant Dixon. In the corner, right ankle crossed over his left knee as if he doesn't have a care in the world, is Greg, his face a mask giving no hint of what he's thinking.

Commander Gordon crooks his finger. "Please come in and shut the door, Emily."

I head for the chair next to Senior Sergeant Dixon, my legs turning to jelly-like appendages the moment I sit.

He opens a manila folder and pulls out a thick report. "You're probably wondering what's going on."

"Yes, sir." I don't give any hint that I know him.

"Firstly, I've brought the drug squad up to speed with your assistance in our investigation."

No! *Isn't that supposed to be confidential?* I clench my fingers together and glance at Inspector Matthews. He's pissed; his profile is as rigid as I've ever seen. I would be too if I found out my team had been under surveillance and one of them had been snitching. His eyes are so blue they're almost white. I shudder when he turns them on me. If disappointment was a colour, it would be that exact shade of icy blue. But it's Greg's expression that cuts deepest. His eyes are like a moonless sky. A vacuum. Black—the colour of betrayal.

"Congratulations on a job well done, Ms Saunders." Senior Sergeant Dixon beams at me as if he hasn't just tossed a hand grenade into my relationship with Greg. "Your observations have been instrumental in helping us to identify the officer who's been working with the drug syndicate."

I drag my gaze away from the hollow emptiness of Greg's. "It has?"

"Yes. Your suspicions about Sergeant Seymour were spot on. He had a second phone we didn't know about and was using it to contact Leadbetter's gang. That's the mobile you took a picture of. The numbers were most illuminating."

Commander Gordon's lips twist into what I think is meant to be a smile, but it looks like he has heartburn. "We also retrieved footage from the car park. Unbeknown to Sergeant Seymour, covert cameras were recently installed in the area where he attacked you."

Greg sucks in a sharp breath, his gaze snapping to mine. For a moment, his expression wavers. The love I've gotten to know so well peeks through, only for the shutters to slam down.

"I'm sorry that happened to you, Emily. I must say, your self-defence moves were most impressive." The commander clears his throat and continues. "Earlier video footage showed

Seymour secretly meeting with someone and exchanging money for two small plastic bags. He was arrested late last night."

"Arrogant fool," Inspector Matthews growls. "Not only was he giving away intel, he was buying drugs right under our noses."

"Why was Emily involved in any of this in the first place?" asks Greg, his tone soft but deadly, like a cobra about to strike.

No, no, no. I stare at Senior Sergeant Dixon, telepathically telling him not to answer. Greg can't find out like this. But my silent plea is ignored.

"We were convinced you were the rotten apple, Sergeant Anderson." Dixon taps the A4 manilla folder in front of him. "You were already under surveillance when we noticed you and Ms Saunders were meeting outside work hours. So, we asked her to report back on anything unusual when she was with you."

"In other words, you asked her to spy on me." Greg's voice is gravelly, his expression so full of hatred that I can feel the burn deep in my soul.

Tension in the room skyrockets to code red. Inspector Matthews raises his hand. Greg acknowledges him with a slight nod of his head. Fissure lines spread across my heart as he sends another blast of anger in my direction. I turn away, my throat dry. Why did I keep it from Greg? He'll never forgive me for this.

"Spy is such a harsh word." Dixon straightens his jacket. "We prefer to think of it as observation."

Inspector Matthews crosses his arms and clears his throat. "I'm not happy the Professional Standards Command involved you, Emily, but I understand why they did it." His gaze flits to Greg, then back to me. "I also know you wouldn't have had any choice in the matter."

By some miracle, I don't burst into tears. Inspector

Matthews might be understanding, but he's far from impressed. I doubt he'll want Claire to be friends with me anymore. As for Greg, he's looking straight through me.

"There had better not be any reprisals against Ms Saunders for helping us in our investigations," says Senior Sergeant Dixon, nodding at Inspector Matthews and then settling his gaze on Greg. Don't tell me he's finally reading the room!

A tsunami of rage boils up inside me. Why did internal affairs expose me like this? If I'd known they had no qualms about breaking confidentiality, I wouldn't have hesitated to tell Greg immediately. I blink back tears. I won't show weakness. Plenty of time to cry later.

"There won't be," Inspector Matthews assures him. He turns his icy stare onto Greg. "Knowledge of Emily's involvement will stay within this room."

"Why so glum, Ms Saunders? You should be pleased." Dixon smiles at me, and I want to leap across the room and rip his face off. "Your chances of promotion to the city office or fast-tracking another application for the police academy are very high after your assistance in this case."

In any other circumstances, I'd be doing zoomies around the room, like Silas does when he's excited. Instead, an icy dread seeps into my bones. I don't want spying on the man I love to be the reason I get ahead.

Greg's jaw is set, his eyes firmly above my head like I don't exist. This looks so bad. I can't imagine he'll ever forgive me. Have I lost him forever?

❧

Natalie greets me at the gym, her blonde hair tied back in a ponytail. We don't usually work out on a Thursday night, but I need to release the fear and uncertainty swirling in my gut after internal affairs dropped their bombshell today.

Given what happened last time I attacked the punching bag, I figure fighting a real person should be safer for me. At least I hope so. If I get too carried away, Natalie will knock me on my arse and keep me there until I come to my senses.

"You sure this is what you want?" Natalie's gaze drifts to the faint bruises on my wrists from Seymour's attack. "We could always get a coffee instead. Talk." The question in her eyes is unmistakable but I can't tell her what happened with Seymour. That's police business. And I'm not ready to talk about Greg. The wound is too raw.

"Nope. I want my muscles to burn."

Natalie drops her bag and pulls out her gloves. "Okay. But if you go psycho on me, I will deck you."

I throw my head back and laugh. This is what I need. No judgement. No expectations. No lies. Just a clean, fair fight. "Thanks, Natalie. Perhaps we can go for coffee after?"

It's her turn to laugh. "I can't see us making it to a café. We'll be lucky if we don't need Scott to pour us into our cars afterwards."

"I'll go easy."

Natalie snorts. "No, you won't. The last time you had that gleam in your eye, I sported bruises for weeks."

That pulls me up. "I'm sorry. You don't have to do this. I can work out with a bag."

She grabs my arm. "It's fine, Emily. I'm looking forward to beating your arse up." She squeezes. "But I'm also here if you want to talk."

Tears sting my eyes, and I blink them away. Maybe it's time to let people in.

I gulp some water and go through my stretches. Natalie does the same.

Scott's coaching what looks like a beginner in the far corner of the room. It seems so long ago since I started out, but it's only been three years since I took up kickboxing. I was hooked from the first lesson. It gave me the focus I craved.

And the skills to gain confidence in myself after failing to get into the police academy.

Scott finishes with his student and strolls towards us. "Evening, ladies. I wasn't expecting to see you tonight."

I shrug. "We wanted a workout."

"Mmm ..." He points at the mat. "Don't make me kick your arse, Emily."

I glance at Natalie. "Why is everyone so interested in my backside?"

Scott makes a show of leering at me. "Because it's a mighty fine specimen."

"Ha!"

His expression sobers. "I'll spot you two. Make sure you don't get carried away."

Great. Now, we have a babysitter. Still, once the fighting starts, I'll forget Scott's watching.

Natalie and I warm up with a few easy kicks and punches. The smack of leather on leather settles my stomach, bringing a sense of calm to my fractured mind.

I bounce on the balls of my feet. Centre myself.

Natalie regards me with understanding eyes. Fuck that. She'd pummel me into the mat if she knew I was a liar.

I signal I'm ready to start. Natalie acknowledges. And then it's on. I fight like my life depends on it. Show no mercy. One after another, I thump my fists against Natalie's gloves, kick my feet against them.

Thwack!

Thwack!

Thwack!

Natalie's like a rock. Strong. Unyielding. Absorbing my anger. My disappointment. The fear that I might have lost the best thing to ever happen to me.

Instead of being satisfied, my body buzzes, demanding more. My punches speed up and my vision tunnels to Natalie's gloves and nothing else. The gym could collapse around us and I wouldn't notice.

"Stop!" Scott's commanding voice pierces my red haze. "That's enough, Emily."

I lower my hands. Wipe the sweat off my face with my arm. Scott's expression is grim as he regards me from the edge of the mat. I ignore him. Kill joy.

"What do you say, Natalie? Game to bring out the nunchakus?"

"Nope." Natalie steps away and rips off her gloves. "I'm buggered. Not all of us have the stamina of a whirlwind."

Scott tosses Natalie a bottle of water, then turns to me, his eyes glittering. "I'll spar with you."

"Really?"

"Yes. That fire you're sporting needs to be doused before you burn yourself."

"It's under control," I say, which is bullshit, and from the way Scott shakes his head, he thinks so too.

I remove my gloves and take a swig of water while Scott retrieves the nunchakus from the safe. They're prohibited weapons, but we have the permits to use them.

My hands tingle from the sparring with Natalie, and I crack my knuckles. Scott hands me a helmet and fingerless gloves. Once they're in place, I take hold of the nunchaku, grasp each rod and pull until the chain is tight. It's been a few months since I last worked with them.

I spin the nunchaku in the air. Scott mirrors my movements. We circle each other, flicking our weapons out. Metal hits metal, but they're light taps. Warming up.

We dart in. Out. Testing each other's weaknesses. Waiting to see who will lunge first.

Scott shoots forward, his biceps bulging as he swings the nunchaku at full power. Mine collides with his, sending a lightning bolt of pain through my wrist and up my arm. I jump back with a yelp. Ouch. That hurt.

He crosses his arms and looks at me expectantly. And just like that, the fire goading me extinguishes like a bucket of water has been dumped on my head. Scott's reminding me I've broken the cardinal rule. Never lose control. Which is what I've done from the moment I stepped onto the mat.

The red haze in my mind clears, allowing logic to replace emotion. I can fix this mess. When Greg calms down, he'll see that I had no choice. That professional integrity meant I couldn't divulge my involvement with internal affairs, no matter how much I wanted to. So, I went looking for the real culprit to prove his innocence. He won't like it, but he's a detective. He'll understand the need for secrecy. Won't he?

I let the nunchaku hang from my hand and bow. "Thanks."

"You're welcome." Scott takes the nunchaku from me. "Feel better?"

"Yeah." Much better. I need to see Greg. Make things right between us.

As if my thoughts conjured him up, I spot Greg in the gym's entrance. His hair is mussed up, and his tie is loose like he's been pulling at it. *Has he forgiven me?*

I rip off the headgear and gloves and bound towards him, but slow down as I near. His expression would have a category five storm veering in the opposite direction. It doesn't look like forgiveness. I stop a foot away, my stomach cramping. "Hi."

His gaze flicks to my wrists. His face softens to less stormy for a moment, then reverts to cyclone proportions. "Em."

Tension swirls around him, the vein at his temple pulsing to its own beat. If he was a stranger, I'd be preparing to defend myself. I take a deep breath. "What are you doing here?"

He glances past me. "You led me to believe you were a newcomer to self-defence." His voice is soft but laced with steel, like it was in Inspector Matthews' office.

Bile creeps up my throat. I never should have let him assume I was a novice. "Umm …"

Greg eyes me like I'm a criminal. "Nunchakus are illegal."

"Not if you have a permit." I curl my fingers into tight balls by my sides. "I can explain."

Greg shoves his hands into his pockets, giving an air of nonchalance, but his body remains coiled. Ready to strike. "By all means." He leans against the wall, his glittering dark brown eyes boring into mine.

"It's complicated."

"Lies usually are."

I wipe my sweaty palms on my legs, a burn across the knuckles reminding me I've put them through quite the workout. I feel the weight of the stares behind me: Natalie, Scott, the rest of the people in the gym. "Can we talk somewhere more private?"

"No. I don't trust myself with you right now."

His words punch my stomach harder than any of Natalie's strikes. Trust is everything. I resist the urge to double over and move to a corner of the room where spare equipment is kept. It isn't private, but it's a discrete distance from everyone else. Greg follows.

I sit on a discarded weight bench. Greg continues to stand.

I rest my hands on my lap and look up at him. His eyes are hard chocolate spheres. God, I hope he understands. "I had two boyfriends who were intimidated by my kickboxing. They told me it wasn't feminine. So, I learnt to hide it. No guy wants to go out with a woman who can kick his arse. Even you said so."

He snorts. "Maybe your old boyfriends didn't like being lied to."

Damn it. My stomach aches like it's been pummelled for the last hour. How I wish I'd handled things differently. "Internal affairs swore me to secrecy. I had no choice."

He stares at me, his body as still as a statue. A minute

passes. And another. It's eerie, even a little creepy, the way he keeps staring, saying nothing. "Greg?"

He blinks. "What about sleeping with me? Was it all a ruse to get closer? Get access to my home and look for evidence I'm dirty?"

"No. Of course not." I reach for him, but he bats me away. "Internal affairs only contacted me after you and I made love. I felt awful not being able to tell you the truth."

He steps closer, and I cringe at the fury in his face. "It seems the promise of a promotion or a position at the police academy, *something I had no idea you even wanted*, helped soften your resistance and any guilt you might have had in lying to me."

The fissures in my heart deepen. "Greg, this isn't the place to discuss this. Can we go to my unit and talk?"

"What's there to talk about?" He lifts his right forefinger. "First, you lied about rock climbing." His middle finger goes up. "Then I find out you've been snitching on me to internal affairs." His ring finger joins the other two. "And now I find out you're a kickboxing ninja." He shoves his hands into his trouser pockets and steps back. "You've played me for a fool."

My muscles sag. What have I done? The most amazing man I've ever met, a man I admire and respect, feels like a fool because of me. I have to fix it. "Internal affairs were very insistent that I tell no one, warning there'd be consequences if I did. Inspector Matthews understood I didn't have a choice."

"Bullshit. You had a choice. You just didn't trust me enough." He turns away as if to storm off, then pivots. "This is why I don't do relationships, Emily. I have no time for liars, and people inevitably lie. It's in their nature."

And that's the point at which my heart splinters into a million tiny pieces. I'm Emily. Not Em or Red. Emily. The way Greg's looking at me, I'd doubt he'd squeeze the brakes if he was driving and saw me in his headlights. He's that pissed. And I get it. I know he's been hurt by those closest to him. He needs to see past the lies and how good things have been between us. I have to make him understand.

"What we've shared has been real, Greg." I choke back tears. Please don't let me start bawling. Not in front of everyone. "Our relationship is too special to throw away."

"Special?" He spits the word out like it's poison. "I'm far from perfect, but the one thing I've prided myself on is honesty. Something you seem to be missing, Emily. There is no relationship between us. There can't be, because without trust, there's nothing. Only one person using the other."

My body is numb. I can't believe this is happening. "But I love you."

Greg slaps his palm over my mouth. It's firm and warm, and from the dull sheen in his eyes, I know it will be the last time I'll ever feel his touch. "No more lies, Ms Saunders. It was fun while it lasted. I'd wish you good luck in your career, but with your silver tongue, you won't need it. The sooner you get that promotion, or a position at the academy, or whatever the hell it is that you are so determined to have, and out of my life, the better."

With one last searing look, he swivels and strides away, the shattered pieces of my heart trailing after him.

Chapter Thirty-Three

Greg

The pub's packed tonight thanks to the appearance of a popular cover band. The crash of drums and the thrumming of a bass guitar drown out the din of the crowd. But there's no suppressing the roar in my head.

I take aim at the dartboard and throw. "Bullseye!"

"Bullshit." Jake chuckles and slaps me between the shoulder blades. "You could have taken someone's eye out with that piss-poor aim."

I blink. Shades of red, green and black zoom in and out of focus. One dart clings to the edge of the felt. Three more lie on the floor beneath. Fuck. How many beers have I had?

Jake collects the darts and shoves me into a seat. "I think we'll give the game a miss tonight."

"I was just getting warmed up." I empty the remains of my beer, the cool liquid soothing my parched throat. I need more. My legs wobble, so I press my palms on the table to help me stand.

"Ah, ah." Jake grabs my arm and forces me back into my seat. "No more booze. How about you tell me what's going on inside that ugly head of yours?"

"Nothing." I cross my arms and glare at him. Yeah, it's childish, but I don't need a lecture from Jake.

"You were an arse all day, barking at anyone who dared look at you. And the way you froze Emily out at this morning's meeting was unprofessional. It's not her fault internal affairs approached her when they saw her helping you with the dog."

I drum my fingers on the table. It wasn't one of my finest moments, but learning that the only woman I've imagined settling down with has been lying to me has left a gaping knife wound in my chest.

Em had bags under her eyes, suggesting she'd slept poorly. My first instinct had been to hug her and bury my face in her hair. Forgive her. Proof of how screwed up I am over her. When she asked how Jimmy was going, I snapped. All I could think was, liar, liar, liar. I told her his welfare was 'police business' and of no concern to a civilian. My tone was low and cutting, the one I use when I'm interrogating crims. Her cheeks turned tomato red. Jake's right. It was a bully move. But he doesn't know what she means to me. Or meant.

I slam my fist on the table. Love is a mug's game.

Jake scratches his jaw like he's trying to figure me out.

The band starts up with 'A View to a Kill' by Duran Duran. Jesus, I hate eighties music. But given it's the theme song to a James Bond movie, it's on point. What the hell. I might as well tell Jake. He's my best mate and I'm going to spill my guts at some point. Might as well be now. He's less likely to hit me in a public place.

"Emily and I were dating."

Jake rips his beer coaster in two. "Jesus, Greg. What did I say?"

"I tried to resist her, but fuck, Jake, I'm only human." I scrub my fingers through my hair. "She pushed all my buttons and more."

Jake tears another strip off the coaster. The vein at his

temple looks ready to erupt. "So, you banged her despite me telling you to keep your sex life away from work?"

My blood boils. I don't like the way he's insinuating I disrespected Em. "It wasn't like that. We've been seeing each other for nearly two months."

"Eight weeks?" Jake's jaw drops, and he throws what remains of the beer coaster onto the table.

"Seven weeks, if you want to get technical."

Jake takes a deep breath and leans back in his chair, arms crossed, his gaze piercing mine. "You like her."

Where the hell's he going with this? I rub my eyes. Lack of sleep is catching up with me. "Of course I do." Or did. "I wouldn't have slept with her otherwise."

"True, but you like, like her. You've never dated the same woman for more than a week."

"It's over now." I shrug like it's nothing when it's everything. "She got what she wanted. It's obvious she was using me."

"I doubt that." Jake scoops up the shredded coaster pieces and arranges them in a neat pile.

I thump the table again, scattering the pieces. I ignore the glare he sends my way. "You're not listening to me. For all I know, she only slept with me to get closer, so she could search my house and look for evidence to give to those internal affairs pricks."

Jake picks up a piece of coaster and rubs it between his thumb and middle finger. "They only contacted her a few weeks ago."

I snort. "Do you believe anything those arseholes say? Em and I have been dancing around each other since she started working at the station. Then four months ago, *she* came onto *me*. I'd say they spoke to her a lot earlier than that."

Jake's hand stills. "I thought you said you started dating Emily seven weeks ago?"

Fuck. "I need a drink." I push out of my seat, but Jake pulls me back down.

"Explain."

I should never get drunk with this fucker unless he's drinking, too. "We almost hooked up at your engagement party."

Jake's expression darkens. "Is that why you disappeared during the speeches?"

I shrug and look away from his death glare.

"Claire better never find out. She was beside herself when you went missing. If she knew you'd been getting it on instead of …"

He leaves the words hanging. Even confirmed bachelors know that messing with a bride-to-be's celebration is suicidal.

The woman herself skips across the room and falls into Jake's lap. I look away as they share a kiss. I'd rather face a sharp blade than witness the love and devotion between these two right now.

I clear my throat when they don't come up for air. "Jake, Claire, I'm right here." And wishing I was doing the same thing with Em. If only she hadn't lied to me.

They break apart, and Claire turns to me, her shimmering green eyes as unwelcoming as I've ever seen them. "Greg." She picks up a piece of the beer coaster. "I see you're doing what you do best."

"What do you mean?" The fucking mess on the table is her husband's, not mine.

"Drinking." She glances across the bar. "Breaking hearts."

I follow her gaze. Em. I close my eyes and take a breath. Reopen them. She's here with Claire's friend, Jules, fancy cocktails in front of them and brooding expressions on their faces. Em's obviously spilled the beans to the girls. How much has she told them?

"With respect, Claire, it's none of your business. Em knew the score."

Claire blanches at my tone. "I wish Emily had listened to you, Jake." Jake slides his palms down her arms, soothing her. I'm the one who's been wronged, and yet they're making me out to be the bad guy.

My head spins. Wait. What did she say? "What the fuck does that mean?"

Jake grabs my collar. "Watch how you speak to my fiancé."

I slap his hand away. "What the fuck does she mean, *Jake*?"

A tic starts up in Jake's jaw. The music dulls to a soft din. "I warned Emily to be careful. That getting involved with you wouldn't be good for her."

I hope he can see the hate in my eyes because right now, I've never hated anyone more. Betrayed by my girlfriend and my best friend. Fuck them both.

"I'm sorry, Greg. I assumed she would be just another fling."

"You assumed wrong."

"Let me explain—"

"No." I jab my finger at the band. "Fuck off and dance with Claire."

He gives me a long, hard look, but I won't be sucked in by his shining blue eyes. "We'll talk later."

Like hell we will. I swivel to stand when I spot Monica. "Hey, stranger."

"Greg."

For the first time all night, my neglected smile muscles get a workout. Monica's poured into a body-hugging cream dress that makes her red hair shine. I wonder which lucky guy she'll be taking home tonight.

I stand to give her a kiss on the cheek, but I stumble and pull her onto my lap instead.

"What in the world?" Monica slaps me away. "Let me go, you big oaf."

"Sorry." I scoot across the bench seat and give her space.

Monica pinches me hard on my bicep and slides into the seat across from me. "I have a date, you arse."

I rub my arm. "I said, I'm sorry."

"Detective Sergeant Anderson. I wish I could say it's a pleasure." Commander Gordon looms over me, his eyes shooting daggers. "But I don't take kindly to seeing my date man-handled by the likes of you."

Jesus Christ. I should never have come out tonight. Tossing myself off a tall building would have done less damage.

"Good evening, sir." Somehow the words form without slurring.

I widen my eyes at Monica. *What the fuck*, I mouth to her. The commander's married.

She pats the seat next to her, and the commander slides in. Great. Fucking great. "I'm selling Peter's house for him."

"It looks like you're doing more than that." My throat swells. At this rate, I'll be out of a job by Monday. Then again, maybe that's a good thing. I won't have to report to that Judas, Jake. Or see that liar, Em.

The commander jerks like I hit him.

Monica's pupils narrow to tiny points. "You're drunk, Greg."

"Yes, I am." I grab my bottle of beer only to realise it's empty. I shove it aside. "You know me too well."

The commander stiffens. What the hell am I doing? I might as well hand my badge in now. Monica places a hand on the commander's, calming him. "Greg and I once dated, but we're friends, Peter. Nothing more."

I smother a smile. One weekend of fucking like bunnies isn't exactly dating, but I'm not going to correct her. That would have Commander Gordon reaching across the table and ripping my throat out. What I had with Em was dating. I glance at her table, but she's not there. Did she see Monica on my lap? I should go after her. But then what? It won't change the fact that she lied.

The commander stares down his nose at me. "Not that it's any business of yours, but my wife and I are in the middle of a divorce."

"Oh. My apologies." I tug at my collar. "I've had a bit too much to drink. I'll leave you lovebirds to it." I slide out of the seat, grabbing the table's edge to steady my balance.

"I hope you're not driving, Detective Sergeant," says Commander Gordon, his tone as severe as I've ever heard it.

"Nope. I've got him, sir." Jake drapes his arm across my shoulders.

The fuck he has.

I let Jake help me out of the pub and then pull away. The icy breeze slaps my face and clears the fog in my head. "I'll get a taxi."

"Greg—"

"No, Jake." I jab my finger against his chest. "You don't get to be my friend now. Friends don't go behind friends' backs. You had no right to warn Em away from me. No right at all."

A taxi pulls up. At least something's going my way tonight. I slide into the backseat and slam the door. "Cammeray," I tell the driver. He seems to sense the urgency and peels away with a squeal of rubber on the asphalt.

The motion of the taxi does weird things to my stomach. I rest my head against the window. I'm not usually this irresponsible with alcohol when I'm in public. Then again, this is the first time I've fallen in love as an adult and had my heart ripped out and shredded into tiny pieces.

Another first with Em.

And a big mistake.

One I'll never make again.

Chapter Thirty-Four

Emily

The incessant buzzing of my mobile pulls me out of a broken sleep. I blink my eyes open. Sunlight streams through the cracks in the curtains, telling me it's way past sunrise. I slept in. Again. I fumble for my phone, my heart racing. Could it be Greg?

"Hey, sis,"

"Hi, Ethan." His name comes out as a pitiful croak. I push myself to a seated position.

"You sound like you're still in bed?"

I don't have the energy for my brother this morning. "It's been a tough couple of days."

There's silence on the other side of the phone and silence in my bedroom. But there's no silence inside my head. It's alive with whispers of *what if, and if only.*

"Is this about the secret you were going to tell Greg?"

"It's over between us." I press a hand to my heart. It's still beating despite feeling like it's been beaten up with a set of nunchakus. "But it's cool. We were only fooling around." The lie tastes like ash as it spills from my mouth.

"I'm sorry. Do you want to talk about it?"

I crawl out of bed and open the curtains. Let the light

chase the gloom from my bedroom. If only it was as easy to cleanse the darkness from my heart. "No. We had a good time together, and now it's over."

"You seemed pretty serious about him."

My shoulders slump. "I was." I straighten the sheets and quilt. Smooth the creases on the pillow. If I pressed my nose to it, I'm sure there would still be traces of Greg's scent.

"So, you're just giving up?"

Since a glass of wine is out of the question at this time of the day, I shuffle into the kitchen and turn on the jug. "It's too late. He's already moved on. He hooked up with an old girlfriend at the pub last night."

"What?"

I yank the phone away from my ear and put him on loudspeaker. "Ouch, Ethan. That nearly busted my eardrum."

"Sorry." His voice lowers to a quiet rumble. "Are you sure you didn't misunderstand what you saw?"

I wish. "Nope."

"Bugger. Then he never deserved you, sis."

I measure out tea leaves. Try to keep myself anchored in the moment instead of replaying the image of Monica sprawled on Greg's lap. "Thanks."

I hang up and pour hot water into the teapot. There's nothing like a cup of Lavender Grey to make the world a little more bearable. I throw some bread into the toaster, and by the time it's cooked, the tea is ready.

Tears prick my eyes, and my hands tremble as I sip the warm brew. Memories of my last night with Greg play on repeat in my mind. *The love* in his eyes was as clear as a canola field in full bloom when he asked me to move in with him. And I destroyed that love with my lies.

This is all my fault. And I don't know how to fix it.

I've been running from my parents, from myself, ever since I left home. And yet, where do I go when my heart breaks and I no longer know what I want?

Home.

Dust swirls around my car as I leave the asphalt and turn onto the private gravel road. Fields of green span to the left and right. It'll be a carpet of yellow flowers in another couple of months. The house comes into view, the galvanised roof reflecting the sun. My heart speeds up. I had so many plans when I left home. Get my psychology degree. Become a cop. Kick some criminal arse. It all came true except for the cop part. Although, after what happened with internal affairs, I'm not sure I want to be a police officer anymore.

As I manoeuvre the car alongside the house, my mother steps off the verandah. Her hair is peppered with silver high-lights, but her jeans and jumper reveal a youthful figure. A wave of emotion comes over me. Despite feeling trapped growing up, I've missed the familiarity of home.

The moment I step out of the car, I'm enveloped in Mum's arms and the heady fragrance of vanilla and cinnamon. We're both of similar height, aka tiny, and it feels weird to hug someone of the same stature. Greg is twice my size, and being in his embrace always made me feel delicate and protected.

"Emily, it was a wonderful surprise to get your call." Mum pulls away and looks me over. There are new worry lines on her forehead. Can she tell I've been crying? The tears I shed on the drive are long gone, but mothers seem to know.

"I've got two weeks' leave and thought I'd spend some time with you."

Her brow furrows. She always could smell a lie. But in true mum style, she says nothing. "You must be tired and hungry after the trip. I've just finished baking an apple pie."

She bustles me inside. A mist of flour covers the kitchen bench tops, and an array of clean and dirty pots and dishes litter the oak breakfast table. All that's missing is broken furniture and it would resemble the aftermath of a cyclone. Despite my melancholic mood, my face breaks into a smile. Mum's an outstanding cook, while my skills are limited to boiling an egg, but we both share a penchant for messiness.

Mum pours tea and cuts two generous helpings of apple pie, lopping dollops of cream on top. I sit at the nearby table and tuck into it the moment the plate is in front of me. The pastry is crisp, and the apple soft and sweet. "They don't make pie like this in the city." I lick my lips and wipe crumbs from my face.

Mum smiles. "It's good to see you haven't lost your appetite."

"Nope." Although, that's not entirely true. My appetite's been missing in action since Greg confronted me at the gym last week. But the fresh country air and Mum's delicious cooking have reignited it.

Ethan strolls in, dark smudges underneath his eyes. I drop my fork and slide off my chair. "Hey, little brother."

The smile he attempts rings false, and his eyes remain a flat, murky brown. Something's up.

"Hey, to you too." He wraps his arms around me and nearly breaks me in two with his hug.

I pull away and clasp his hands. They're calloused from working the farm and sweaty. "What's wrong?"

He glances at Mum. Her cheeks have paled to the colour of the flour. She grabs my empty plate and dumps it in the sink.

Ethan crosses his arms. "I told them about Simon."

Oh.

Mum wrings her hands out. "Your father didn't take it very well."

"Understatement of the century." Ethan slumps into a seat at the table. "His face darkened to the ugliest ruddy colour I've ever seen. I thought he was going to have a heart attack."

"You just took us by surprise." Mum dishes out a slice of

apple pie for Ethan. Her answer to all life's problems is pie and freshly brewed tea.

"So, where's Dad now?" I ask.

"He's here." My father's soft voice drifts across the kitchen. He lingers in the doorway as if he's unsure if he's welcome. His short back and sides haircut is more silvery white than grey, and the lines on his face have multiplied since I saw him at Christmas. He holds his arms out. "Do I get a hug, Emily?"

Tears prick my eyes. "Of course." I take the few steps towards him and throw myself into his embrace. He squeezes me tight, and I feel like a child again, all my problems forgotten. Only they're not.

He kisses the top of my head and lets me go. "It's good to see you, love."

Ethan scrapes his chair back. "I'll get going."

"No," says Dad, his tone gruff. "I mean, wait. Please."

"Why?" Ethan's chin lifts, and his eyes harden. "So, you can tell me to get the hell off *your* land again?"

My father's shoulders sag. "I'm sorry. I shouldn't have said that."

"But you did." Ethan steps towards Dad, his hands balled into fists by his sides. "You said there was no point keeping the farm for me if I was going to shack up with some other bloke. You'd rather sell up and retire."

My jaw drops. How could Dad say that to Ethan? And what about me? Isn't the farm part mine as well?

My father holds out his hand. "Let me explain."

Ethan shakes his head. "I think you were clear enough."

"Give your father a chance." Mum wedges herself between them and both men take a step backwards. She might be half their size, but her voice carries authority when she speaks. "In our defence, we thought you were interested in one of the Lawson girls. We had no idea that you ..." Mum shrugs and lowers her head.

Ethan waves his hands in the air. "That was you and Mrs Lawson trying to match make. I only went out with Kelly to shut you up."

Dad grabs Mum's hand as if for support. She slips under his shoulder. "I was wrong to react the way I did. I have no excuses except you caught me by surprise and my brain went haywire."

"This is why I've never told you." Ethan glances at me. I smile and nod to let him know I've got his back. "I still remember how you stopped doing business with the farm supplies store near the railway line five years ago when the owner came out gay."

My father's brow crinkles. "That's not true. It was because Phil lost distribution rights for the spare parts on our machinery."

Ethan's breath hitches. "Not because he was gay?"

"Of course not."

That's a relief. I've been telling Ethan for years that he can trust our parents with the truth, but he'd been too scared of their reaction to risk it.

Dad takes a deep breath. "I'm sorry you couldn't trust us before now."

Ethan grips the back of a chair. "So, you're okay with it?"

"No," says Mum with a whisper.

Ethan stumbles back as if she slapped him, his eyes watering. Mine do the same. I can't believe she said that.

She shakes her head. "What I mean is, we want you to be happy. That's all we want for both of you. It's just …" Her voice catches, and she swipes at her eyes. My parents are traditional in their values, but I'd expected them to react better than this.

My father kisses the top of her head. "What your mother is trying to say is we'd hoped there might be grandchildren one day."

Fire sweeps up my spine, along my throat, and across my

face. This is why I left home. It's like Mum and Dad are living in the fifties.

"Christ, Dad, I'm only twenty-one." Ethan paces, his work boots thumping loudly on the timber floor. "I'm not ready to have kids." He stops and squares his shoulders. "But if and when I do, there's no reason I can't adopt."

"Is that all you and Mum care about, Dad?" The words shoot from my mouth before I can stop them, but I'm not sorry. This has been a festering wound in need of cleansing for too many years. "You've been hassling me to find myself a *nice man* and have a family ever since I finished high school, and throwing women at Ethan, hoping to get him to settle down when he should be out enjoying himself." I stomp the tiles with my foot. "Why can't we be good enough just the way we are?"

My parents gape. I've never raised my voice to them. Ethan steps towards me, but I bat him away.

My hands shake and tears spill from my eyes. I don't want to disappoint my parents, but I can't keep pretending that their attitude doesn't sting. I hug my arms around my stomach and, to my horror, burst into tears. So much for finding comfort at home.

No one says anything for a beat until Mum leaps into action and bustles me into a chair at the table. She passes me a box of tissues, and I sob into my hands, equal parts angry, sad and embarrassed. The soft sounds of Mum boiling the jug and making more tea drift around me. Ethan and Dad remain silent.

Finally, I feel strong enough to face them all. I wipe my eyes and blow my nose.

Mum places a hot cup of tea in front of me, steam wafting off the surface. "You want to tell us what's really going on?"

I take a deep breath. Sip my tea. Avoid Mum's concerned gaze. "Why wouldn't you offer the farm to me?"

Dad sits on the chair next to me. He smells of hay and grease, transporting me back to my childhood. "You made it clear you wanted to move away. Make a name for yourself in the city. I thought you said you were happy to inherit your grandmother's old house in town and leave Ethan with the farm?"

"I did. But what if I changed my mind?

"Then I'd revisit the will."

"But I'm just a woman."

My father shakes his head. "I don't understand where this is coming from, Emily."

Tears spill down my cheeks. Of course he doesn't. He wasn't the lost little girl watching her parents gush non-stop over the baby boy they brought home from the hospital. The way they spoke about him, in hushed tones, I wished I'd been born a boy.

"It doesn't matter, Dad."

He squeezes my hand. "Emily, your mother and I are so proud of what you've achieved. You're the first person from our family to go to university. The first one to work for the police force, and the first to earn a black belt in kickboxing."

"You didn't come to my graduation." I'm acting like a pouty teenager, but how can he say he's proud and yet never bothered to be at the most important event of my life?

"Sweetheart, we had a terrible drought that year. So many problems with sick and dying sheep and crops. If we could have left the farm, we would have."

Mum plonks a photo album on the table. "This is our brag book, Emily. I don't know why we haven't shown it to you before. I put it together when you left for uni. It was my way of keeping you close after you left."

"All our friends have seen it." Dad opens up the album. "Many times over."

Ethan play-punches my shoulder. "They don't have one for me, sis. Told you that you were the favourite."

"Hush," says Mum. "You're both my favourites."

I turn the pages, tears blurring my vision. There's a photo of my high school formal. I'm dressed in black pants and boots instead of a dress like the other girls, although I'm wearing a sparkly pink top. Then there's my graduation photo where the smile is so bright it's blinding. The photo I sent them when I became a black belt is next. As I flick through the album, I see there's even a photo of me driving the tractor when I was five. I wasn't tall enough to reach the clutch, let alone strong enough to push it in, but I could steer.

"I thought you hated me driving the tractor, Mum?"

She traces a finger across the picture. "I did. But that's because I was petrified something would happen to you. You were so tiny and fearless."

"You didn't think it was men's work?"

"Yes." My eyes widen. She taps my nose and smiles. "But only because *I* didn't want to do it. It says everything about me, not you. Our love has always been unconditional. I'm sorry if you felt it wasn't. We'll love you whether or not you keep working in the city or return home. And whether or not you get married or have children."

"But you said ..."

Mum kisses the top of my head. "That's me being a selfish old woman."

I roll my eyes. She's only sixty-two. "You're not old."

"No. But I still remember how overjoyed I was when I finally fell pregnant with you after years of trying." She snatches a tissue from the box and dabs her eyes. "I guess I've become a little obsessed. Worrying you might have the same trouble."

Mum pushes a slice of apple pie towards me. "Are we good?"

I slip off my chair and hug her. Breathe her in. Swallow to stop more tears from falling. "Never better."

"It's good to have you home, kiddo, whatever the reason." Dad ruffles my hair, his gaze thoughtful. "But if you're having man trouble, you let me know and I'll take my shotgun out for target practice."

Oh God. Trust Dad to see through me. I bark out a laugh. "You don't need to do that."

Mum swats him on the chest. "For goodness' sake, Daryl, don't be ridiculous."

Dad winks at me. "I wouldn't hit anyone. Just scare them into thinking twice about hurting my little girl."

"No guns, Dad." Why he even owns a rifle is beyond me. My father has no desire to harm wild rabbits or kangaroos, and even if he did, he has a woeful aim.

I'm not ready to talk about Greg. Not yet. Maybe never.

Dad gives me a hug, then turns to Ethan. "It's time we met this young man of yours. How about you invite Simon over for a Sunday roast?"

Ethan's jaw drops. "You mean it?"

"Absolutely. I'm sorry I reacted the way I did when you told us. We'd like to meet the man who means so much to you."

I smother a smile. Our conservative dad's in for a shock when he sees Simon's piercings and tatts.

I sip my tea. It's cold now, but that's okay. The kitchen is toasty warm, with sunlight pouring through the window above the sink and love consuming the room. The truth, as I've believed it, has been turned on its head. All my life, I've felt second best to my brother. It's why I've strived so hard to prove myself at school and then work. To be noticed as more than a womb. I could have avoided so much pain if only I'd faced my fears instead of running away from them.

Chapter Thirty-Five

Greg

Home looks the same as always: white picket fence, stone-washed brick walls, pink and purple flowers poking up from charcoal-grey pots, thanks to my industrious gardener. But a pervasive sense of emptiness seeps through my veins as I approach the front door. I shove my key in the lock, my fingers as numb as my heart. After a weekend of drowning in my misery, I've spent the last week avoiding Jake. Em's been easier to ignore. She took two weeks' leave without notice. I'm sure Jake helped push through the approval. The fucker. It's hard to know who I'm angrier with —Em for not telling me about internal affairs or my best friend for warning her to stay away from me.

I kick off my shoes and continue into the living area. Silas' snout is pressed against the glass of the back sliding door. Idiot. I unlock it and he falls face-first into the room. Despite the storm raging inside, a smile cracks on my face.

"You're such a goofball, buddy." I rub the top of his head. He looks up at me with one adoring eye. Em had the same pleading look in hers, but how much of it was real? Silas, on the other hand, makes no secret of what he wants. Although, I don't kid myself it's me. Any person will do, as long as they give him food and a walk.

I stride into the bedroom. If I linger in the living area, I'll end up on the lounge with a whiskey in my hand and an unhappy dog at my feet. I've learnt the hard way over the last two months that a well-exercised dog means a good night's sleep.

I peel out of my shirt and suit and drape them over the bed. Silas bounces through the doorway while I move stiffly, feeling every day of my thirty-nine years. I was a fool to imagine I could have more with Em. Have I learnt nothing from my parents? Sure, Jake and Claire are happy, but they're caught up in a sex-fuelled haze. Who's to say they're not sitting in court in five years fighting over property and alimony?

I pull on jeans, a T-shirt and a jumper. "I hope you appreciate this, buddy."

Silas grins and shakes his head like he understands me. This is what I'm reduced to—talking to my four-legged side-kick. "Come on, boy."

There's a knock as we reach the front door. My heart does a little jig. Stupid organ. *Could it be Em?*

I clip Silas' lead around his collar and grab the knob. I'm not sure I want it to be Em. It's touch and go whether I'd slam the door in her face or drag her into the bedroom and fuck this sick sensation out of my chest.

Silas whines and licks my hand. "Yeah, she did a number on me, buddy."

I swing the door open, the dance in my ribcage petering out to a slow shuffle. "Troy. What are you doing here?"

"Hello to you, too." My brother steps back, narrowly avoiding Silas' tongue.

Silas strains against the lead. He'll make my life hell if I don't follow through on the walk now. "I was taking the dog out. Want to join us?"

Troy smooths the front of his pinstripe suit jacket. He's even more particular than I am about what he wears, and earning three times my salary, so I'd guess there was little change out of five grand for the suit.

"Sure." His voice kicks up an octave, which tells me he thinks it's the worst idea ever.

I lock the door behind me. "Don't be a pussy. Your clothes can be dry cleaned."

The irony isn't lost on me. Two months ago, I'd have been as meticulous as Troy. I still am, to some extent. But Silas and Em have shown me it's okay to be messy. And with Em, that messiness translated to the bedroom and the most intense sex of my life.

I yank on Silas' lead and regret stabs me in the arse when he yelps. It's not his fault Em lied her way into my bed. And my heart. I need to remember women are for fun. Nothing more. I'll leave the relationship shit to others.

Silas stops at the gate and sniffs the mailbox post. He cocks his leg and squirts what will be the first of who knows how many pee messages to the rest of the canine community.

"I still can't believe you've got a dog." Troy steps in beside me, and we meander down the street.

"Yeah, well, I don't know how much longer." And isn't that a kick to my guts? First my girlfriend. Then my best mate. Next will be my dog. Soon, my life will be back to the way it was, minus Jake.

Great. Fucking great.

"So, how come you dropped by, Troy?"

He tugs at his tie and looks straight ahead. "I told Felicity about the photos."

"What?" I didn't think he had it in him. "Do you need a place to stay?"

"No." He stumbles. "Obviously, she wasn't happy, but once she stopped screaming at me, we talked."

"Good on you. Owning up to your mistakes isn't easy."

"I didn't want to be looking over my shoulder, waiting for the photos to turn up. You might have put Sophie behind bars, but that doesn't mean I'm safe." Silas stops and investigates a hedge. He does this every walk. It's clear he thinks there's something hiding in there, but he's still yet to find it.

"So, what happens now?"

"We still have a long way to go, but I'm hopeful we can work through it. Felicity's seeing a psychologist for her depression, and we're going to start couples counselling. Plus ..." He takes a deep breath, and his expression tells me he can't believe he's saying it. "I'm quitting politics."

"You what?" I never saw that coming.

Troy grins, his chin wobbling ever so slightly, telling me he's freaked out. "I want to see my kids grow up. I can't do that if I work sixty-hour weeks and travel half the year."

"Have you told Dad?" Silas jerks his head out of the bushes and darts in front, nearly bowling Troy over. "Silas, heel." My tone is firm, and for once, the crazy dog listens to me. He falls back into place on my left side. If only Em could see him now. Obeying my command. And doesn't that cut through my chest with the efficiency of a sharp blade?

Troy wipes his hand across his forehead. "Let's just say you might be the favourite son now."

I snort. "Not in this universe."

We reach the dog park. Silas whines. "Wait." I release him from the lead. "Okay."

He charges towards a black labrador. I wave at the owner. Cassie, I think her name is. She's a marketing manager for a cosmetic company, her make-up and hair always immaculate, even when walking her dog. She waves back, keeping a respectful distance, her gaze drifting to Troy. The last time I saw Cassie, I was here with Em, who all but pissed on me to make it clear we were together. Cassie got the message loud and clear. If any other woman had staked her claim on me like that, I'd have kicked her arse to the curb. But with Em, it made me want her more.

That's one of many warnings I should have heeded that I was in over my head.

"Is everything okay, Greg? At work. With Emily." Troy's tone is neutral, but his eyes have that politician-like steel in them, the one where they smell blood. I should know because cops have the same look.

Taking Em to Dad's party was a mistake. Now the family will expect me to settle down. If not with Em, then with someone else. "We broke up."

"I'm sorry. She was nice." He shoves his hands in his trouser pockets, as comfortable as I am about feelings. "Do you want to talk about it?"

"Nope." I cross my arms.

"Greg …"

"I'm not doing this with you, Troy."

"What happened?"

Jesus. He's impossible. "It was never meant to be forever. We've had our fun. Now it's over."

"And it sounds like you wish it wasn't."

I kick a stone across the grass. "Let it go, mate."

"Well, I'm here if you need to talk."

A massive ball of white fur whizzes between us. "Sorry," yells the red-faced teenager chasing after it. "Come back here, Midas."

I grin and brush the hair off my jeans. At least Silas' fur is darker. White would show up on everything.

Troy pats furiously at his trousers. "Bugger." He scrapes the hairs off, then pulls a bottle of sanitiser out of his pockets and drowns his hands in it.

"You realise there are probably more germs on your kids' snotty faces than on that dog's fur?"

"Interesting. I never thought I'd see the day a dog tamed you."

I turn away from the knowing look in his eyes.

He nudges me in the ribs. "Are you sure you can't keep him?"

"Yep."

Silas rolls on the ground with the labrador, a massive grin on his face. He loves the freedom of the park, playing with the other dogs. He won't get that when he returns to Jimmy. "His owner's expected to be discharged from hospital in a few days. Silas belongs with him."

My eyes fill with tears. Fuck. When did I become such a pussy? I blink them away before Troy notices. I don't want to go back to the way it was before Silas. Before Em. Or before Jake. But it's not up to me.

Chapter Thirty-Six

Greg

The hospital lift takes its sweet time arriving at the third floor. It would have been quicker climbing the stairs with a broken leg. Not that I have anywhere else to be. Only a mountain of admin and a scowling Jake waiting for me back at the station.

Em's desk is wiped clean as if she's never returning. But things couldn't look more different at my house. The spare toothbrush still sits on the vanity next to mine, and a ratty T-shirt she used to wear while washing Silas is tucked under my pillow. Her scent lingers in the fabric, and like a creepy stalker, it comforted me while I lay in bed with a stinking hangover on the weekend. I'll grow some balls soon and toss her stuff.

The doors open, and I shut down any thoughts of Em. I've never had trouble letting go of women in the past. The little redhead will not be the first one to break me.

I falter in the doorway of Jimmy's room. A woman sits on the bed tapping on her phone, honey-blonde hair brushing her shoulders. She's a stunner. In another life, the one before Em, I'd be asking for her number.

"Where's Jimmy?"

Her head snaps up, and she slips off the mattress. Her chin lifts, and she stares me down. "He's having a shower. Who are you?"

"I'm Detective Sergeant Greg Anderson. And you?"

She breaks into a smile. "I'm Jimmy's daughter, Natasha." She steps forward and shakes my hand. "Nice to meet you, Detective. Dad never stops talking about you."

Jimmy's never mentioned a daughter. What the hell's he been doing on the streets? "Don't believe everything he says."

"It's all true, Sarge. If it wasn't for you, I wouldn't be here." Jimmy exits the bathroom. His crackly voice is the same, but everything else is so different I hardly recognise him. His dark brown trousers and check shirt are clean and pressed, his face is shaven, and the wiry mop on his head is combed. But it's the sparkle in his eyes that arrests me.

"Jesus, Jimmy, you scrub up well."

"Thanks." A pink hue brightens his cheeks. "It must be all the hospital food."

I snort. "More likely, no alcohol or weed."

He glances at Natasha. "I don't know what you're talking about, Sergeant."

"It's okay, Dad." Natasha hugs him. "That was the past."

While I'm pleased to see Jimmy's looking fit and healthy, there's an ache in my chest because he'll want Silas now. I'll miss the goof ball.

"I never knew you had a family, Jimmy. Are you going to help him out, Natasha?"

"Yeah." She squeezes Jimmy's arm. "We lost touch, but I'm here now."

Natasha picks up her handbag. "I'll get us some coffee while we wait for the discharge papers. Would you like one too, Detective?"

"Nah. I'm good. Thanks."

She smiles and strides out of the room, her delicate musk perfume drifting behind her. I almost wish I fancied her. It would be proof that Em hasn't totally ruined me.

"I'm happy for you, Jimmy. Looks like you and Silas can finally have a proper roof over your heads."

"Yeah." Jimmy shuffles to the bed and lowers himself down. "About Silas."

"I'm sure you've missed him." I cut him off. This hurts bad enough as it is without drawing it out. "He'll be over the moon to see you." And I'll be all alone.

Jimmy's eyes redden. "I can't keep him."

"What?"

"Natasha's allergic to fur. She has one of those spoodle things. The ones that don't shed hair."

My pulse quickens. "So, you can't take him?"

"Not if I want to live with my daughter."

"And do you?"

"Yeah." A tear slides down his cheek. "I'll miss Silas like crazy, but he likes you, Sarge. Knowing he's in a good home makes it easier to let go."

My heart beats like Silas' tail when he's excited, but the fear that I'll screw it up has me backing away. "I never said I'd keep him forever."

Jimmy studies me like he's trying to read my mind. "He seemed so happy when you brought him to see me."

"He is happy." And I want to keep him, so what the fuck am I doing?

"Then what's the problem?"

Jimmy's as tenacious as Silas when he gets his teeth into a bone. Or one of my expensive woollen blankets. "If it wasn't for Em, Silas and I would have dug graves for each other in the backyard by now."

"So? You've got your pretty girlfriend to help."

I slump on a chair next to the bed and hang my head. Girlfriend. Before Em, that word had the power to shrivel my balls. Now, I want more than a girlfriend. I want a wife. Kids. Everything Jake's got.

"Sarge." Jimmy pats my shoulder. "Has something happened?"

I lift my head and sigh. "We're not together anymore."

"Why?"

"It's a long story."

"In other words, you stuffed it up."

"No." I glare at him. He raises an eyebrow, daring me on the wily bastard. "She did something I can't forgive."

The wrinkles across Jimmy's forehead deepen. He scratches his chin. "I can't imagine that little sweetie cheating on you."

"Not that." Christ, the thought of her with another man boils my blood. "She lied about something important."

"Did she have a good reason?"

I rub my eyes. I think I preferred Jimmy when he was drunk. Lucid Jimmy's a pain in the arse. "What is this? I'm the cop. I'm the one who does the interrogating."

"Then it's past time you were on the other end. Did she have a good reason to lie?"

Fair question. Em would have gotten into a lot of trouble if internal affairs found out she'd broken the code of secrecy. She could have lost her job. They can be vindictive bastards. "I guess so."

Jimmy rubs his hands down his trousers and squeezes his legs, the bony knuckles on his hands going white. "Sarge, I have thirty years on you. Thirty years of making stupid choices. I'd hate to see you do the same thing."

He gestures towards the door, his expression sombre. "My little girl was eight when I walked out on her and her mother with just the clothes on my back and the scarf Natasha gave me as a Father's Day gift. I'd been on a bender and came within an inch of hitting my wife, the woman I loved. Alcohol had me in its clutches, and I couldn't get myself free. Didn't want to. Instead of tackling my demons, I joined them." He jabs at his chest. "Spoiler alert, Sarge. Worst decision ever."

"Shit, Jimmy. I'm sorry."

"Don't be. I'm telling you so you won't make the same mistake I made. I saw the way your girl looked at you, and more importantly, I saw the way *you* looked at her. Don't run from the woman you love because you think it's easier than facing your demons. There's nothing easier about living with regret."

"It's too late." I rub my eyes, the weight of too many years convincing myself I'm better alone dragging me down. "But I'd be honoured to take Silas." I've already lost the girl. At least I get to keep the dog.

Jimmy shakes his head and pins me with a look that peels away my layers like their tissue paper and exposes the secrets of my soul. "I never took you for a coward, Sergeant Anderson."

My jaw clenches, and I push my chair back. Jimmy's spent thirty years in a stupor on the streets and now he's Yoda? If it was anyone else, I'd tell them to mind their own fucking business. But for all his sage words, Jimmy's vulnerable right now. I'm many things, but a bully isn't one of them.

I give him my business card. "Call me when you get settled. You're more than welcome to visit Silas anytime."

He clasps my hand. I resist the urge to peel it off me. If he gives me more advice, I won't be able to hold my tongue, and I don't want to hurt him.

"Thanks, Sarge." He squeezes my fingers. "For everything."

Tears prick my eyes. I've become a soft pussy since Em. I hug his bony frame. "You take care of yourself."

I flee the room like the coward Jimmy accused me of being.

Is it too late?

If Em saw me accidentally pull Monica onto my lap, and I think she did, then she's more likely to use my balls for kickboxing practice than listen to an apology. But Jimmy's right. I've been ignoring my demons since I was fourteen years old. Since the old man fucked us over. It's time to stop.

Chapter Thirty-Seven

Greg

I text Jake and tell him I'm taking a week's leave, effective immediately. He can kiss my arse if he says no, but he texts back straight away with an OK and to call him if I need anything. No questions. Just acceptance. I don't respond. I'm not ready to forgive him. Not sure if I can. Em had good reasons for what she did, but Jake ... he should never have interfered.

The sun is a glimmer of hope to the east as I bundle Silas into the car. He's surprisingly obedient. It's as if he senses the critical nature of this mission—win back Em at all costs.

Unfortunately, Silas' stomach isn't on board with the trip. I pull over to the side of the road for the fourth time in three hours. Fucking dog's thrown up in the car twice, and the putrid fumes of vomit saturate the interior. Who knew dogs got car sick? If Em was here, she'd know. But she isn't. I'm not sure how a pukey-smelling dog will win her back. Should have left him with Jake and Claire. Then again, it's hard to stay mad at him when he looks so miserable.

I snap Silas' leash on. He bounds out the door and towards an embarkment where he proceeds to munch on grass like he's a born-again cow. I ruffle the fur on his head.

Poor bugger. Once he's finished grazing and throwing the grass back up, I pour water into a bowl and let him have a couple of sips.

"Ah, ah." I pull him away. "Not too much, buddy. Last time I let you drink your fill, it ended up in the backseat."

I clip Silas back into the car and manoeuvre onto the road. Luckily, Em's parents' phone number was publicly available; otherwise, I may have broken the rules and looked them up in the system. Em's brother, Ethan, answered the phone. He gave me the address, but not before he made a few threats to cut off certain appendages if I made things worse with Em.

According to the GPS, we're less than ten minutes away when I turn onto a gravel road. My stomach heaves. I could blame it on the spew-filled air, but it's got more to do with anticipating Em's reaction when she sees me. And what about her parents? Has she even told them about me?

A sage green weatherboard house comes into view, and the churning in my gut reaches hurricane proportions as I realise that the long list of firsts with Em continues to grow. I've never chased a woman. And I sure as hell haven't voluntarily put myself within striking distance of a woman's parents before. Silas pants and whines like he knows we're closing in. I take a deep breath so I don't start copying him. Despite the fear seeping into my bones, I've never been more confident I'm doing the right thing. That Em's worth fighting for. Embarrassing myself for. Taking a beating for.

We come to a halt next to a four-wheel drive, dust wafting into the air. A red kelpie bounds towards the car. Silas growls. Shit. He's usually good with other dogs.

A man steps onto the verandah. A wide-brimmed hat shields his eyes from view, so I can't tell if he's happy to see me or pissed. But he's not carrying a rifle, so I take that as a good sign. I step out of the car and stretch my legs. The dog runs over and sniffs my jeans. Silas barks through the open window. Crazy mutt is looking more and more like a liability.

The man ambles across the short distance. As he nears me, I recognise it's Em's brother, Ethan, from photos in her apartment. He tips his head. "Greg, I presume."

He's eighteen years younger than me, yet the way he studies me under that hat makes me feel like he's the adult and I'm a teenager.

I swallow, my throat drier than the dust coating my car. "Yeah. You must be Ethan. Did you tell her I was coming?"

"Nope." He glances at Silas, then back at me. "She's still pretty upset."

"I've been an idiot. I'm hoping she'll forgive me." Silas' barking picks up. The kelpie sits obediently at Ethan's feet. "Is it safe to let my dog out?"

"Sure. Tom'll be fine with him."

I grab the lead from the front and open the passenger door. Silas is too quick for me, slipping past and barrelling towards the other dog.

I hold my breath as the two dogs size each other up. Silas is friendly, but you can never tell.

A few seconds is all it takes for Silas and the kelpie to decide they're friends, and then a game of chase is on.

Ethan screws his nose up and steps back. "What's that stench?"

I slam the car door shut, trapping the offensive odour inside. "That would be Silas' vomit. He doesn't travel well."

"It hasn't smelt like that all the way, has it?"

"Nope. Only most of it."

"Wow. You deserve a second chance just for that."

I shove my hands into my pockets. She has to forgive me. "Do you think Em will give me one?"

"Hard to say." Ethan shrugs. "You might as well come inside. Em's in town. She should be home soon."

My dog rolls in the dirt while the kelpie watches. Lovely. "What about Silas?"

"He can come too."

I call Silas and he trots over, his face covered in drool and filth.

Ethan laughs. "That's why we only have short-haired dogs. That's going to be a bitch to wash out."

I shrug. He can be drenched for all I care, as long as I get Em back.

The house's interior is airy, and the mouth-watering smell of lamb wafts down the hallway, greeting me as I step over the threshold. Silas' nose twitches.

"You're in luck," says Ethan. "After a week of making us eat vegetarian, Mum's cooked a roast lunch today." Ethan shudders. "Em can finish the leftovers."

I hide the smirk that twitches at my lips. He clearly isn't a fan of his sister's dietary preferences.

We enter the kitchen, and my heart does a double take. Em's mother's the spitting image of her, only with grey hairs and wrinkles that suggest a lifetime of laughter. She looks up from where she's stirring a pot on the stove. The lines on her face deepen as she looks me over.

"Mum, this is Em's friend, Greg."

She drops the wooden spoon and wipes her hands on a nearby tea towel. "I see."

I tug at the top of my shirt. It's suddenly very hot. "She doesn't know I'm here."

Silas trots towards Em's mum and sits at her feet, his head lifted, his one eye looking up at her with adoration.

"Oh, my. And who is this adorable creature?"

I choke back a laugh. Like mother, like daughter. Red dust coats Silas' fur, and I have an awful feeling he has dried vomit stuck to his whiskers. He's as adorable as me after a heavy night out. "This is my dog, Silas."

She pats his head, and he nuzzles into her hand. "Aren't you a pretty boy?"

Silas beams, his tail thumping the floor. "What happened to him?"

"He was defending his previous owner from some thugs. Took a broken bottle to his eye."

"Oh no." Em's mum's hand flies to her mouth. "That's awful."

"Yeah. I reckon he would have made a good police dog." It's bullshit, but there's no harm in talking Silas up.

"Are you a police officer?"

So, Em hasn't told her parents anything about me. That doesn't bode well. "Yes, Mrs Saunders." I resist the urge to shuffle my feet like a little kid.

She glances at Ethan and surprises me with a smile. "Welcome to our home, Greg. And please call me Judy."

Chapter Thirty-Eight

Emily

The trip into town was as painful as it gets. Happy couples prodding at the stinging wound of loss in my chest. Everywhere I walked, there were people holding hands or pushing prams. It was a constant reminder of all that I've ruined with my lies. The sun shines brightly, not even the tiniest wisp of a cloud muting its brilliance—a perfect winter's day. But it does nothing to lift my mood.

There's no escaping the truth. I miss Greg. His naughty humour and cheeky smile. The way he took control without undermining me. Until he dumped me without giving me a chance to explain. I know I hurt him, but I'm still reeling from how fast he fell back into Monica's arms. I thought we'd shared something special.

I thought wrong.

And then there's my job. There's no guarantee I'll get a promotion or be accepted into the police academy, and I'm not sure I want either option, anyway. But how can I keep working at the station and seeing Greg every day?

As I near the house, my pulse speeds up. Even under all the dust, I recognise Greg's Audi parked next to Ethan's four-wheel drive. What's he doing here?

The front screen door slaps open, and the man himself steps onto the verandah. He exudes strength and self-assurance, his blue jeans and long-sleeve T-shirt accentuating the bulging muscles of impressive quads and biceps. Heat pools in my centre while my cheeks burn with embarrassment. He looks like he walked off a photo shoot, and I have bags multiplying under my eyes and the beginning of a potbelly from Mum's cooking.

I step out of the car. My confidence has taken a dive after all the horrible words Greg said in the gym, so I shove my hands into my jacket pockets and rock on my heels.

"Are you here to yell at me some more?"

Greg jumps off the verandah and walks slowly towards me, his stride hesitant. "I'm sorry about that, Em." The rumble of his voice settles between my legs and in my chest. He's apologising? Does that mean he's forgiving me?

But what about Monica? If I hadn't seen her in Greg's arms at the pub, I'd be throwing myself at him right now. I'm not sure if I can forgive him if he's slept with her, even if my lies drove him into her arms.

The screen door slams shut. I glance past Greg and see Mum and Ethan watching, their jaws flapping in the breeze. Ethan has Silas by the collar. My heart softens at the goofy boy. I've missed him almost as much as I've missed Greg.

Greg takes a step closer. "I love you, Em."

My heart stalls. A week ago, I would have given anything to hear those words. Now, all I can see is a redhead who's everything I'm not sprawled across Greg's lap.

"And what about Monica?" I'm proud of how well the question leaves my mouth. The words are clear, and I don't burst into tears. I'm making progress.

He lowers his gaze, and my heart sinks into the red dirt. Some things can't be undone. "I wondered if you saw us at the pub."

I blink away tears. I've shed too many already. "Yeah. You looked pretty cosy." And it was all my fault.

He reaches his hands towards me, and I take a step back. "Em, it was an accident. I was only saying hello, but I was drunk. I stumbled and Monica fell on top of me."

A warm shiver of hope tickles my spine. "Why should I believe you?"

"Because it's the truth. You could ask her yourself; she was less than impressed with my behaviour." He glances at Mum and Ethan, then lowers his voice. "Internal affairs is a cop's worst nightmare … It was a lot to process."

The warmth in Greg's eyes is in stark contrast to the harsh, dead look he gave me at the gym. I want to throw myself into his arms and smother him in kisses, but I need to get everything out in the open first.

I shuffle closer, my arms at my sides. "I'm so sorry. I wanted to tell you; I just didn't know how. If I could go back and do things differently, I would. I'd tell you about my black belt. About internal affairs." I flex my fingers and give him a coy smile. "About all the ways I know how to immobilise a person."

His face lights up with a smile. "I love your fire, Em. Your passion."

I gulp in breaths, my chest heaving. Greg's driven hours to see me. He's brought Silas with him. He wouldn't come all this way if he didn't care.

My limbs go weak. "I'm sorry I hurt you."

He tucks a curl behind my ear. "And I'm sorry for telling you, I'd be glad to see the back of you. It was cruel and wrong. And a lie."

Tears prick my eyes. Damn it. "Do you really love me?"

"More than anything."

His declaration buries itself deep in my chest, chasing away the disappointment. The lies.

"And I love you. So much." I launch myself at him, wrapping my legs around his waist just like I did that first night. He catches me with ease, his large hands cupping my butt. He smells like sweat and sandalwood and ... ew, something less pleasant. I wrinkle my nose. What has he been doing?

Who cares? He could have rolled in sheep dung and I'd still rub myself against him. I melt into his strength. His pupils dilate as our lips touch. It's a gentle caress, tentative. Searching. Feeling our way back to each other. But gentle's never been our thing. I close my eyes, the intensity in his gaze too much to absorb, and thrust my tongue into the heat of his mouth, my hips undulating against his groin. He meets me thrust for thrust, our tongues duelling for control, his fingers digging into the soft swell of my arse.

It's like we've come full circle to the beginning, the night of Claire and Inspector Matthews' engagement party. Only this time, there's no uncertainty. I love this man with all my being and he loves me.

Barking brings me back to my senses. Greg tears his mouth away, and I gulp in air. A cough reminds me the dogs aren't the only ones watching us. I slide my legs down until my feet touch the ground, my face burning.

Greg's hands move to my waist, and he tugs me to his chest, resting his chin on my head. He kisses my hair. "You okay?"

"I will be," I mumble into his shirt. "Do you think we could just stay like this until they go away?"

He chuckles and lifts my chin. His brown eyes are the softest I've ever seen, warm melting chocolate soothing the ache in my heart. "Since when did you become a coward?"

"Since my mother witnessed me dry humping a man like a horny teen." I clutch his biceps. "Is she still there?"

"Yep. And, given the daggers shooting in my direction,

I'm guessing the bloke marching across from the barn is your father?"

My legs go weak. "I'd say so." This is not the best way to introduce the man I love to my parents. And love him, I do.

Greg drops his arms and threads his fingers with mine. He squeezes softly, letting me know he'll back me up if I need him to. I turn to face the house. Mum, Dad and Ethan all have identical stances, their heads tilted to the right, regarding us with impressive poker faces. Although, Greg's right. Dad looks like he's deliberating whether this is a shotgun moment.

Silas wriggles, and Ethan lets go of his collar. My beautiful boy bounds towards us, and I crouch down to meet his kisses. "Hey, gorgeous. I've missed you."

I'm rewarded with a wet cheek and a whiff of that odd smell again. Time to face my parents. I stroke his fur and straighten.

Greg and I walk to the verandah, hand in hand. It's not more than a dozen steps, yet it feels like a mile.

"Mum, Dad, Ethan, this is Greg."

Greg sticks out his hand.

"We've already met." Mum grins. "But let me greet you properly." She pulls him in for a hug. That's a good sign. I release a stale breath from my lungs.

Ethan gives him a little wave. "We met earlier."

"I haven't had the pleasure." Dad crosses his arms, his tone suggesting it's anything but a pleasure. My stomach drops. No, no, no. Please don't make a scene. "Mauling my daughter in front of her family isn't the best way to make a good impression."

"No, sir." Greg swallows, his throat working overtime. He gives me a small smile and stands taller. "I love your daughter, Mr Saunders, and I intend spending the rest of my life showing her how much I love her."

My legs wobble at his sincerity.

Dad looks at me. Tears well in my eyes. I lean against

Greg, seeking his warmth. His strength. Dad regards us both for a few more moments, then holds his hand out. "Welcome."

They shake hands, and my father steps back, his nostrils flaring. "What *is* that smell?"

Greg grimaces. "Sorry about that. My dog doesn't travel well. Got sick a few times on the way here."

Silas nudges Greg's leg like he knows he's being talked about. Poor boy. I make a mental note to get some anti-nausea tablets from the vet.

"Come inside. Lunch is almost ready." Mum ushers us into the house. "Is Simon far away, Ethan?"

"No. He should be here in a few minutes."

I squeeze Greg's hand. "We'll be in shortly, Mum."

My father's eyes narrow. "Don't wander far. Lunch will be served the moment Simon arrives."

I smother a grin. What does he think we're going to do? "We won't be long."

Dad huffs and follows Mum and Ethan into the house. I pull Greg around to the side garden. It's shaded from the sun and private.

My heart bursts with happiness. Life has never felt more right—my parents have accepted Ethan's boyfriend, accepted Greg after the mess that was me when I arrived here a week ago and accepted me for who I am all these years, even though I didn't know it.

I press a finger to his mouth. "There's something I want to tell you."

"Okay." He licks the tip of my finger, his hooded eyes promising all sorts of wicked treats.

"Don't distract me, Greg."

He clasps my hands to his heart. "I can't help it, Red. I thought I'd lost you."

And I thought I'd lost him. I stretch up on my toes. Greg bends to meet me and captures my mouth with his. I dip my tongue between his lips, and we affirm our love with languid strokes of our tongues, soft caresses and gentle sighs. As much as I want to sneak away to the barn for a quickie, that might earn Greg an introduction to the end of Dad's rifle. Even my father couldn't miss at close range. Not to mention, the drone of an engine and crunch of gravel signal the impending arrival of Simon.

I rest my chin on Greg's chest. Since I was a little girl, striving for a career has been my whole life. Now, it's only a part of it. "If I get a promotion, I'm turning it down."

He cups my jaw, his brown eyes swirling with love. "Does that mean you're applying to the police academy?"

"Nope."

"But isn't that what you wanted?"

"I thought so, but the shadow of internal affairs would always be there. Sullying any success I might have."

"Em, that's not true. You—"

I hush him up with another kiss, one that fills me with a warm glow. "I've done a lot of soul-searching, Greg. I've been so focused on proving I'm as good as a man that I've missed the truth. I'm already good enough. I always have been."

Epilogue

Greg

Sweat pools under my armpits as I up-end the plastic rubbish bin onto the floor and rummage through the contents. They have to be here somewhere.

"What the fuck are you doing?" Jake's gruff voice echoes inside the tiny bathroom.

"I've lost the rings." My hands shake harder than any kid I've seen on ice. The most important day of my life and I'm fucking it up. The old man would give me one of his boorish lectures if he knew. Fortunately, he had a "prior engagement". Thank fuck. My mother and sister also made their excuses about some yoga retreat in the Himalayas they couldn't possibly miss out on. I don't care. Troy and Felicity turned up. And I have Em and her family, and Jake and Claire.

Jake laughs. "Jesus, mate. You're losing it."

"It's not funny. I've searched everywhere and nothing." I pick up a wad of toilet tissue that looks like it might contain bodily secretions of some sort. I'm wearing gloves, so it's not as if I'm at risk. After all the filth I've encountered over the years, there's no way I'm taking chances with germs, even if it's a rubbish bin in Em's parents' house.

Jake waves his hand at me. "I've got the rings, you moron."

I jerk my head towards him. "What?"

"You gave them to me for safekeeping."

"Oh. That's right." Thank Christ. The thumping of my over-zealous heart quits its drum solo. I shove the rubbish back into the bin and snap the gloves off. Then wash my hands twice for good measure. "I guess I'm more nervous than I realised."

Jake slaps me on the back. "I never thought I'd see the day."

"Yeah. Me neither." We jostle past each other and into Emily's old bedroom. It's complete with posters of *The Matrix* and *Die Hard*. No surprises there. Em's staying in a nearby cottage, the same one we'll spend our wedding night in before flying out to Vanuatu for our honeymoon. She wanted to follow the tradition of not seeing each other on the wedding day until she's walking down the aisle, her parents' not-so-subtle hints cementing the idea. Tonight can't come soon enough.

"I'm proud to stand by your side today, Greg." Jake squeezes my shoulder, his expression sombre. "I'm sorry I ever doubted you."

My throat stings like it's been scrubbed clean with a wire brush. To think I almost threw our friendship away when I learnt Jake had warned Emily away from me. "Your intentions were honourable. You couldn't know how much I'd fallen for Em. Hell, it took me a while to see the truth." My voice cracks, and I pull him into a bear hug. "There's no one else I'd want standing at that altar with me today but you, Jake."

Could I sound any sappier? We put some distance between each other. Clear our throats.

I check my bow tie in the mirror. Adjust the rose on the lapel of my tuxedo jacket. Jake stands alongside me in an identical black suit and matching smile. Marriage to Claire agrees with him, and no one deserves happiness as much as Jake does. I hope I'll be half the man for Em that he is for Claire.

Silas peers up from his bed on the floor, his one eye telling me he thinks the black bow tie around his neck is a crock of shit. Not my fault, buddy. It was all Em's idea.

Mrs Saunders pokes her head through the door. "Ready?" She beams at me. I hardly recognise her in a stunning cobalt blue dress with her make-up and hair all done. While Em's dad was a little harder to win over, always cleaning that blasted rifle when I was around, Mrs Saunders has been rooting for me from day one.

"Yes, ma'am."

She leads the way into the garden where a marquee has been set up. Em wanted a small wedding at home with close friends and family, although it looks like half the local town was invited as well. Jake and I walk up the aisle, white seats on each side, rose petals scattered along the grassy middle. Silas trails behind. If I hadn't seen it with my own eyes, I wouldn't believe a dog could sulk. But sulk, he does.

Smiling faces greet us. Em's sparring partner, Natalie, and her trainer, Scott, wave at me. I give them a nod. It's taken me a while to get used to seeing Em sporting bruises caused by her 'friends'. It goes against my protective instincts. But I've learnt to accept that Em thrives on the adrenaline rush and is more than capable of looking after herself. Not to mention, she would have my balls for interfering. And not in a good way.

A few of the team from the station made it and are already helping themselves to the champagne. Although, I doubt they'll get too messy. Not when the boss, aka Jake, is here. Dylan gives me the briefest of grins before turning his attention to a pretty brunette. I give the kid full marks for trying. One notable absence is Laura. Em thought she declined the invitation because she has a crush on me. Her face turned a delightful red when I explained that Laura swings both ways, and in this instance, her interest lies in Em's direction, not mine.

When we reach the front row, Jake peels away to kiss Claire. The floaty light pink dress she wears accentuates her bulging stomach. I swallow a lump in my throat as she fights her heavy midsection to stand. Warmth suffuses my veins as I imagine my pint-sized rocket round with our child. I'm such a goner. So many firsts with Em, I've lost count.

Claire kisses my cheek. "I couldn't be happier for you, Greg."

I mumble my thanks and move away before I do something stupid, like cry, and stand at the makeshift altar, an archway covered in pink and white climbing roses. Silas sits at my feet, pawing at the bow around his neck and refusing to look at me. Ungrateful sod. He's lucky he's even here. If I had my way, he'd be locked away with the other dogs. Okay, that's not quite true. But I wouldn't have him at the altar with me. Or would I? As Em said, Silas brought us together and should be part of our big day.

The celebrant, a vibrant woman with a spiky platinum silver hairdo, winks. "You're just in time. The bride's on her way."

My heart kicks up a beat. Part of me feared Em would come to her senses and call it all off, but it's really happening. Jake nudges me, and I turn to look up the aisle as 'Beautiful Crazy' by Luke Combs starts up. Em warned me this would be country music all the way. Em's brother appears, and there's an audible gasp. He looks stunning in a white tux. Tears fill my eyes. I blink them away. Em doesn't have any close girlfriends, so she asked Ethan if he'd be her man of honour. She chose well. Simon, dabs his eyes with a tissue from the front row, where he sits next to Mrs Saunders. Who knows, Ethan and Simon may be next.

Ethan shakes my hand when he reaches us. I pull him in for a hug. It's not tradition, but who cares?

Then, the music changes and the lilting strains of Keith Urban's 'Memories of Us' fill the speakers. A shiver runs down my spine as Em comes into view. Fuck me. She's dazzling in a shiny white satin dress, although the plunging neckline and split up the front reveal more creamy flesh than I want anyone seeing but me. I smile and shake my head at the white lace ankle boots on her feet. She sashays up the aisle, one small step at a time, her fiery curls peeking out from under an Akubra hat. No veil for my girl.

Silas scrambles to his feet and lets out a whine. I pat his head. Yeah, buddy, she's perfect. And she's ours. And we're well and truly hers.

Jake digs me in the ribs. Shit. I fumble to take Em's hand from her father. He grins at me and slaps my back before sitting beside his wife.

Em clasps my fingers tight, the blue of her irises brighter than the sky above, tears dancing at the edges. Happy tears, since her smile's even more blinding than her eyes.

I wrap my free hand around her waist and pull her close so I can feel every inch of her delectable body. The celebrant clears her throat, reminding us we're supposed to step apart, but I ignore the not-so-subtle warning. Instead, I lower my head and capture Em's mouth with mine. She responds with a breathy moan, encouraging me to deepen the kiss. I oblige, my tongue slipping between her lips. The guests break into catcalls and wolf whistles. Em presses harder against me, her fingers digging into my biceps, silently begging for more. Jake joins the celebrant with the throat clearing. I guess it wouldn't be a good look to start dry humping each other at the altar. I smile and reluctantly release Em's lips.

Her cheeks are pink, those beautiful eyes shining with love and trust. Reflecting my absolute devotion back at me.

"Love you, Detective."

I straighten her hat and brush her cheek with my fingertips.

My friend.

My lover.

And soon to be my wife.

Who knew getting married would feel so right?

"Love you too, Red."

Bonus Scene

If you're not ready to let Greg and Emily go, then sign up for my newsletter. Not only do you get the free e-book, *Breaking the Rules*, you get exclusive access to a short wedding night bonus scene for *With or Without Trust*.

https://karenlieversz.com/newsletter/

Also by Karen Lieversz

Breaking the Rules (Free e-book for newsletter subscribers)
https://karenlieversz.com/newsletter/
With or Without Panties (Book 1 in the Hot Cops Series)
With or Without Vows (Book 3, coming late 2024)

BREAKING THE RULES

A steamy small town romance

Rules are meant to be broken.
Aren't they?

After being screwed over, both literally and figuratively, Grace's dreams of making it big in the city spiral into one giant nightmare. She returns to her home town vowing to follow one simple rule – never trust a man. It works just fine until sexy Sergeant Owen Mason starts waving his badge at her. Flexing those massive biceps. Smiling.

Stupid rules.

The attraction is instant for Grace and Owen, but past hurts and a drug investigation that takes an unexpected turn threaten to keep them apart.

Now Grace and Owen will need to decide just how many rules they're willing to break for love.

Free e-book at https://karenlieversz.com/newsletter/

WITH OR WITHOUT PANTIES

A steamy opposites attract romance

It's what's underneath that counts.

Solo parent Detective Inspector Jake Matthews has dedicated his life to cleaning up the streets of Western Sydney. But when the beautiful blonde with sexy green eyes walks straight into his path, responsibility is the last thing on his mind.

Even if it's the one thing he can't escape from.

When Claire Thompson breaks her golden rule—never *ever* wear ugly underwear—a near miss with a hot cop's SUV reveals her embarrassing secret. Lucky for Claire, the handsome inspector finds her rule-breaking captivating.

The universe doesn't.

Before the all important first date, an office drug bust puts Claire on the wrong side of a jail cell door. The evidence is damning, and Jake treads a narrow line between duty and his growing feelings as he sets about proving Claire's innocence.

Jake and Claire will need to reveal all their secrets — along with Claire's panties — if they're going to have any chance of breaking their self-imposed rules and finding their happy ending.

With or Without Panties, *the first standalone book in the* Hot Cops *series, is packed with sizzling heat, misbehaving canines, and a dash of suspense.*

Acknowledgments

It feels surreal to have the second book in my *Hot Cops* series published. I'm still pinching myself. A massive thanks to my beta readers, Carrie, Emma, Antonella, Georgia, Kat, and Michele. Their feedback and insight were invaluable. I'm so grateful to have such talented writers and friends supporting me. I'm also very lucky to have a wonderfully supportive ARC team. They are the final eyes before this book makes it's way into the big wide world.

A special thank you to Kim Lambert from Romance Writers of Australia for being incredibly generous with her time and ideas during a plotting course where I workshopped this novel. And thank you to my local cop source, Terry, who helped guide me on police protocol which I may (or may not) have always followed 😊

I'm so fortunate to have outstanding editing support in Kelly Rigby. She is the red pen behind the words and did her best to keep the "fucks" to a minimum (while I did my best to argue why they had to stay 😊). Her structural and line/copy edits were key to making this the best possible story it could be. The fabulous Jo Speirs then cast her eagle eye over the final product, picking up the sneaky little typos and inconsistencies that slipped through. Thank you ladies! Then, there is my amazing cover designer, LJ. I appreciate her patience as I obsessed over every tiny detail. The cover is perfect for Greg and Emily.

None of this would be possible without support at home because, like many authors, I maintain a full-time job on top of my writing. Thank you to my husband for his unwavering support and patience and to Juno, our kelpie/staffy, who ensures I am regularly exercised.

Lastly, and most importantly, a huge thank you to you, my reader, for choosing to read *With or Without Trust*. Given the huge selection of books available, I'm honoured and humbled that you chose mine.

If you enjoyed *With or Without Trust*, please consider leaving a review on Amazon and/or Goodreads. Reviews are a wonderful way for readers and authors to find each other.

Thank you!
    Karen xx

About the Author

Karen Lieversz writes contemporary romance and women's fiction with heat, humour, and a dash of irreverence.

A born and bred country girl, Karen spent her childhood making up stories and reading to the cows, who proved to be avid listeners. Drawn to the city lights, she now lives in Sydney, Australia, with her husband and four-legged trainer. When Karen's not glued to her laptop, you can find her walking her dog or kicking her heels up on the dancefloor.

Keep up to date with Karen's Hot Cops Series and other misadventures by following her on Instagram *www.instagram.com/karenlieversz* or join her mailing list at *www.karenlieversz.com/newsletter* to receive advance news on her upcoming books and exclusive content, as well as receive a copy of the free steamy Hot Cops Novelette 'Breaking the Rules'.

* 9 7 8 0 6 4 5 8 5 5 6 3 0 *